SKY BREAKER

~TALES OF THE WANDERER~

LEE C. CONLEY – DAVID GREEN – J.E. HANNAFORD – DAMIEN LARKIN – DEREK POWER – C. MARRY HULTMAN – H.L. TINSELY – C.F. WELBURN

AF347707

Books by the Authors

Lee C. Conley
The Dead Sagas:

A Ritual of Bone, A Ritual of Flesh

David Green
Empire of Ruin:

In Solitude's Shadow, Path of War (coming July 15th)

Nick Holleran Urban Fantasy Series:

The Devil Walks in Blood

J.E. Hannaford
Black Hind's Wake

The Skin, The Pact (coming September 2022)

Damien Larkin

Big Red

Blood Red Sand

DEREK POWER
Filthy Henry Series:

The Fairy Detective, The impossible Victim,
Accidental Legend, Stolen Stories

Duplex Tempus

C. MARRY HULTMAN
Face of Fear

All the Children Shall Lead

After the Hurricane:

These Walls Will Fall

The Haugarian Chronicles:

The Soldier's Song (Coming September 2022)

H.L. TINSLEY
The Vanguard Chronicles:

We Men of Ash and Shadow

The Hand that Casts the Bone

C.F. WELBURN
The Ashen Levels:

Fledgling, Journeyman, Adept, Hero, Paragon

The Linguist

I Shall Return With Winter

First Edition
Published By
Fables
An imprint of Nordic Press
Kindlyckevägen 13
Rimforsa, Sweden.
2022
This is a work of fiction. Similarities to real people, places, or events
Are entirely coincidental
Sky Breaker – Tales of the Wanderer
Ebook: 978-91-987508-0-5
Paperback: 978-91-987508-1-2
Hardcover: 978-91-987508-2-9
Written by
Conly, Lee C., Green, David, Hannaford, J.E., Larkin, Damien,
Power, Derek, Marry Hultman, C., Tinsley, H.L. & Welburn, C.F.
Cover Design by
David Green
Formatted by
C. Marry Hultman
Edited by
Charlotte Langtree
Copyright © 2022 Nordic Press

www.nordicpresspublishing.com

Contents

The thing about portals is this; you really need to know what you're doing when you open one. If you try to conjure one to just throw something through, it must open somewhere specific and only for a short period of time. Opening one to, effectively, nowhere is a bad idea. Particularly if you throw in whatever you want to get rid of and don't seal the portal back up immediately.

You see, the magic required to open an uncontrolled portal is, oh, how to explain this to a mortal mind? It is like throwing a stone into a lake; ripples happen. Not lovely rings on the surface of water, no. Proper ripples, truly fantastic ripples. Ripples through the very fabric of time. Because if you don't seal up that 'trash portal' almost straight away, it spawns many more portals. Ones that open anywhere and anywhen.

Portals that, if you know what you are doing, allow you to go through to different points in time and change history how you want. Which I do, I really do. After those druids flung me into this no-place, this place that connects all portals, I had several seconds to come up with my revenge plans. It was so simple, really.

And look at it there, the prime portal. Those foolish druids meddled in magic they did not truly understand. Hilariously, it is this stupidity that will allow me to attain godhood. I could never open so many portals on my own, but now that they are opened, I'm sure as Hell going to use that power to my advantage. The energy released by closing a small portal must go somewhere. Back into the ether? Why, that seems like a waste of good magic. But into my body, imbuing me with the very energies of reality itself? That seems like a much better place to store such forces. All I must do is close all the smaller portals to achieve what has been written about me in prophecies since I was born. My very birthright, you might say. Immortality as a god.

Which is where you come in, boy. The druids firing me into this void removed my corporeal form but did nothing to my spirit. Then, along you come, with a body for me to borrow so I can step back into the world and start shutting the portals down.

Now, don't worry. This will only hurt for a second.

-The Wanderer, before it began.

SWAMPERS

C.F. WELBURN

I

JOB SATISFACTION

If there was one thing Ewin hated more than working Harvest, it was working Harvest with a hangover. He peeked out from around the mossy tree, leant back and took another swig from the wineskin. There was no avoiding the work but topping up from the night before helped take the edge off. The horn blew and he dragged himself to his feet. He could already hear Gower hollering. One of these days, perhaps he'd tell the arrogant bastard where he could shove his orders. Today was not that day. Leyre would kill him if he lost this job. He fixed a grimace on his face and slunk back to the line.

"They want more every year!" Breeg complained as together they hauled a huge pallet of ground wheat across the muddy brick road towards the iron gate. "They'll want us to send 'em up a castle brick by bloody brick next, you'll see."

Sometimes Breeg's whining grated on Ewin, but today he was in complete agreement. The demands were getting ridiculous. On both ends of the line. No doubt the workers up in the mountainous Yre complained as much as they did down here in boggy Yew.

But that was the way it was. Ewin had been five when the Rent had opened, and seven when some over-paid genius had learnt how to connect the two specific Rents. Yew had become barely recognisable in the interim. Apart from the swamp stench and hum of mosquitos—nothing could quite get rid of those.

"It'll bring trade in," his father had said happily in those first days, when he still lived.

It had brought in more than that. The big oak in which the Rent had appeared was still there; the other trees around it had been chopped, snapped, swept aside and burnt to make room for an iron fence, roads, brick warehouses and the stone mansions of those who profited most. The small winding lane was now wide enough for four carts to be drawn abreast. Wealthy overseers had moved in with their families and made Yew their own, treating the former residents as little more than drudgeons. *Swampers*, he heard them say. It made Ewin ball his fists. It made him and his friends curse them in their cups, and then glance over their shoulders in case they'd spoken too loudly. It made them rue the day they had played too close to that old, unremarkable oak with the strange crack running through its bark…

He was part of the last generation who would remember the marshy backwater Yew had been, little more than a boil on Tregate's swollen arse. But there were only three such portals in the whole of Penryth, and that made Yew special. It went from hole to hub, from bog to bustle. The swamp dwellers became resources. Dirty hands for cheap, dirty labour.

Oh, it put food on his table. Allowed him a drink with his mates of an evening. Even if the amount of shit they had to put up with usually dominated every topic of conversation.

As if reading his thoughts, Breeg piped up.

"Comin' down the Ivy at knock-off?"

"For a quick one."

"Leyre keeping the purse strings tight, eh?"

"As always."

Breeg had no such concerns. The stout, black-toothed urchin of a man was loyal and kind, but if he ever got married, it would be to someone who lacked a sense of smell. And possibly sight.

"Tomorrow's a big day," Ewin continued. "Don't want to overdo it."

They looked at each other and laughed. They had this conversation every year. They never learnt.

"Oi, less chatter! Got three carts backed up!" Gower stood one leg on an old stump, looking down at them; his constant frown of irritation creased more deeply today. They nodded, knowing better than to complain. It'd do no good. There were plenty of others who would jump at the chance for a steady, if frugal, wage. Slackers were quickly replaced with keener folk from Tregate's slums.

They saw to the three carts, and three more after that, leaving the goods at the iron fence which stood in a wide circumference around the oak. Nobody was allowed within a hundred meters of it these days. It was almost unthinkable that as children they had been able to walk right up to it. Had dared each other to throw things into it! Of course, that's how all of this had started, when poor Yacob had squeezed into the crack. Yacob had died, the Rent had been born. That was some thirty years ago. Yacob's parents had been compensated, but never recovered. They were both dead now anyway. Nobody cared. Once it was realised how profitable the Rent could be, the Tregations arrived in droves and put in security and restrictions.

It was a vague memory now, but sometimes when Ewin arrived home in time to put his son Jenri to bed, he'd recall that distant day their friend had entered the crack, screamed and been dragged away into a swirling darkness.

II

LAST ORDERS!

"Bloody hell!" someone shouted, bursting through the door. It was Iker, and he looked pale.

Ewin, Breeg and Badger looked up from their drinks. Badger had been in the middle of one of his long-winded explanations of how those in Yre had it better than they did. If it wasn't for Iker's horrified face, Ewin would have been glad of the distraction.

"What's wrong?" he asked.

"Kael," lanky, straw-haired Iker said, struggling to catch his breath. "Got him, it did."

"Got him? What got him?"

"Dunno. A thing snatched him. Came right out of the Rent!" Iker's legs were trembling.

"Sit down," Ewin insisted, making room. "Drink!" he called to Wane. The ruddy-faced barkeep winked and reached for an empty mug. "Start again, slowly this time."

"I… don't know. It was just there, an arm, a snake thing… then he was gone."

There was silence as the four friends looked at each other. The four who had been there thirty years ago when Yacob had gone. Sweaty, dirty Breeg; fat, slow Badger; skinny, gap-toothed Iker; and himself, weary, irritable Ewin.

"Well, what was it? An arm or a snake?" Badger asked.

"Who gives a shit?" Ewin said with a scowl. "Kael's gone?"

Kael, despite being a Tregation slummer, had not been a bad'un. Drank with them sometimes.

"One minute he was there loading up, the next—" Iker made a slashing motion with his hand, then stared around with haunted eyes. "If me boot hadna come loose, would've bin me."

Ewin was about to ask more when suddenly the Ivy's door crashed open and a huge bulk filled its frame.

"There you are!" Gower growled. It wasn't clear until he had stormed over just who he was talking to. His boots were too clean, his long grey trench coat not stained, or creased enough. His face shaven, though showing a day's worth of stubble.

Iker glanced up, his grimy forehead glistening.

"You think you can just up and leave?"

"Sorry, sir," Iker mumbled. "I didn't know what to do… I panicked—"

"You abandoned your post. Left the gates open. Did you sign out?"

"But Kael…"

"Idiot got careless. I told them to hire people capable of wiping their own arses! Bloody useless."

"A man's dead," Ewin blurted.

"You got something to say, Ewin?" Gower glared. Ewin shrank, raised his mug to his lips and shook his head.

"That's what I thought," Gower said with a sneer. "Right in the middle of bloody Harvest. Drunk more than likely, like the rest of you sorry sots!" He cast his eyes around the room. Men like Gower did not frequent the Ivy. The ceiling dripped. The smoking lamps had blackened the crooked walls. Seeing him here was like discovering a silver in a handful of grubby coppers. Nobody spoke. Breeg chewed his lip, Iker stared off, Badger looked at his feet and might have passed wind, Ewin groaned.

He wanted to tell his stupid self to shut up, but just couldn't.

"It was no accident. He was snatched by something. Tell him, Iker."

Iker was mumbling and seemed not to hear him.

"Snatched? By what?" Gower snarled. "The cable goes directly to Yre. Nothing bad there, except the cold and bearded women!"

"I'm just sayin' we shouldn't jump to—"

Gower's face reddened. Ewin closed his eyes. Dammit. Somebody needed to speak up, but why was it always him? Badger and Breeg didn't have families. He had Leyre and Jen-ri. His wife had warned him repeatedly about sticking his neck out. The initial anger on Gower's face melted into a cruel smile.

"Congratulations Ewin, you've just been promoted. Report to the gate at dawn, you're in the Sanctum now with Iker here."

Ewin's stomach tightened, "I, erm… No, I think—"

"I don't give a fuck what you think. And don't expect more pay. You lost that boon for speaking out of line. You might be inside, but you'll get your regular wage. I'll sort someone more appropriate out once Harvest is done; for now, you're up. Don't disappoint me." He shot one last look around the bar. Even Wane was gawping, his pretence at cleaning a nearby table ridiculous in its blatancy. "Anyone spreads these rumours of something 'snatching' anyone will be docked wages and taken to Tregate for slander. And don't drink too much. I've seen your faces. Any of you slacking tomorrow will be out of a job once Harvest is done." He glared once at Ewin and Iker, turned on his heel and left.

"Bloody hell, Ew," Breeg said, but Ewin already had his hand up.

"Another round, please Wane," he said. He might regret it later, but suddenly did not want to arrive home whilst Leyre was still awake.

III

THE INNER SANCTUM

At dawn Ewin reported to the iron gate. He was forced to sign something he couldn't read. When he asked what it was, Nobby, the Tregatian guard, just scowled.

"I look like a bloody teacher to you? Just sign it and get to work."

Ewin frowned, just enough to show Nobby he had a spine, but not enough to warrant a reprimand, then he signed. Not like he had much to lose. Except his life, that was. Accidents were rare, but yesterday's incident had left them all on edge. Nobby snatched his pen away and wiped it on his trousers before putting it back in his pocket. Ewin bit his tongue. Nobby by name, knob-head by nature, as Iker sometimes joked down the Ivy. Ewin saw why. He bowed his head and passed through the gate.

Iker stood waiting for him, already preparing the ropes and hooks and pallets and all other manner of implements they were responsible for. He looked up and tossed Ewin a pair of gloves but did not stop working.

"How you feeling?" Ewin asked, fitting the gloves one by one.

"Like crap," Iker said. "Give us a hand, will you?"

Ewin nodded and stooped to thread a rope around several stacked crates.

"You don't think it will happen again, do you?" Ewin asked.

"Just stay back behind the lines and do what I say."

Ewin nodded. Just get the job done and get out of there. That suited him fine.

Gower and his fellow overseer, Vykers, stood waiting, clipboards in hands.

"Look sharp!" Gower said. "Got a big day today. I trust you've been over everything with him?" he asked Iker.

Ewin nodded. Iker hadn't, but no need to cause his friend any more grief. How complicated could it be? Pick up the orders from the gate, move them to the Rent, attach them to the cable, stand back and watch… That was it, wasn't it? Oh, and try not to die. Stay behind the line, he reminded himself. Gower grunted and pointed to the path.

"I got it from here," Vykers said. The Sanctum overseer was reputedly even stricter than Gower, and the cruel slant to his eyes and unpleasant twist to his lip seemed to confirm it. The grey hair around his balding head put him somewhere in his fifties, an age most swamp dwellers from Yew would be lucky to reach.

Gower grunted, glared at them and left the perimeter. Ewin peered towards the huge tree and saw the Rent for the first time in over thirty years. Strange, since he spent almost every day hauling stuff to be fed into it. It shimmered up and down the length of the broad trunk, equal parts black and silver, like dark water catching the moonlight. It was exactly as he recalled. Similar to the Great Rent in the sky, but closer, more palpable. Time had not made it any less mesmerising. He thought of Kael, then of Yacob, and shuddered. He looked at the white safety line painted on the ground. It wasn't as far away from the Rent as he would have liked. Another quarter of a mile would have done it.

He focused on the mundane stacks of pallets and boring list of work. That helped. It was just a normal day. A routine shift. Kael had been careless, he told himself. Yacob, unlucky.

Back then, when Ewin and his friends had been free to come and go as they pleased, the Rent had been a place for adventure and mischief. They'd kept it secret for a few weeks when they had discovered it. Little more than a strange crack they had pried open with sticks and sharp stones. They'd thrown things in; acorns, Badger's shoe… nothing had come back. They knew to be careful. They'd heard of the other Rents in Penryth. Everyone had. The Great Rent in the sky was as commonplace as the moon. But the fact that one would appear right here in Yew was unthinkable. They were proud. It was their secret! Until Yacob died… Then they had to tell. Running, screaming, crying to the adults.

Everything had changed after that. The church had swooped in to condemn it, but in the end the ambitious businessmen of Tregate had bribed, coerced and bought the rights. It wasn't long before Tregate Transportation was turning a profit and becoming richer and more powerful by the day. Of course, a healthy percentage of the profits went to the crown. As long as King Shitface got his royalties, the corrupt company—who employed everyone from the privileged overseers down to the overworked underpaid labourers—could pretty much do as they liked.

Once scientists and technicians had established a direct link between Yew's Rent and the Rent up in Yre they were able to lock it in place with an iron cable. As long as whatever they sent was attached securely, it would end up there on the other side of the Pinnacles. If something passed through unattached, then it was anyone's guess where it might go. Like Yacob. Like Kael. Like Badger's shoe…

Sometimes things emerged that were definitely not from Yre. A large fish that Ewin heard someone call a shark arrived on one occasion. A metallic object with a flashing screen appeared once. It had beeped for about a day before going dark and silent. The church had gone mad on that one, and rumours of zealots burning down part of the university up in Tregate even made it back to Yew. A yellow and black striped animal that resembled a horse appeared once, screaming, its entrails hanging out. That was another reason for the fence.

They weren't just concerned about keeping people out, but keeping things in. Ewin might fantasise about punching that Nobby bastard's lights out, but he slept better knowing he was there.

The cable proved to be reliable, and the Pinnacle mountains were arguably just as perilous to cross on foot, so trade began. Farming produce for the most part was sent from Penryth: fruits, wheat and wine. From Yre, they received things which had been almost priceless before salt, heavy and sharp; silk, light and soft; and furs from white bears for when the cold seasons came. It was a good arrangement; everyone benefited. Ewin had a job, got paid. The stew that Leyre cooked tasted better with salt, his bed was warmer with furs... But others benefited more. He'd seen Gower's and Vyker's houses from outside. They must have had about ten rooms and had glass in the windows. What the owners, or even the controlling Captains, must get was beyond Ewin's reckoning. Unimaginable sums to folk who had grown up trading roots and frogs.

"Those pallets aren't gonna fetch themselves," Vykers snapped, snatching Ewin from his bitter thoughts. He shook himself and, together with Iker, hurried back to the gate, leaving the balding overseer smoking his pipe and mumbling unflattering remarks.

By noon, any fascination with the Rent had worn off. Ewin was too tired. If he had thought work outside the gate had been relentless, then this was worse. Ensuring the pallets were linked up properly took the most time. And Vykers was constantly breathing down their necks, double checking everything. He'd not even been able to take a sip from the wineskin he'd smuggled in under his overalls. After a while, Ewin even began entertaining the notion that falling into the Rent might not necessarily be a bad thing.

Then there were the orders that came back through. How could salt weigh so much? By the end of the shift, he would struggle to lift a single grain of it.

The only benefit to being so busy was that the time passed swiftly. Even lunch had been eaten sat perched upon a splintered pallet, planning their next task. There was no sneaking off here. No midday nap or clandestine drink.

Before Ewin knew it, the horn was signalling the end of the shift.

"The Ivy?" Iker asked, running a dirty hand over red-rimmed eyes. Ewin nodded as enthusiastically as he was able.

"Pick up those tools before you even think about leaving!" Vykers growled from where he stood checking lists at the gate.

"I've got this," Ewin said, waving Iker off. "Get cleaned up."

"Gotcha. First round's on me then."

"I'll keep you to that," Ewin said, turning to gather the things they'd used: a knife, a pair of clippers, a glove with a hole in it and a pile of cut string. He rubbed at the base of his spine when he straightened. He would kill for a drink, but right now Leyre's cooking and his bed were more appealing. He was bending to gather what he had missed when his eyes caught on something in the Rent. There was a shape that seemed to stand just inside… Had they not pushed a pallet through properly? Or had Yre sent something which had got jammed? The thought made him groan. If Vykers saw it, they'd be called back to work…

It was already getting dark. The overseer was concentrating on a clipboard, so Ewin decided to just leave as quickly and as unobtrusively as he could. He cradled all the tools in his arms, looked once more at the Rent and froze. That wasn't a pallet. It was moving. It began to take form. A very human form.

"Kael?" he mouthed, wordlessly. Then he recalled something about a tentacle and, even though he was far beyond the white line, he stepped back. He glanced over his shoulder. Iker had left the compound, and Vykers had wandered off to speak with Nobby. Ewin turned back. The shape was clearer now, emerging as if from black water. It was a person! What the hell? He realised he was gripping the rope cutter tightly, ready to swipe at the thing. But when it stepped out, it fell to its knees. It was a boy, no older than five or six.

"Are… are you alright?" Ewin asked, which all things considered, seemed a silly thing to ask.

The boy looked up and Ewin's knees went weak. The cutter and everything else clattered to the dirt floor.

It was Yacob, red-haired, thin, pale, freckled… and he hadn't aged a day in the thirty years he had been gone.

IV

BREAKING AND ENTERING

"It was him, I'm telling you!" he hissed across the table at the Ivy.

"Yacob?" Breeg said, sharing an uncertain look with the others. "He's dead, Ew. Been thirty years."

"I know how long it's been Breeg. And I know what I saw."

"We agreed never to talk about that again," Iker said coldly.

"I don't give a shit what we agreed!" Ewin said, slamming his fist down. A few eyes, including Wane's, swung to their lamplit corner. "He's back," Ewin finished in a lower, more sinister tone.

His friends regarded him as though he were mad. Or drunk. Or both.

"You sure you're not just tired?" Breeg asked. "Maybe you should get some sleep—"

"I'm not tired. Well, I am. I'm bloody knackered. But that's not it. It was him, I swear it!"

"And he's still there?"

"Aye. Couldn't get him out. Bloody Vykers was right behind me. I told him to hide behind the tree. That we'd be back for him tonight."

"We?" Iker said, setting his beer down.

"Tonight?" Badger groaned, so tired his mug looked about to slip from his hand.

"We must. If he's still there in the morning, they'll find him. Then he'll be off up to Tregate for sure. Scientists will cut him up. Like that shark. We'll never see him again…. and we owe it him, don't we?"

There was a long silence. They didn't even meet one another's eyes. Finally, Iker cleared his throat.

"Maybe it's not for us to decide," he said. "I mean, thirty years, Ew! How can he not have changed? It must be a trick. We should warn the overseers. It's not natural."

"The bloody Rent ain't natural, but that doesn't stop us from shoving stuff into it day in, day out! We have to do something!"

"What if it's that… thing I saw?" Iker said. "We can't trust it!"

"He was our friend Iker! We can't leave him there."

No one spoke. Someone at the bar laughed. The sound seemed to come from very far away. Ewin took a drink and continued. "We have to help him. At least get him out of the Sanctum until we can figure out what has happened. Hear his story."

"Doesn't matter anyway," Breeg said. "If he's inside, nowt we can do about it."

"There must be some keys somewhere, right Iker? You've been in there the longest. You know about spares?"

Iker shrugged.

"Only keys I've ever seen are on Vyker's belt. 'Spose Gower has a set, too. Good luck with that. Even Nobby has to get their permission."

"Shit." Ewin cursed, looking into his beer. "Then we gotta get them somehow."

They knew where the overseers lived but, more importantly, they knew where they drank.

"Anyone fancy a round in the Canopy?" he suggested.

"You're kiddin'," Breeg said.

"Count me out," agreed Iker.

"Ain't got enough money for that place," Badger, rather pointlessly, added. He barely had enough money for this place.

"Come on!" Ewin said. "I can't do this alone… Look, I'll get the keys. I get caught, it's on me… I'll speak with them. Say I want to transfer back to the perimeter. That someone else would do a better job than me."

"I dunno, Ew…" Breeg said.

"We owe it to Yacob. And if it doesn't work, then so what? I'll take the blame… and you'll get a free drink." He regretted those words as soon as they'd left his mouth, but there was no taking them back. That would be a day's wages, easily. He'd worry about explaining that to Leyre later. Say he was robbed, maybe.

"Well, if yer buyin'…" Badger said, shrugging his heavy shoulders. Ewin scowled. The tight bastards.

Breeg and Iker looked at each other, ruefully shook their heads and drained their drinks.

"This goes wrong, it's on you," Iker said.

"It won't," Ewin said. "And thanks for the support. You need anything from me in the future, it'll cost you a few bloody beers."

"Forget the drink." Breeg said, lowering his head sheepishly. "You're right… we owe Yacob this much."

"Aye," Iker said, putting his face in his hands and exhaling.

"I'm still getting my beer though, right?" Badger asked as they were leaving.

The Canopy sat half a mile up the hill, on the main road out to Tregate where the houses were stone instead of wood, and the water flowing instead of stagnant. People in clean clothes stood back and eyed them suspiciously.

"How much you gotta earn for a place round 'ere?" Breeg asked.

"More than you'll ever get," Ewin said. "Now, concentrate. Follow my lead. We'll go in, get a drink. Act all natural like. Let's see what the situation is." The four friends nodded and pushed into the well-lit inn. Several heads swivelled and as many noses wrinkled. Ewin ignored them and headed straight for the bar. It was bright, busy, spotless. A minstrel plucked away at a lute in the corner, and the wooden floorboards were polished instead of covered with sawdust and mud.

"Four beers," he said.

"I'd see your coin first," the landlord said.

Ewin frowned and upended his purse on

the bar. "That good enough for you?"

The landlord grunted and scraped the coin into his hand.

Yes, he was definitely going to tell Leyre he was robbed. With these prices, it was hardly a lie. He turned to survey the bar while they waited for the drinks, attempting in vain not to look out of place. His fingernails were filthy. Breeg's trousers were held up by a length of brown string. Badger's armpit odour engulfed him even from here. Even Iker, who had worked the Sanctum for many years and was the wealthiest amongst them, looked like he'd never seen soap; his scraggy yellow hair gave him the look of a scarecrow from up at the farms.

Ewin was relieved to see the overseers were present, but equally as disquieted when he noticed Gower was on his way over.

"What in the Great bloody Rent are you doing in here?"

"Same as you," Ewin said, nodding to the beers which were still being poured.

"I know how much you fuckers get paid," he snarled. "You been skimming off the pallets, eh?"

"Nope. Just a special occasion."

"Oh yeah? One of your huts hasn't sunk into the swamp today or something?"

"No," Ewin said, feigning a smile and clocking the bunch of keys on Gower's belt. "Breeg's birthday."

"Hmpf," Gower said, losing interest. "Well, what you want? A fucking cake? Just drink up and get off. Get enough of your ugly mugs all day at work without having to see them here."

The landlord was setting the beers down one by one and Badger, wasting no time, grabbed the nearest.

"Which is another reason we came," Ewin interjected as Gower was already turning. "I appreciate the promotion, but Breeg here is a better man for the job. Since it's his birthday and all, I suggested I might have a word with you."

"And you think you're worth the extra paperwork, huh? Get out of my face. I've had enough of you lot today–"

Just then Badger dropped his drink. A timely accident. Badger would never waste beer. Neither was he the sort of fellow to come up with so impromptu a ruse. Nevertheless, it had the desired effect. It shattered on the floor, splashing Gower's clean shoes and the bottom of his well-pressed trousers. The noise died down and the minstrel stopped playing.

"You bloody idiot!" Gower spat. "These shoes are new. Take off your shirt!"

"What?" Badger asked, slack mouthed, still gaping at his hand where his beer had been.

"Your shirt! Now, or you're sacked."

Badger, slow to comprehend, did as asked. If they hadn't looked ridiculous enough before, the half-naked swamp dweller's hairy, fat belly, sealed it. "What are you waiting for? Clean 'em!" Gower snapped. Badger's face sagged, and he knelt to clean and buff the black shoes. It was a pathetic sight.

"Tomorrow you'll be on loading duty all day."

Badger could do nothing but glumly nod and wait while the overseer inspected his shoes.

"It'll do. Now, drink up and get out. I don't want to see you in here again."

The landlord nodded in agreement. "You heard him, gentlemen. Time to go."

Gower nodded to the barkeep, scowled at the miscreants and stomped back to where

Vykers, Nobby and a handful of guards sat drinking.

Badger wrung the beer from his shirt and squeezed back into the sorry, sodden garment. If anything, the beer seemed to have cleaned it. The others downed their drinks before he could even think to ask for some.

"Let's go," Ewin said, looking knowingly at Breeg.

"Yep," Breeg said, patting his pocket to the jangle of keys.

They struck directly for the gate. If Gower discovered the loss and put two and two together, they'd best not be caught there.

"It's that one," Iker said, pointing at the largest key. "Let's get this over with." Something about his tone suggested he wasn't expecting to find anything waiting for them. Except perhaps a right bollocking.

The gate gave a scandalous creak and they hurried to where the Rent shimmered like a starry night. Badger and Breeg were spellbound; after a hard day's toil, Ewin and Iker were numb to it.

"Now's not the time," Iker snapped, then

turned to Ewin. "Where the hell is he?"

Ewin whistled. Nothing happened. He began to worry the boy had fled back into the Rent. Then, slowly, a small figure stepped out from behind the tree.

"By the Great bloody Rent…" Iker said.

"Bloody hells," Breeg said. "Yacob, is that really you?"

Badger just stared, his mouth marginally more agape than normal.

"It's OK," Ewin said, signalling the boy to step forward. "You remember us, right? We've changed somewhat, but it's us!"

Yacob, still for all appearances a five-year-old boy, nodded, but did not approach.

"Come on, we'll look after you. We promise!"

But Yacob's eyes had drifted to the gate. They turned as one to see Gower striding across the gap, drunker, angrier, his musket drawn.

"You bloody scum! I knew it! I swear you'll all swing for this—" he stopped short when he saw Yacob. "Bringing your bloody sprogs in here, too? What the hell do you think this is?"

"He came out of the Rift," Breeg explained, as if all of this was simply going to go away.

It wasn't. Ewin looked around, panicked. Iker caught his eye and nodded.

"Get him, lads!" Iker cried, and they rushed the big overseer. Gower had time to pull the trigger. There was a bang and cloud of smoke as his musket went off. Badger grunted and grabbed his neck. Blood pumped from between his fingers.

"Get your filthy hands off me," Gower roared, bringing down the butt of the pistol on Breeg's skull. Breeg clasped his head and fell to the side. Badger didn't like that. He didn't like that at all. He grabbed Gower in a bear-hug and began to squeeze. The overseer grunt-ed and dropped his firearm, kicking at the big man's shins. Badger didn't seem to notice; he was losing a lot of blood. Gower gasped as they staggered and lurched closer to the Rent. They'd already crossed the white line.

"Guards!" Gower called into the night. It was no good. The guards were all in the Cano-py where he had left them. Ewin and his friends weren't the only ones breaking the rules. Bad-ger had his back against the Rent now. "Stop, you fat fuck!" Gower wheezed. "We'll both—"

"Badger, get back!" Ewin cried, reaching for his friend's arm, but the big man was drenched in blood and looked about to pass out.

"Help me!" Gower gasped, but it was too late. The black light surged and bubbled at their backs, engulfing them. Badger vanished first, then Gower, his shiny shoe the last visible thing before the Rent shimmered and they were gone.

"Shit!" Ewin cried, rushing forward, skidding to a stop a metre from the opening.

Breeg just stared from the ground, his face running red.

"Let's get out of here," Iker said, shakily.

Ewin nodded, picking up the musket and tossing it through into the Rent. Then he remembered why they had come. He turned to see Yacob staring into the void.

"Yacob! Quick, we must go!"

Yacob turned, and for the fleetest of moments it looked like he was smiling.

V

COLD STEW

"Badger…" Breeg was mumbling, once they'd scrambled away into the trees. The left side of his grubby face glistened with blood.

"Bloody idiot," Iker said. "What'd he get so close for?"

Ewin looked past his friends, scanning the wood.

"Let's focus. That shot will have been reported. Badger… Badger's gone. Let's take care of this situation before we can deal with that!"

A lantern flickered through the trees and they shrank back further.

"What do we do with him?" Breeg hissed, jabbing a blood-stained finger at Yacob, who had still not uttered a word.

"He goes with you."

"With me?!"

"Just for tonight. Look, I can't take him back to mine. I'm gonna be in enough trouble as it is."

"Ewin's right," Iker said. "We've both got families, and you…"

"And me, what?"

"You know… Come on Breeg, you know it makes sense. Just until tomorrow."

"And then what?"

"Tomorrow's tomorrow," Ewin said. "Look, we'll go to work as normal. Act as though nothing has happened. It's Harvest, everyone's too busy covering their own arses to start worrying about anyone else."

"I think when Gower doesn't turn up, Vykers will start to worry."

"So what? The fat bastard fucked off back to Tregate for all we know. We've got jobs to do, let's just do them. All of this will blow over. Yacob, you ok to go with Breeg? Tomorrow we'll talk."

Yacob nodded.

"Good," Iker said. "About time someone started explaining what the hell's going on around here."

Another lantern appeared and voices this time.

"Let's go," Ewin hissed. "We get caught out here, we're all done for. Breeg, leave Yacob in your house tomorrow; after work, we'll sort it. Ike, I'll see you at the gate first thing. Remember, just act natural. Nobody has seen us. The guards were off getting drunk, they'll get it in the necks more than us if any trouble is reported. Just carry on as normal."

"As normal," Iker repeated, hollowly.

"If you say so…" Breeg said, not nearly as convinced.

They waited for the voices to fade, nodded in solidarity and spread out into the night.

Ewin got home as stealthily as he was able, hoping Leyre was asleep. She wasn't.

"Where the hell have you been?" she said, sitting at the table, watching the door as a spider watches its web.

"Leyre!" he said, attempting to sound pleased. "I thought you'd be asleep."

"You said you'd be home early. Stew's cold and… what's wrong?"

"Nothing. Nothing's wrong." Leyre knew him too well, and even he could hear the guilt in his voice. Plus, he was sweating. Why was it so hot in here? He tried not to meet her eyes and went to examine the stew.

"Don't lie to me, Ewin. What's happened? Are you drunk?"

"No," he scoffed, hanging his jacket on the hook behind the door.

"But you have been drinking."

"Not much. Just with the lads after work. We had a big day, I'm sorry… I'll warm the stew up. You get to bed."

"Not until you tell me the truth. You're sweating. Have you been running?"

"I hurried back when I realised the time."

Leyre squinted. "You seem off."

"Well, maybe I am. It's not easy working the Sanctum! Bloody hell, what a first day! I thought they had it easier in there, but I was wrong. Actually, I think I'll go straight to bed."

"Without eating?"

"Got a big day tomorrow. I'll be glad when Harvest is over. And with what happened to Kael, Vykers is really busting our balls. Things will get back to normal soon, I promise."

"Like you promised you'd be home early?"

Ewin gave an apologetic wince. "Jenri's ok?"

"In bed. Waited up for his father. Again."

"I'll make it up to him, I promise…"

She sighed and sat back. Then her eyes drifted to his neck.

"Is that blood?"

"Erm… no."

"My gods Ewin, that's blood, isn't it? You been fighting?"

"No! I got a scrape on my neck at work this morning. I'd forgotten about it. Can we just leave it?"

"Let me take a look."

"No."

"Sit down, Ewin!"

"It's fine. I—"

"Sit down now, or I'll give you more than just a scratch to worry about."

Ewin swallowed and obeyed. Leyre stood, stooping over him.

"There's nothing here…" she said.

"What?"

"There's no scratch. Whose blood is it, Ew? Tell me now!"

Ewin sagged, put his face in his hands. He hadn't wanted this to happen… Slowly he looked up, met Leyre's eyes and sighed.

"Something… bad happened," he said.

"Bad? At work?"

"Sort of."

"Start talking!"

"Badger… he… he's gone." He actually felt a lump in his throat saying it for the first time.

"What do you mean, he's gone?"

"Into the Rent."

"Into the… What the hell? I didn't think he was even in the Sanctum."

"He wasn't… look, sit down."

"I'm fine!"

"If you want the truth, I'll tell you. But sit down."

Leyre scowled but dragged a stool over.

"You remember Yacob?"

She frowned, searching.

"Yacob, the Yacob?" It had been a long time, but everyone who had lived in Yew back then remembered the story. "I remember him, aye. Why?"

"He's… back."

"What!? But that was years ago."

"I know."

"Where has he been? How do you know it's him?"

"He's not changed Leyre! He's exactly the

bloody same!"

"Frogshit."

"It's not. He's at Breeg's."

"What the hell's he doing there?"

"We couldn't think of anything else."

"I can't believe this. Did nobody else see him? What about the overseers?"

Ewin rubbed his eyes.

"There's more isn't there?" Leyre asked. "What happened? Whose blood is that?"

"There… was an accident. Gower went into the Rent, too."

"Gower?! Your boss, Gower?"

"Yes."

"Oh gods, Ewin. What have you gotten into?"

"We went back to get Yacob, and Gower followed us. Pulled his musket. Badger got shot. The blood must have hit me."

Leyre began pacing. Pacing was always bad. "We're fucked."

"What do you mean?"

"They'll hang you, you know that? And Jenri and I will lose the house… What the fuck, Ewin?!"

"Don't worry. Nobody saw us. Nobody

else knows! And thanks for being more concerned about the house than me!"

"Don't worry?" she grabbed the nearest thing, which happened to be the ladle in the stew pot and began hitting him with it. "You stupid idiot!"

"Shh," he hissed, grabbing her wrist. "You'll wake Jenri."

"I don't care!"

"Please! The less people who know about this the better. Tomorrow we will carry on as normal. Don't wake the lad. Don't get him involved."

The words sank in and Leyre let the ladle clatter to the table. "You need to get your stories straight. Who else knows?"

"Just Breeg and Iker. And now you."

"So, this can be fixed..."

"Yes. We just need to keep calm."

"Yes. Keep calm..." she walked over to a jug of bullrush wine, poured herself a mug and took a big drink. Ewin almost asked for some, but thought better of it. "So, everything else is normal. You didn't arouse any suspicion or do anything out of the ordinary."

"No," he said, uncertainly.

Leyre clasped her head. "What did you do?"

"We may have gone for a drink in the Canopy."

"The Canopy? What the fuck were you doing up there?"

"We had to get the keys. Yacob was trapped. You know what they'd have done to him at the university. Same thing they did to that shark."

"I don't give two shits about Yacob. I was three when that happened! I give a shit about the other boy. You know… your son?!"

"I'm sorry. But I couldn't just leave him there."

"Why the hells not?! And I assume you were seen in the Canopy?"

Ewin recalled the shirtless Badger. "Probably," he said.

"Probably? You either know, or you don't!"

"Yes. We were. Vykers was there. And a couple of guards from the gate. Nobby, and Kal, I think."

Leyre rubbed a hand over her face, stood and began pacing some more. "You have to blame Breeg."

"I'm not blaming Breeg."

"He's a slob. He's got nothing to lose. They'll find the boy at his house… You and Iker, you can just claim that it was his idea."

Ewin thought about it. It had been Breeg who had taken the keys. It had been Breeg who had been wounded by the musket's butt. It was Breeg who was sheltering the boy… But no, he couldn't.

"We'll find another way."

"There's no other way."

"Let's just see what happens. I'll go to work in the morning and—"

"Oh, you'll go to work alright. I'm not losing this house for anybody."

"Just stay out of this Leyre. I don't want you doing anything."

"I'll do what's necessary. Cleaning up after you, as always."

"Don't—"

"I'll speak with Vykers. Tell him how Breeg was acting all odd. How he attacked you."

"How he what?"

Ewin's head snapped to the side as Leyre brought the ladle across in a two-handed swing.

His vision darkened and he grasped his split cheek, where the skin burned.

"You bitch," he said, examining the blood on his hand, feeling a tooth twist loose.

Leyre stood back, chewing her lip. "Yes, that ought to do it," she said, and reached once more for the wine.

VI

BUSINESS AS USUAL

Ewin's hands were sweating as he approached the gate. Nobby barely acknowledged him. He was probably worrying about losing his job.

"Sign in," he said absently. Ewin did as asked and slipped through the gate before Nobby could ask him anything.

Iker was already suited and uncoiling some rope. "Mornin'," he said.

"Mornin'," Ewin answered.

"What happened to you?"

Ewin touched his swollen face and grimaced.

"Leyre." Before his friend could smirk, he added in a hushed voice, "She found out, Ike. She knows."

"What? How?"

"She was on me as soon as I came in."

"What's she going to do?"

"Nothing. Don't worry. The plan hasn't changed."

No point in worrying him. They could hardly discuss it here, in any case.

Iker didn't look convinced. "If you say so."

"I do. Now, hadn't we better get working?"

"Aye." Iker said, still distracted. "Let's start with that pallet there. Pfff, gonna be a long day."

Ewin nodded and moved to the pallet. For once, he was actually glad of the work.

An hour passed before Vykers came stomping through the gate.

"You two!" he shouted. "Stop what you're doing and get your arses over here."

Ewin and Iker, in the process of shifting a heavy bag of beans, set it down and approached in silence.

"We're about done with Ull farm," Iker said, too keenly. "We'll be onto Tobias's next."

"I can see where you're up to," Vykers said, tapping the clipboard. "That's not why I'm here."

"It isn't?" Iker asked.

"Where the fuck are your friends? We're men down and losing time."

"Friends, sir?"

"Come on, you can't have many!" Vykers snarled. "The fat fuck you were with last night and the grubby little shit. Badger, Breeg? Those swampers!"

Now Iker's and Ewin's confusion became genuine. They had expected Badger's absence to be brought up, but Breeg's?

"Erm, I'm not sure, sir. They're not at their posts?" Iker asked.

"Why would I be asking if they were at their bloody posts?" Vykers said, furious. He swung his gaze on Ewin.

"What've you got to say for yourself? You worked outside with them."

"I… I don't know, sir. I mean, yes, we were with them last night, but I came straight here this morning. Have you checked their houses?"

"We're two men down, Gower's off sick, it's Harvest and Captain Trell is on his way down from Tregate. No, I haven't fucking checked their houses!"

Ewin looked down at his dirty boots, and fidgeted. So, they were covering for Gower, trying to keep this under wraps. He felt a glimmer of hope that they might get away with this. Unless Leyre fucked it all up, spouting uncalled for accusations.

"Then, I don't know, sorry, Sir. We've been flat out since we got here."

"Bloody useless. Well, what are you waiting for? Get back to it. You've lost five minutes and there's three more farms to get through before knock-off. If you're behind when Trell gets here, I'll dock your wages by half."

"Yes, sir. Of course," Iker said, as they both nodded and backed away.

"And if you see your sorry-arsed friends before I do, tell them they're out of a job. Should have just hired slummers. Told 'em it was a waste of time using you lot."

Just as he was finishing his tirade, Nobby came rushing down the path.

"Quick, sir. You need to see this."

"What is it? Gower?"

"No. He's still… sick," Nobby said, sparing a furtive glance for the workers.

"Then what?"

"Think I know what happened to one of 'em."

"Really? Oh, this better be good." Vykers snarled, before swivelling his head to where Ewin and Iker were watching.

"I can't hear enough work going on in here," he growled and followed Nobby out through the gate.

It wasn't until lunch that they found out what had happened. They didn't have much of a break, so signed out quickly and rushed towards Breeg's house. What they found made them stumble to a halt. A smouldering ruin of collapsed wood was all that remained. A couple of guards were picking through the wreckage.

"You!" Vykers yelled, spotting them.

"What happened?" Ewin asked, looking around.

"Looks like your friend won't be getting the sack."

"What do you mean?"

"Dead, ain't he. Burnt alive."

"Burnt? Breeg?" Ewin couldn't believe the words were coming out of his mouth. Iker stood in stunned silence at his side. "But how?"

"Was wondering if you could tell me that. Your mate have any enemies?"

"You what?"

Vyker's looked mildly annoyed at the lack of respect. "Anyone want him dead?"

"No." Iker said. "Breeg never hurt a fly. He was a good man...."

Ewin was no longer listening but searching the crowd. He caught Leyre's eye. She nodded once and slipped away. What had she done? He moved to follow her.

"Where'd you think you're going?" Vykers asked. "I ain't done with my questions."

"I'm sorry, there's something I need to—"

"Not until I'm finished. Did Breeg have a son?"

"No," Ewin said.

"That's what I thought. Yet the neighbours saw a boy fleeing the house shortly before the fire was reported. Any idea who that might be?"

"No," Ewin and Iker said.

"Bullshit! He was your friend; he was with you last night and now he's dead. Trell will be here in an hour, and the whole day is turning into a shitshow. I swear if one of you doesn't start talking soon, you'll both be off to Tregate in a cage for sabotaging operations."

Ewin swallowed, looked at Iker. His friend was just staring at the smoking ruin and shaking his head.

"Well?"

"Erm, the boy was called Yacob," Ewin said, slowly, not knowing where to begin or even less where to finish. "He was our… friend."

VII

THE FIVE FRIENDS

They'd been five friends once, then four for a long time. Now just two remained, and they sat in a stuffy office with Vykers looming over them.

"So, that's it?" the red-faced overseer said, once Ewin and Iker had finished their convoluted tale. "That's your story? That's what I'm supposed to tell the captain?"

Ewin shrugged. It had been the truth. Well, as close as they could come without mentioning the Rent and Badger's and Gower's demise. He looked at the door. He needed to get out of here and speak with Leyre. Despite what the neighbours claimed to have witnessed, he wasn't entirely convinced his wife hadn't had a hand in it. He ran his tongue over the gap where his tooth had been.

"Are you listening to me?" Vykers said, snapping his fingers in Ewin's face.

Fortunately, Iker came to his aid. "Yes. We'll do what we can to find the boy."

"Before the captain arrives!"

"Yes, erm, we'll try, sir."

"Don't try. Just do it! I've already had to stick a couple of greenhorns in the Sanctum, Gower's not around, one of your friends is still missing, the other dead, and here I am expecting a visit from my superior on the busiest day of the bloody year with nothing but ghost stories to tell him! Oh, you'll find the boy and you'll explain this whole debacle. Meanwhile, I'm another two workers down. If I miss my quota, you can be sure as shit, I'll pay it down the line threefold. Do I make myself clear?"

"Yes, sir," they mumbled.

"I said, Do. I. Make. Myself. Clear?!"

"Yes, Sir!" they answered, livelier.

"Then get out and don't come back without this boy."

They nodded, scrambled to their feet and scurried through the door.

For a moment Iker and Ewin hung outside beneath an old rotting tree, pathering on the mossy green cobbles.

"Do you think he did it?" Iker asked.

"Yacob? I... No, why would he?"

"Are we even sure it is Yacob? I mean, he's been gone thirty years, Ew. How could he just turn up like this? And why hasn't he aged?"

Ewin shook his head. Who knew how the Rents worked? If the top scientists up in Tregate's university were stumped, then asking a swamper who'd been wearing the same clothes for three days was as futile as it sounded.

"Let's just find him," Ewin said, looking around.

"Easier said than done," Iker said, scanning the gnarled trees.

"We know he fled from Breeg's; he can't have gotten far. He's a boy, for Rent's sake. Where's he gonna go? I'll start by checking round my house, you start at yours. If we find no trace, we'll meet back at Breeg's and see if we can find any clues."

"OK," Iker said. It wasn't much of a plan, but that didn't matter. Ewin just wanted to get home as soon as he could. "See you back at Breeg's," Iker shouted, but Ewin was already running.

He arrived at his door to find it locked. "Leyre!" he shouted, banging on the wood.

"Open up!"

The lock clicked and the door opened a sliver. Leyre's face appeared in the gap, but she looked right past him, into the trees, before stepping aside. "Get in, quick."

He did as asked, frowning as she quickly locked the door behind him. "What's going on?"

"You tell me," Leyre said.

"Last thing I know you're going to talk about Breeg. Now he's fucking dead!"

"It wasn't me."

"Then who was it?"

"It was Yacob."

"Bollocks. He's a boy."

"He was outside the house, just before you arrived."

"What?!" Ewin said, rushing to the shutters and peeking out.

"He's gone now. He was watching the house from the treeline, disappeared when he heard you coming."

"What did he want? Did he say anything?"

"You think I'm gonna open the door and have a chat? That's not Yacob, Ewin. Get your head out of your arse! He's been dead three decades. The boy was with Breeg, now Breeg is dead. Now he shows up here. Forgive me if I sound like I am going out of my fucking mind!"

Ewin ran a hand through his stubble, stooped to look through the shutters again, then back at Leyre. Then he noticed Jenri sitting in the corner, arms wrapped around his pulled-up knees.

"Jenri," he said, trying to soften his voice. "Sorry, didn't see you there…" He glared at Leyre. "What's he doing here?"

"I couldn't send him to school, could I? Not with a murderer on the loose."

"Is it true, Pa?" Jenri said, eyes wide. "Your old friend came back through the Rent?"

Ewin frowned at Leyre, but he only had himself to blame. The house was small, the walls flimsy. Jenri had probably heard every word of their conversation the night before.

"I… I don't know, son. We're looking into it. There has to be some sort of explanation."

"Why was he here?" Jenri asked, lip trembling. "Did he want to set fire to our house, too?"

"No, no. Of course, not. Nothing like that.

Likely he was just hungry. He's a boy. Younger than you. He's probably frightened. You have nothing to fear. Not whilst your mother and I are here."

"But how can he be younger than me, if he was your friend when you were little?"

"I don't know. Nobody knows how the Rent works, not really. I mean, they fluked the transport link up to Yre, but nobody knows what really happens if you go through unbound."

"But why is he still small?"

Again, Ewin shrugged. "Time might work differently in there. Maybe for us it was thirty years, but for him it was a minute. We don't know. We need to find him and speak to him."

"You're not going out there, are you?"

"I have no choice. I have to find him. The captain is arriving from Tregate this afternoon."

"Don't leave us," Jenri implored.

"You'll be safe with your mother." He looked at Leyre, who had a knife on the table in front of her. He'd felt what she could do with a mere ladle. And all of this was probably just some mistake anyway. "Where was he?" he asked her. "Before he disappeared?"

"Over there, to the right," she said, pointing. "Ran off round the backside of Peat Bog."

Ewin chewed his lip for a moment before his eyes widened. "Shit."

"What is it?"

"Nothing. I mean, probably. But Iker's house is that way."

"You don't think he'll try to—"

But Ewin didn't let her finish. He grabbed another knife from the drawer and unlocked the door.

"Keep it shut," he said. "Don't open it for anyone short of me or Captain Trell himself!"

"Be careful, Pa!" Jenri called. Ewin paused on the footstep, forced a smile, then turned and took off.

He ran until the air burned in his lungs. His foot sunk in the bog once and, with a sucking noise, pulled his boot off. He leaned against a tree to wiggle it back on, looked around and ran again. When he reached Iker's house, there was no sign of trouble. He hid the knife in his belt, pulled his tunic down and knocked.

Rae, Iker's wife, answered.

"Ayup, Ew. Thought you were working the Sanctum with Ike?"

"Afternoon, Rae," he said, trying to sound like he wasn't breathing so hard. "Oh, yeah, that. They had to put someone else on the job. I wasn't up to it." He indicated the split on his cheek and swollen eye.

"I can see, nasty."

"Slipped. Looks worse than it is. Look, I know he's at work, but did Iker pop back for lunch?"

"No. Ain't seen him since this morning. Are you sure you're ok? You wanna come in? Got some tea on."

"No. Thank you," he said, already backing away. "I'm sorry to have bothered you."

"Well, you see Iker, tell him to come straight home tonight. Been out three nights straight." She raised a brow letting him know who she thought was to blame.

"Will do," he said over his shoulder.

The plan had been for Iker to come back here; where the hell was he?

Ewin began backtracking. He stumbled to a halt at the edge of Peat Bog where a series of footprints meandered. Large and small. He followed them, his knuckles white about the knife's hilt. Abruptly, the large footsteps stopped, and the small ones led away and vanished where the mud turned to leaves. He looked around, noticing the bog itself had been disturbed. Something had been thrown in. His eyes fell upon a shape in the reeds. As the details took form a gasp escaped him. He stumbled closer until his feet began to sink, sweat running down his back. Iker's upturned face emerged from the bog with mouth, nostrils and eyes crammed full of the foul black sludge.

Ewin staggered back and clung to a tree to stop himself from falling. A twig snapped behind him, and he spun, but there was no one there. A moorhen fluttered from the rushes, making him flinch. He had to get out of here, back to where there were people… He clasped the knife and ran.

VIII

SECRETS LIKE SPLINTERS

"You alright?" Wane asked, from behind the bar. Ewin nodded. Everyone he met seemed to ask him that today.

"Drink," he stammered.

"Erm, ok. Bit early, int it?" Wane said with a frown. "Brown or pale?"

"Don't care. Which is strongest?"

"Pale."

"That. Make it two."

Wane arched a brow, but did the honours.

Ewin finished it and slammed it down before the second one was ready.

"Ha," Wane said. "Been that kind of day, has it?"

"Aye," Ewin said, accepting the second mug.

"Shouldn't you be working?"

"Day off."

"At Harvest?"

Ewin shot Wane an angry mind-your-own-business glare. The friendly barkeep waved a dishcloth apologetically.

"You're normally with the others, that's all…" he shrugged and left Ewin to drink his second beer in peace.

But there was no peace in Ewin's mind, for his thoughts churned and tumbled. Across the past few days and back over the last thirty years. To what had happened that day… It had been a prank. A joke. Five boys playing. Nobody had known… He shuddered, took another drink and stared off unseeingly across the empty tavern. Yacob had been the smallest of them, the one they left out when there was only four of something. The last to get an invite to an adventure. The one who was made to stand close to the glowing crack in the tree… The one the boys had jostled and shoved…. Whose fault had it been? He could hardly recall. He'd blanked it from his mind. He'd been five for fuck's sake. They couldn't have known what would happen! But the guilt had been there, buried like a splinter all his life. They'd made up a story to tell their parents, about how Yacob had been angry and entered the tree in a sulk. They'd agreed to never speak of it again, and for thirty years they hadn't. Yacob's death was quickly overshadowed by the opening of a new Rent in Yew. The four boys grew up in a place that hardly resembled that distant time.

The door flew open and Ewin almost leapt from his seat. It was Vykers and his ruddy face was redder than normal.

"There you fucking are!" he yelled. "I might have known it. Oh, you're sacked for this. I want you out of your shitty little house by the end of the day. Unless you can give some answers. Where's your lanky friend? Where's this boy?" Vykers grabbed Ewin's filthy shirt and pushed him up against the bar so that his stool clattered to the floor and beer smashed between his feet.

"Dead." Ewin gasped, struggling to stay upright. Vyker's grip slackened a little.

"You what? Who's dead?"

"Iker."

"Iker's dead?" Ewin could but nod. "How? Where?"

"Peat Bog."

"Bloody hell. Is this connected to the fire?" Ewin nodded.

"And your other friend, the fat one. You

know what happened to him too, don't you?"

Ewin nodded again.

"Speak, man, before I shoot you here and now!" Vyker's hand trembled over his musket and, although being shot without a trial seemed farfetched, Ewin was not about to test it.

"When we got the boy from the tree, Badger fell in—"

"What? How? Wait… it was you, wasn't it? You bastards. We heard the shot. What've you done with Gower?" Now the musket was in his hand and levelled at Ewin's chest, quivering. "Tell me, you son of a bitch. You kill him, too?"

Ewin considered his answer as Wane slipped out of the backdoor.

"It was an accident. He shot at Badger, they fought. It was over so—"

"You expect me to believe a boy did all of this? It was you, wasn't it, you piece of swamp shit!"

"Me—?"

Vykers raised his musket and shot up at the ceiling. A shower of dust came down. "You're the only one left. There's no sign of this boy. And even if he exists, you expect me to believe he emerged from the tree? That he was capable of killing Gower and all the other scum friends of yours? Oh no…" Vyker's face was flushed, his finger on the trigger, twitching.

At just that moment the door swung inward and a sweaty Wane filled the door.

"In there!" the barkeep said, breathlessly. He stepped aside and a man in the cleanest clothes Ewin had ever seen stepped into the room. His shoes shone in the dull light, his buckles and buttons gleamed.

"Stand down, overseer," he said.

Vyker's face paled as he swung to face the man. "Captain! Oh, thank the Rent you're here—"

"What's going on?"

"This fucker killed Gower. Tried to sabotage Harvest."

The captain paused, his lip twisting as he examined the overseer's sweating face, the spittle on his quivering lip. "And you thought to come in here and shoot him?"

"What? No, I was just—"

"Give me your gun."

"Why? I—"

"Give me your gun now, or I'll take everything from you."

Vykers hesitated, bowed his head and then handed his musket to Captain Trell.

"Now, we're going to have a little sit down and calm ourselves. Then you are both going to tell me everything. Is that clear?"

Ewin and Vykers looked at each other, then back to the captain. They both nodded.

"Good," Trell said, glancing over at Wane. "Fetch me a drink."

"Of course, sir. Brown or pale?"

"Just water," the captain said flatly. "And if it tastes even remotely of this fetid swamp, I'll have this place burned to the ground, too."

Wane swallowed and disappeared to try to track down the closest thing to clean water such a dive in Yew might possibly possess.

IX

BY MURDER SEALED

Captain Trell didn't utter a word until both men had finished their accounts. He did look briefly towards the bar after taking a sip of his water and gave the faintest of grunts, to which Wane's shoulders sagged in relief.

"Is that all?" he said, once they were done. If the captain was fazed by anything he had heard, his stony, grey-moustached countenance hid it well.

"Yes, sir," they said, simultaneously.

"Good. Then, Vykers, you've a job to do."

"Yes, sir."

"I'll be doing my rounds a little later than planned, but hope to find all to schedule, despite the utter circus you seem to be running around here. We'll speak later, and I'll also be wanting the names of all the guards who were supposed to be on duty that night."

"Of course, sir."

"Oh, and I shouldn't need to remind you that not a word of any of this goes any further, should I, overseer."

"No, sir. I'll keep it to myself," Vykers said glumly. He left the Ivy looking like a broken man. A man who was probably on his way back up to Tregate once Harvest was done, and whose pension would be significantly less than he had been planning.

Once he was gone the captain sat regarding Ewin in silence for some time. Ewin shifted, glanced towards the door.

"Oh, you're free to go, too," Captain Trell said. Ewin frowned and began to rise. "Once—" he said, making Ewin freeze and sink back down "—we clear something up."

The drink Ewin had come in for to calm his nerves was by the by now. Almost being shot and then interrogated by a captain of Tregate had just added varying spices to what was already the weirdest and worst day of his life.

"This friend of yours. You sure it's him?"

"I don't know. Looks like him."

"Bring him to me."

"But—"

"This," Trell said, spreading his clean-nailed hands, "needs to go away. Word gets out and it'll be hell. Your account will be proved or disproved at the university but, in the mean-time, we've got an operation to keep running. If the Rent gets shut down for even a day during Harvest, the financial loss would be… unfortu-nate. I may have the power to save you today, but lose the crown money and you'll have your guts pulled out slowly with a hook. Do I make myself clear?"

Ewin swallowed and nodded.

"Good. Find the boy and bring him. I'll be lodging at the Canopy. You have until mid-night. And try not to die, as seems to be the order of the day. Do this, and I can't promise you a pardon, but I might be able to go some way to see that your wife and boy avoid any repercussions."

Ewin nodded again. There really were no words for what he was feeling.

"Very well. You may go."

"Thank you, sir."

The captain waved him away as though la-zily dispersing a cloud of gnats.

Ewin squinted at the low sun that peeked through the swamp's stunted trees. A small crowd watched him from across the lane, having likely heard the shot and rumours of the captain's arrival. He bowed his head and made his way home as quickly as he could.

If it hadn't been for Jenri or the fact that he'd never been more than ten miles from Yew in his life, running might have been tempting.

No. This was his mess. He'd started this. Long ago, in another life. And if there was the smallest chance of being pardoned and that his son and wife might keep a roof over their heads, then finding and capturing Yacob was his only chance. He checked the knife in his belt and rushed down the lane. Old folks tutted and shook their heads at his truancy; children stopped to stare. Ewin ignored them all. His reputation was not as important as his life.

It was gloaming when he reached his house; lamplight flickered through the closed shutters. He went to bang on the door, but it stood ajar. His breath caught in his throat.

"Leyre?" he called, brandishing the knife and peering inside. There was no answer.

"Leyre!" he repeated. "Jenri! Are you there?"

Nothing.

He took a deep breath and kicked the door so that it swung inward. The pot was boiling, the lamp was lit… but there was no one there. He noticed the bedroom door was shut. He crept over and pressed his ear against the wood, listened. He had to hold his breath to hear over his ragged breathing.

"Is anyone there?"

Still no answer. He closed his eyes, said a quick prayer then booted the door open.

Something hit him in the face, clawing, flapping. He let out a startled cry, stumbled backwards over a stool and down to the hard boards with a grunt. The crow flapped around the rafters for a moment before knocking over a vase and escaping through the door. Lying on his back, heart thumping, Ewin gave a nervous laugh. He clambered up and moved towards the bedroom. Shit, the window was open.

Then he noticed a torch in the trees. He leant out.

"Leyre! What in the Great Rent are you doing?"

She rushed over. "Jenri's gone, Ew!"

"What?"

"I heard a noise from his room. When I entered, his window was open and he was gone."

"Why would he leave? He was terrified."

"I don't know. I heard voices. I thought he was talking to himself, you know, how he does. But I think it was someone at the window."

"Yacob," Ewin said, feeling a chill on his neck.

"Perhaps they just wanted to play," she said hopefully.

"Iker's dead," he said, his words sounding hollow.

"What? Iker!?"

"Drowned in the bog."

"But Badger, Breeg…" she trailed off and looked at him. "Are you next?"

"I don't know."

"But why? Isn't he like five? And what's he want with Jenri?"

Ewin shrugged. "To get to me, I guess. And who knows what the hell happened to him in that void. I don't think he's five anymore."

"Where've they gone? Think Ew!"

"I…" But he knew in that instant where they had gone. Back to where all of this had started… "Stay here!" he yelled, already heading back through the house.

"Where are you going?" she called after him.

"Get inside. Lock the door and close the window. Wait for Jenri; he might come back."

"But Ew—"

He didn't hear anymore; he was out the door, leaping through rustling leaves and squelching mud, his pulse thundering and imagination running riot.

He arrived at the gate just as it was being locked. He hung back in the trees, catching his breath, watching. Nobby was there, Vykers too. Captain Trell was talking to both of them. He did not look pleased. He gestured towards the guard hut, and the two reprimanded, soon-to-be-former employees walked towards it with their heads bowed. The captain followed them like an executioner might the condemned. Under other circumstances Ewin would have taken pleasure in that. Not tonight. A movement at the gate caught his eye. It was Jenri and the slightly shorter Yacob. They were opening the gate. Fuck. They had Gower's keys. He'd thrown them off into the woods that night, and Yacob had seen him do it. The two boys entered, closed the gate behind them, but did not lock it. Sparing a glance for the hut where the captain's stern voice could be heard, Ewin ran at a crouch and slipped inside the Sanctum.

He had only been a minute behind them, but when he arrived only one figure remained silhouetted against the swirling Rent.

"Jenri!" Ewin cried. "Get away from there now!" He grabbed his son by the shoulder and pulled him back away from the vortex, dropping to a knee to look him in the eyes.

"Are you ok? What did he do to you?!"

"Nothing, Pa." Jenri said. "He just wanted to play. Said this is where you used to come when you were little."

"It's not safe here," Ewin said, looking around. "Where did he go?"

Jenri shrugged and pointed towards the Rent.

Ewin took a steadying breath.

"We must get home," he said. "We'll talk there. Your mother's worried sick."

"OK," Jenri said, then suddenly pointed over Ewin's shoulder towards the Rent. "He's back!"

Ewin spun, raising the knife as the small figure rushed towards him. The blade hit Yacob in the throat. The boy cried out and fell to the ground, clutching the wound, gurgling.

Ewin stood back, his hand trembling. "I'm sorry," he said. "For everything. But you will not hurt my family!"

"No. I won't," Jenri said from behind him.

Ewin turned to see his son regarding him with a sad smile. "Jenri? Why are you smiling?"

But even as he finished his sentence, Jenri's face shifted and it was Yacob that stood before him.

Ewin spun to see the pale, lifeless face of his son staring up from the mud.

"No. No!!!" he cried, whirling upon Yacob. "How? Why?"

"You know why."

"It was an accident. A game. We were five! We didn't know the Rent would open up! We didn't...." Ewin began to sob, his shoulders shaking.

"The accident has been forgiven. But the Rent... That is something I cannot abide." As Yacob finished his sentence, his eyes glimmered amber.

Ewin blinked. "You're not Yacob."

"Does it matter?"

Ewin splayed his bloody hands. "Yes, it fucking matters! Who are you? What do you want!"

"I just told you. I'm here to close this Rent."

"But… I don't understand. If that's all you want, why kill us?"

The boy smiled. "I don't make the rules. I just do what I must. The Rent was opened with murder, and so too must it be sealed."

"But you yourself are a murderer!"

"Who have I murdered?"

"Everyone, you fucker!" Ewin snarled, leaping forward and stabbing the knife down. The boy moved to the side and was suddenly behind him, his back against the Rent.

"I wouldn't try that again," he warned, almost playfully. "Now think clearly. Badger was shot by your overseer. We saw it ourselves, right here. Your friend Breeg went home, got drunk, knocked the lamp over. I didn't wake him. I left him there in the burning house, but I didn't cause it. Iker ran from me. Right into that bog. I watched as he called for help, tried to claw his way out. I didn't interfere. So, you see, my hands are clean."

"Bullshit! My son's death is on you!"

"Who is holding the knife? Whose hands are covered in blood?"

Ewin looked down and let the blade slip to the floor. When he looked up his vision was blurred with tears.

"But the Rent is still open. I live. You've failed!"

The boy with the amber eyes smiled. "I must go," he said. "I've much to do. This has been… interesting." He stepped back towards the Rent.

"Wait!" Ewin called out, but the boy did not heed him. As the black light bubbled about him, his shape became not that of a boy, but of a man. The black puddle swirled until all that remained were two points of amber light. "Come back!" Ewin cried, rushing toward the vortex and skidding to a stop at the threshold.

No! That was what the fucker wanted. For him to fling himself into the void and end it. Well, he'd not win so easily.

Suddenly, he heard a gasp behind him, and wheeled to see Leyre. Her mouth hung open as she stared from the Rent to her husband and finally to the small body on the ground.

"Jenri!" she cried, rushing forward, dropping to her knees to cradle the boy's head in her lap. When she stood her eyes smouldered.

"Leyre. Wait! I can explain—"

She leapt screaming upon her husband, bringing the knife down again and again.

Ewin gasped and writhed, but soon stopped struggling. He twisted to face the tree and, as the world and Rent faded, two amber eyes blinked and were gone.

Darkwhale

J.E. Hannaford

Oh, the rare old whale, mid storm and gale
In her ocean home will be
A giant in might, where might is right,
And Queen of the boundless sea.

Tulak's water spout showered Tom in sparkling, icy gems. He entwined his fingers through the harness, his knuckles white with determination, and took the deepest breath that he could. He *had* to make it up in one piece this time. The entire town had turned up on the cliff-top and now stood, a collective of antici-

pation all watching, waiting for him to fail –
again.

Tom Surfborn, the boy who couldn't speak
to whales… He'd heard the chatter behind
hands and the murmurs all through his youth
and now, as boys in their eighteenth and nine-
teenth seasons vied for the right to ride, he
would undertake the trial again.

His father had passed first time, and his
father's father the second. In the remembered
history of his family, no one else had needed five attempts to pass their Whalerider test.
Five seasons of pointing fingers and whispers,
of hints and suggestions that he should head
inland and try his luck with the hogs instead.
Not that he had anything against the Hogrid-
ers. They were fierce and brave, mounted on
beasts of war, defending the edge of the marsh-
es against the outside world. But the Surfborns
had always been Whaleriders. Until him.

Water pressed down on him now, the pressure building as they descended, and the water darkened as light struggled to penetrate the
depths. Tom's lungs ached with desperation to
release a breath, but he would hold on – until
he fainted if he had to. Tulak levelled out and

cruised along the sea bed, rolling from side to side, her great flukes powering them through the water. Tom looked around, trying to spot anything recognisable in the darkness; a fish passed close, fins grazing his arm in a gentle caress before speeding off into the darkness once more.

Bubbles he couldn't hold any longer escaped in a narrow stream from Tom's lips. If Tulak didn't rise to the surface soon, it would be five failures.

Until he showed he could stay aboard for the test dive, he'd not be allowed to bond his own calf, and he'd never be considered a true Surfborn. Tom kept a tight grip on Tulak… his fingers were slipping. It was over. Again. His heart sank as he accepted that he had to release the handles.

A high-pitched whistle carried through the water and Tulak began to rise. So fast – too fast. Maybe he *could* do it. Waverider save him – if she leapt and breached, Tom wasn't sure he had enough strength left to hang on. Light rippled through the water, brighter and brighter as they rose. Tom allowed himself to exhale faster, easing the burning pressure in his chest, willing Tulak upwards, desperate for air.

They broke the surface, water running from their bodies, whale and man, if not in harmony, at least still together. Waverider be blessed! He'd done it.

Tom let out a whoop which died on his lips as he realised that only a single person had watched him surface.

The village was almost silent. Water lapped against the whale-boards and the shore. Tulak's flukes splashed behind him, but far above in the sky a crackling noise like a glacier breaking apart filled the air. He searched the cliff top for his family. They faced away from him, staring upward.

Only Neana, Matriline of the Pod, looked his way. She offered Tom a toothless grin as she scratched her whale's twisted silver horns.

"Well done, Boy, it's about time!"

"Thank you, Neana," he replied. "Thank you, Tulak."

He raised his gaze skyward. Instead of the flickering red and purple aurora that decorated spring skies like sparkling gems, a rent in the fabric of the sky yawned across the horizon. Its edges glowed like the evening sun, while the gap in the middle was darker than a midwinter night. The air was eerily quiet. No gulls shouted their raucous haggling over scraps, and the pod of whales floated in silence around the trio on the whale-boards. Each individual's horned head was raised, intelligent eyes joining those of every other living thing to stare at the rift.

"That was a long dive but, for now, we'd best go join the rest. That sky is a bad omen if ever I saw one," Neana said.

They walked up the steep hill, the cobbles slippery under Tom's whale-seed oil covered feet. Rather than supporting Neana, he found that it was her strong grip that stopped his otherwise inevitable slide back to the whale-boards. A life on the whales gave you a grip like no other. His shark-leather suit was loose and flapped as he walked; only bonded riders were allowed their own. He tugged it to a better position to walk with and, despite the looming rift in the sky, Tom found himself grinning. Bonded riders like he would be soon. He ran to his family as they reached the top.

"Did you see?" he asked. "I did it, I passed."

His father frowned. "Did Pod Chief Farran give you the blessing of the Waverider? No.

Then you haven't passed. And, if you didn't pass this time, I'll not be letting you fail again and bringing our name even further down the pod rankings."

"Neana saw, she'll vouch for me," he said, trying to remain calm, his fists clenched behind his back. His own father denying him? He had been certain of his final acceptance. Tom's head hurt with the unfairness of it. Neana wasn't with him now. He searched the crowd and spotted her in conversation with Farran Whale-singer, the Pod Chief. She pointed back at Tom. Farran shook his head. Neana frowned and stomped away to join a group of other Whaleriders.

He caught his mother staring after her, her lips tightly pinched together. At least she had seen the exchange. His father stared stubbornly at the sky, as though his growling and grimacing would cause the rift to seal itself back up. If it knew what was good for it, the rift should try, Tom thought grimly.

Hours after its appearance the rift hung, unchanging, across the horizon, the glow at its outer edge pulsing gently. Folk had drifted back to their homes; slowly at first then, as hunger bested curiosity, fires bloomed, and smoking hearths sent their signal of apathy for the new arrival skyward.

In contrast to the lazily spiraling smoke, the clan elders were a whirlwind of action. Messengers bearing the carved horns of the First Whale knocked on each door, a sign for the whole clan to gather at the boards.

Whalport's clan hut was, as with all the other buildings, woven from dried kelp. Each summer the residents gathered to re-weave it when the riders brought the harvest in. Its matted walls stank in the rain and the huddle of leather-clad Hog-riders awaiting their arrival wore open expressions of disgust.

Tom doubted their town smelled a whole lot better, but the two societies needed each other. In this semi-frozen land they called home, the residents of Runof Springs relied on the sea for their food, and the residents of Whalport relied on them for supplies of whale-seed. The rich fats in the underground stores of the plant provided a nourishing, if bitter, food source in lean times, and the thick oils of the seed pods were used to coat Whaleriders to keep them warm on long dives.

Every now and then, a ship would visit Whalport, trading leather and fine needles, rare treasures from the distant south, for whale-seed roots and pods. Tom often wondered where they took them. What other whale-riding societies were far beyond the mountains and the horizon? Maybe, when he had his own whale, he'd find out.

The harsh tone of the Sounding Bell rang, and quiet murmuring faded to silence. Farran climbed to one of the higher rocks while the Passel leader clambered up to stand alongside him. She was taller than Farran, her muscles bunched with tension, and she kept glancing upwards.

"May the mounts of ocean and land be guided by the hand of the Waverider, may his amber-eyed soul fill our seas with bounty and our borders with peace. May we live with nature and never set against it," Farran intoned, opening the meeting

"Waverider keep us safe," the entire hall replied.

Farran gestured to the Passel Leader. "Fierce-tusk has brought us news relating to the umm… happenings of today. I think it would be better if she told her tale than I." He stepped down, leaving Fierce-tusk alone.

She scanned the room, her eyes resting on the older members of the clan longer than the rest, eventually settling on the trio of Matrilines in the front row: Neana, Vrex and Rona.

"This is not the first rift," she began.

Rippling whispers flowed around the room, but she raised a gloved hand. Charisma dripped from every word of her intense narration as she leant into the story, drawing her crowd in. It was easy to see how she had become a leader.

"On the last full moon, when the sky rippled with promise, I led a patrol along the edge of the glacier, towards the meltwater channel. A late snow had coated the top of the ice, and we wanted to be sure that all was as it should be. We left, armed with picks and enough food for several days. The way was difficult; deep snow packed around our hog's hooves and there was little grazing available. We are used to these conditions in winter, but this late into spring…" She paused and shrugged.

"The first rift was small. It opened ahead

of us, and we scrambled to keep the hogs under control. It smelled strange – almost hot. Around it, the ground melted. Snaggle-tooth poked a stick into the blackness and, when she withdrew it, the stick was hot. Not just a little warm, but it smoked, almost igniting. There was noise. Voices in strange languages shouted. We prepared to fight. Then, as suddenly as it appeared, it vanished." She clapped to emphasise the action and children at the front jumped.

Fierce-tusk leant closer to her audience, her gestures becoming more expansive.

"The second one was a few days later, at the base of the meltwater stream. We'd cleared an ice blockage and were resting the hogs for the return journey when the sky split at the top of the glacier. A huge bird emerged, its wings generating clouds of snow as it took off. I'm certain some went back through the rift, while much more of it landed near us. The bird circled down to our level. It had bright copper eyes."

Neana gasped.

"It gets stranger, Prime Matriarch," Fierce-tusk continued. "It landed behind the glacial edge. I ran towards it, for surely a copper-eyed creature can only be a sign from the Waverider himself?"

The entire hall was nodding now; Tom could hear people nearby quietly agreeing. The blanket of fear had lifted, and the hall was less grim and dark than it had felt upon their arrival.

"When we got there, no bird met us. Instead, we faced a copper-eyed war-hog."

Tom felt the hairs on his arms standing up, his heart rate increasing. Was the Waverider reborn? Had he come to save them again? What great threat loomed that was so huge their god chose to make a personal appearance?

"Did you bring this hog with you?" Farran interjected.

Fierce-tusk shook her head. "Not exactly… It ran towards Whalport, and we pursued, arriving here just as that…" – she gestured upward – "split the sky. We lost sight of it, but the tracks continued right to the edge of the town."

"Waverider is *here*?" a child's voice said, moments before the entire hall broke into uproar.

Tom's ears, still sensitive from his earlier dive, rang and the pain increased until he had no choice but to get away. He edged toward the exit as shouting intensified. The noise was still loud outside but, free of the hall's confines, he could relax slightly. From here, he could see the Whale-boards. Spouts of water rose erratically amongst the pod. Out of habit, Tom counted the whales. Five, six… Tulak, seven… his father's whale, Ghost, the palest of them all, eight… he ticked each off. There were twelve whales. No one was missing. He smiled; one day soon there would be thirteen. Another spout of water rose and a dark grey whale surfaced, its horns twice the size of any other whale in the pod and shining with a coppery metallic sheen.

Tom ran.

Behind him he heard someone call his name. He didn't stop; he slipped and slid the length of the boards to get closer to the whale. It surfaced again, watching him with copper eyes.

Tom gasped for breath, falling to his knees in front of the huge creature. It swam towards him, raising its beaked nose level with his face and regarded him with intelligence.

"Come," Waverider said. "Ride with me."

Other feet slapped against the boards now,

closing in on Waverider. Tom took a deep breath and clambered aboard. Fully clothed, with no whale-seed oil and no harness, he placed his trust completely in his god.

The moment he was aboard, Waverider flipped his fluke and they leapt away from the whale-boards. Behind him, the whaleriders scrambled for their harnesses whilst wriggling into sharkskin suits. Swearing carried across the water as straps wouldn't tighten fast enough and whales spouted in their frustration.

"This is why you learn without a harness first… and why you never rely on one." Neana rode Tulak as Tom sat on Waverider: she was bare of harness and sat effortlessly. Several other riders, all of the Matriline, emerged behind her.

"Where is Waverider taking us?" Neana asked.

Tom shrugged. "I don't know! He just told me to climb on, so I did. I was hardly going to say no."

Neana chuckled, her gums exposed as she whooped with delight, exuding an energy that belied her years. "I do love an adventure. We haven't had anything exciting happen around here for way too long. Just harvesting kelp and an occasional skirmish with boats that get too close. Now, adjust your weight back a little… yes like that, onto your seat-bones more. Good."

"Neana, you have no weapons with you?"

"Pah.… Who needs bits of metal?" She glanced behind her. Tom followed her gaze to see the last whales leaving the whale-boards in the distance.

"Look, boy." She held out her hand and a ball of white fire floated above her palm.

"Magic?" Tom frowned. "But we haven't seen magic in our land for hundreds of years."

Neana gestured up at the rift overhead. "You ride Waverider himself, under a sky rent with power. Is it so hard to believe?"

She had a good point.

"No, but–"

"What would the Pod Chief do if he knew it still existed? Travel to new lands? Start more wars? No, Boy, it's safer to keep any power concealed. Vrex can truly speak to whales – not just sense their feelings, Rona can hold her breath longer than any whalerider I've ever seen. Has to be magic in that."

"What about my father?"

Neana snorted. "He has a strong grip and big lungs. He's nothing special. Sorry, Boy."

Tom glanced back. The rest of the pod were swimming hard and would catch them soon.

"How will I fight?" he asked her, certain that whatever the threat ahead was, it would require battle.

"I don't know," Neana said. "But Tulak believes you're special or there's no way she'd have let you test five times and she's always right. Only in the heat of battle are horns grown and our truth forged."

It was an old saying, but for now, it was one Tom could hold onto. He checked his weight was balanced and held tightly to Waverider's horns as the other riders joined them. The pod surged ahead as one.

Whale song filled his ears as Waverider dived, louder than he had ever imagined it. Its power surged through his soul, an undulating melody led by Waverider and harmonised by every whale in the pod. Tom wanted to join in, to sing with them. He envied Vrex the ability to speak with the whales. Maybe she would tell him what they sang about, if he could ask her quietly. They surfaced, then dived over and over. Each dive deeper and longer as the whales increased their speed, heading for their unknown destination, led by the god of their people.

Day turned into night. They travelled now by starlight and the eerie golden light cast by the huge rift overhead. Tom and Neana led the way, their whales side by side. He'd seen his father and Ghost try to reach the front, but the Matriline had boxed him in. He was glad the trio of women were keeping that distance intact. Whatever mission they were on had to be more important than any argument his father wanted. He was sure there would be one soon enough.

In the distance, another light grew larger. Another rift, near water level. Water rushed from it, red tinged and illuminated by the frayed edges of the rift. The Whales began to slow – all except Waverider. Tom was carried onward, directly towards the churning waters pouring into the ocean.

Percussive sounds of an enormous collision vibrated through the water. Behind him, the pod struggled to persuade their whales any nearer. This close to the rift, a gentle humming dominated over the sound of falling water. Waverider stopped, and Tom stared through in amazement. The sky on the far side was bright yellow, and the waves green and thick, sluggish and soup-like. The level of the ocean was higher.

Heat rolled out of the open rift, much as the Hog-riders had described. Three monstrous creatures swam their way. Enormous scaled plates covered their bodies and armour-plated eyeballs studied him as they closed the gap. Each of the giant creatures had a spine as thick as Tom's leg protruding from its back – like a fin, but more deadly. Huge fangs framed a mouth bearing more resemblance to a pair of horizontal blades than a row of teeth. They fought over a huge and strange carcass floating across the rift itself. Tom realised that its sheer bulk was the only thing that stopped it falling with the water. Each collision pushed it further towards his side and the red waves of blood pouring over it stained the sea.

Where the waters from the rift fell, steam spiralled upwards. One monster turned directly towards him, immense waves trailing from either side of its head as it swam directly at the rift. Tom held tightly to Waverider's horns, praying that the magic of the god would protect him.

At the last minute, instead of battering the corpse, the creature powered up from the water, its huge bulk soaring over and through the rift.

Waverider dived.

Tom gripped the horns tighter as the chemical-rich waters stung his eyes. He closed them, trusting that he would be brought through this in one piece, for surely he hadn't been brought all the way here just to die. What did Waverider need from them?

They emerged on the far side of the rift. The water was still tinged pink but now the flow was moving away from him; from this side the rift was darkness, like the one in the sky above. A speckled starlight gleamed from within it.

Screams carried on the air. That giant monster was attacking the pod!

"Go back!" Tom urged Waverider, but he did not move. Instead, he waited, floating behind the rift.

Tom pulled at the gilded horns. "You didn't

bring us all out here just to die… you're Waverider. Do something, make some magic. Send those creatures back." He kicked at the whale, furious that their god had led people to their deaths. Stubbornly, Waverider remained far away from what sounded like a frantic battle.

"If you won't help – then take me back – let me help them."

It was a foolish idea. As the words left his mouth, Tom knew it. He screamed and dived off the whale's back. Waverider turned his head to study Tom.

"Close the rift," he said, then shook his great body. As the water subsided, a single gilded horn floated towards Tom. Waverider gazed at him through the copper-coloured eyes of a black goose beating his wings and running across the ocean's surface as he gathered speed, then Waverider took to the skies to circle overhead.

The horn was sinking.

Tom took a deep breath and dived after it. It might have magic – even if it didn't, it was a weapon and he had none.

The sea glowed the colour of Waverider's eyes as the rift illuminated the blood-threaded water. Tom gripped the horn and kicked upwards, back towards his pod – whale-less once more. He surfaced near the rift, the hanging corpse hiding him from the immediate sight of the enormous predator which had scattered his pod. He climbed onto the stinking corpse. He scrambled to his feet and, brandishing Waverider's tusk, he shouted to any who could hear him.

"Waverider has gone; he bid us close the rift."

"We guessed that would be a good idea, Boy. Waverider has probably gone for more help. We need to keep these creatures confined or they will eat our seas empty," Neana called back

"Bloody idiot, why didn't you ask him what we were doing before rushing off? Then we could have prepared better, brought more supplies," his father shouted, between dodging an attack from a smaller creature, another unfamiliar fish-like monster. Much like the first, this one had an enormous set of armour plates on its head but was without the spined fin.

From his vantage Tom could see the huge monster rising through the water. "Neana!" he called. "It's below you!"

She moved Tulak quickly, and as the beast surfaced its mouth opened wider than Tom though possible – wide enough that it could have almost fit Tulak's head into one bite.

Neana had clearly had enough. She glanced at the Pod Chief, engrossed in his own battle with the smaller monster, then sent balls of white flame spinning into the open maw of the bigger creature. It thrashed around, flipping its head from side to side in pain, then swung away, aiming for another whale, Farran's.

This time, it didn't miss. The huge jaws clamped down on Farran's whale, biting a chunk out of its side. Farran Whale-singer was thrown from his mount. He grappled with a fluke, attempting to scramble up from the water, but his whale was in so much pain that even their bond was not enough to keep her near the monster. Farran was left in the wake of a retreating, injured whale. He raised his weapon and aimed it at the beast's softer flanks. He tried to stab at it but, without a solid position, it merely pushed him backwards.

Another rider stabbed at the smaller one, successfully wounding it, then reached down to pull Farran aboard. Together they raced after the injured whale. With a clear shot at the injured monster, Neana sent a barrage of white fire until the charred stench of burning fish filled the air and it sank below the surface.

The big one had dived again. It rose below a smaller member of the pod and snapped the whale in two, taking a whalerider in the mouthful. Blood sprayed into the water, and Vrex cried out in shock.

The corpse Tom balanced on jolted. He had been so absorbed by the battle that he'd forgotten that the creature was one of many trying to break through.

Another collision shook him from his feet. He hung on to the nearest part of the body, the heavy bones ridged and grooved, unlike any fish he'd ever seen. This creature blocking the rift was another monster fish – they were eating their own. He poked and prodded the body as he worked along its length, checking below him for the large one's return. The corpse was wedging the rift open. If others had closed on their own after Waverider appeared, then to close this one, the corpse would need to be shifted.

Hand over hand, he worked along the length of its body, careful to keep hold of Waverider's golden horn. Bony plates made for great hand holds and he climbed along it as he would a cliff. The creature's jaw was close to the edge of the rift. If they pushed in, maybe it would twist the whole thing free.

Before they tried, he needed to know if there was any way that they could damage the one rampaging around the pod. Neana was firing bolts of blue magic when it surfaced, and the other whaleriders were stabbing at it with weapons. They had it partially confined now, the whales dancing from its jaws in intricate moves, and the sound of whale song filled the night air.

He scrambled onto the dead monster's head, sitting astride it to edge closer to the eye.

Rona's whale dived.

Neana danced Tulak around, the smaller whales able to outmanoeuvre the larger cumbersome monster fish.

On the far side of the rift, another giant lined up for attack. Tom grabbed as tightly as he could. It went for the softer, rear portion of the corpse but, if they kept battering it like that, the shoal would soon push it free. Where a group of fish that large arrived, there would be devastation. If they bred… It didn't bear thinking about. Tom tucked his feet into a huge ledge which curved over the crest of the beast's head and reached towards its eye socket. While it appeared, armour plated – if he pushed at it – if he shoved it…

He picked up the horn and stabbed downward; it went in. He felt a small wavering hope, tempered with a heavy dose of fear. In order to do this, to kill it, he'd have to ride the living monster. He could do it. If the others could just keep it from diving, he'd kill the beast. He felt his heart pounding, determination pumping through his body.

"In the heat of the battle I wield this horn and forge myself," Tom shouted. Neana turned.

"What do you make?" she called back.

"A monster rider! I need to get closer, so I can jump."

Neana shook her head but gestured for the others to close her space. Then, she drew Tulak alongside Tom. "Talk quickly and loud, Boy."

Tom leapt astride Tulak, and Neana sent her to rejoin the pod.

"We need to push that corpse back through the rift. If we don't, these creatures will continue to break through. If we can unstick it, maybe the rift will shut."

"When we push it through, won't they all rush out anyway? That water looks really unhealthy – it's the same green that Dead-lake turns each spring after the meltwater fills it," Vrex called.

"I'll lead them away. I'll go through the rift too and lead them away." Farren rode up, the trail of blood behind his whale streaming away into the water. "If these creatures start to rampage in this area, our home will not be safe, our pods will be decimated. My position demands the sacrifice."

"For the first time in his life he makes the right decision. Noble, foolish man," Neana muttered almost beneath her breath.

"It will be me," she offered, dodging another attack. The monster missed Tulak's flukes by a handspan. "I'm old and have few years left – I'd be happy to explore a new world for what remains of them." Tulak slipped alongside the monster for a moment, and Tom jumped, wrapping his arms around the huge spine on its back as it thrashed to try and dislodge him. Neana threw him the horn before it tried to dive.

"If you can ride a god, then a monster is easy," she shouted. "It even has handles."

Tom crawled along the head-plates, gripping onto their edges, and was frequently unfooted by the twisting and turning of the beast. He would put a foot into a bony gap, only for the fish to flex towards it and trap him, until inevitably it flexed the other way. Its head was below the surface and it kept trying to descend. Every swish of its tail and swing of its head threatened to throw him loose, the drag of the water against his legs exacerbating the precarious position he was in. Slowly, he edged along its back. He would be over the front of its skull soon, the point at which its jaws would lever open.

It was heading for Ghost now.

"Incoming," Neana called. She sent fireballs at the tail end as it opened its jaws. Tom tucked his feet in tightly and the beast thrashed harder trying to remove him. Bony plates dug deep into his feet with each flexion; it would only take a little more and he'd lose a foot. The great jaws snapped at the whale closest to him.

"The eye, Tom," his father shouted. Tom hefted the horn into his right hand and pushed upwards with his legs. From a standing position, balanced on the monster's back, he brought the horn down into its eye.

In and in it sank, driven by Tom's determination and more strength than he had believed possible. The horn penetrated deep into the monster's head. It thrashed in pain, throwing Tom into the water. Tom was hooked out of the water by Rona.

The Monster dived, barging past the nearest whale. They let it go. He hoped that he had sunk the horn deep enough that the creature would die, and soon. It might be a monster, but it was just trying to survive. He didn't like the idea of anything suffering a long, drawn-out death.

"It's not coming back. It's time to push," Farran urged the pod – a leader to the end. They lined up facing the oncoming monsters, who still battered at the soft, tail end of the corpse. Tail flukes thrashed the water as the whales strained against the bloody mass.

"If the water had been level, this would have been a whole load easier," Rona muttered, urging her whale to give as much power as she could. Farran's injured whale floated just back from the rest of the pod, unable to add her force to the task. He called out a count to coordinate the shoving.

The head began to move away from them, and the tail swung more freely. As it shuddered again, Farran and his whale prepared to dive through the hole. He tried to urge his whale forward, but she was tiring, the blood loss too much for her to make it to the rift.

The monsters on the other side collided with their dead kin one more time. It flexed, then burst free, a green waterfall pouring through the rift freely after it.

"Boy, you deserve the Waverider's blessing. Thank you for giving this old woman a last adventure," Neana shouted, her grey hair streaming in the wind as she rode Tulak through the rift at speed, blasting fire-balls at the confused monsters as she passed.

The rift flickered for a moment. The last of the dead creature slipped into the sea and it closed.

"May it be the best adventure," Rona said quietly as the sea flattened and they were left floating in silence on a red and green marbled ocean.

Ten exhausted and battered whales and their riders swam homeward as the sun rose the next day. They'd travelled as fast as Farran's whale could manage.

Tom switched regularly between Vrex and Rona's whales on the way back. His father remained unwilling to support his claim, or let him board Ghost, even to help Tom to get home – even after seeing him ride Waverider.

Pride and tradition meant too much to him. Tom could see that now. Without Farran's blessing, Tom was no Whalerider in his father's eyes. With Tulak gone, it would be a long time before any other whale was ready to test new riders.

Maybe Vrex could speed it along. Tom was preparing to board behind Vrex when he was mentally shoved with such force and pain that he grasped at his head, letting go of the fin. Darkness closed in and he fell backwards into the water.

He came to, floating at the surface, his father supporting his head, concern etched on his features. He'd leapt in to help? Maybe there was hope for them after all. Another wave of pain crushed Tom. It was excruciating now he was in the water. With his ears submerged, he heard a distant echo of his own pain as whale-song. Different to the voices of his pod, and far below them, a whale cried out in anguish.

Had the monster survived after all? Was it even now hunting down others?

"Can you feel it?" he asked his father.

"I'm not sure what you are talking about, Tom. You fell right off Vrex's whale though, never even made it astride. Flat back. Thought you must have taken more injury fighting that fish than I realised."

Tom said nothing. He suspected that his feet would never bear his weight quite as they used to, but that was a confession for once they were home.

If they got home.

The noise and the feeling grew. Vrex looked anxious, shifting position on her whale.

"There's something coming," she said. "Get out of the water, now."

"With pleasure," Tom replied as his father dragged him towards Vrex's whale before returning to mount his own. *Still?*

The pod formed a protective ring around Farran's injured mount, and Tom was barely out of the sea when a spray of water jetted into the air, followed by a tall, black dorsal fin. The whale dived shallowly, and a black fluke appeared at the surface.

No blood clouded the water, no predator followed it up from the deep. Yet this black whale sang of torment, and Tom understood it. For the first time in his life, he could feel a whale.

The pod started to rumble back. The largest and oldest, now that Tulak had gone, was Vrex's mount. They edged towards the newcomer. Tom was so distracted by the sensations that he didn't have his balance weighted right and slipped back into the water outside of the ring of whales.

The newcomer swam directly at him, picking him up in its teeth and throwing him into the air. Tom flew raggedly, gravity returning him to the water with far less grace and comfort than he would have liked.

Again, the whale swam at him.

"It's a baby," Vrex shouted. "Oh, Waverider, it's only a calf…"

The whale surfaced again, and he saw it then, a jagged wound the shape of the rift on the black whale's side. Waverider was involved somehow, he was sure of it. There were no copper eyes this time, just sad pools of blackness.

He opened his mouth to tell them about the mark – too late as he was dragged underwater by the interloper. The calf pressed against him, anguish filling Tom's brain and leaving little room for conscious thought. He was held gently in its teeth, as they went deeper than Tom had ever dived before. Desperate, he reached back to the calf. A baby – every child needs love…He sent affection, care and kindness, threaded with desperation as the pressure increased and his lungs burned with the effort of holding in his breath. Bubbles streamed from his mouth as he could hold his breath no longer and he fought desperately for freedom.

One more push, kindness, companionship. The grip on his mind lessened. Gentle curiosity probing yet tempered with sorrow. Blackwhale changed direction and slowly, more slowly than Tom could cope with, they began to rise.

They broke the surface of the water far

from the rest of the pod. The calf released Tom and nosed at him gently. Tom placed his hand on the soft snout and stroked it. They floated alongside each other for a while.

He heard shouts in the distance. Quietly, keeping contact with the calf, he swam alongside it. The tentative bond they had formed was fragile, and Tom was wary. He sent reassurance to it and held onto the pectoral fin as the whale began to swim. This whale had no horns, there would be no riding it without a harness. The whale flapped its fluke and swam towards the approaching pod with Tom as high up the pectoral fin as he could get and pressed tightly to the calf's body.

Ghost reached them first.

"Tom, are you okay?" his father hollered across the water. Tom bit back his sarcasm. There were many things he was, but okay was not amongst them.

"Waverider has blessed me with my own calf," he replied instead, gesturing at the wound.

The entire pod had reached them now and the calf was becoming anxious.

The pod parted to let Farran through. He

looked down on Tom, a wide grin on his face.

"That dive was longer than anything I've seen, from anyone but Rona. You rode out here on Waverider. You return to our clan as a Whalerider. With your own calf - if they will have you."

"I think she will. I'll just hang onto this fin for the moment, rather than upset her by climbing on. I think she wants to feel something close to her and she can't swim as fast as the rest of the pod yet."

Farran nodded. "Small steps." He gestured to the others. "Head home. Tell of what happened here. It's a long swim and no calf should be forced to chase for so long. I'll travel with Tom; it's kinder on my whale if I go slowly too."

Vrex smiled. "As new Matriarch…" Her eyes welled with tears, and she wiped them away quickly. "I require the Pod Chief to escort me home. We may swim quite slowly, though. Maybe only as fast as a calf."

Ghost turned a wide circle to swim alongside Tom, and he noticed that his father sat a little taller. "Tom Surfborn is my only son. I would be by his side as he brings a new member of the family home."

One by one the others all found excuses to stay. They swam gently back to Whalport, re-applying the last of the whale-seed oil to the wounds of Farran's whale on the way.

In the distance, the Sounding Bell rang. By the time they reached the whale-boards, most of the village was there. Fierce-Tusk and her riders lined up on the solid ground.

"What did you find? Where is Waverider?" Fierce-tusk called.

"Gone. We were taken to a rift that needed sealing or our community would have been in grave danger," Vrex replied. "Tom, stay with your whale a little longer. She'll get scared with so many people, all this noise," she added quietly.

"What of the rift?" a voice called from the back of the crowd. "If danger came through one, why would it not come through another?"

Farran spoke this time. "I believe that the rift is a symbol of Waverider's trust in us. He has graced our pod with a whale, displaying the very same shape." He gestured to Tom's whale. "I acknowledge Tom Surfborn as the one chosen to ride the marked whale, by both

Waverider and the whale herself. Welcome to the Whalport Pod, Tom Surfborn, Rider of Blackwhale."

Tom stroked the side of Blackwhale, unable to hide his grin. He wanted to shout with happiness but didn't dare scare his mount. He glanced at his father and found his own pride reflected back at him. The Surfborn family legacy would continue after all.

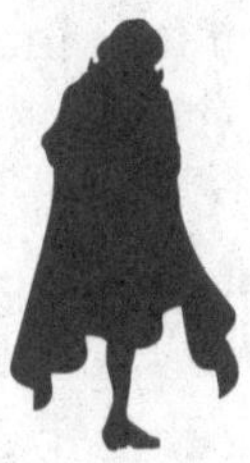

Topher the World

Derek Power

The summit of Mount Karmorg, the highest place on the tropical island nation of Derchripo, was also the holiest spot on the whole island. It was said that only the bravest of warriors, with truly noble souls, could climb The Ten Thousand Steps that brought them to the summit. There, through fasting and prayer, they would eventually be greeted by an appearance from Drom the Confused. Not that Drom himself was confused - after all, how could a god be confused? No, it was the folk who had originally started worshipping Drom who were confused. Mostly because nobody could really agree as to what the god should be about.

Some wanted a protective and nurturing deity, one whom they could pray to for help with their crops and to bring about rain. Others knew that beyond their shores people were, at the end of the day, people. They may come for a friendly visit, but that friendly visit could be at the end of a not-so-friendly sword. For them, Drom had to be a being that could go to battle and seek peace in the chaos of war.

These two somewhat diametrically opposing views resulted in the worshippers of Drom picturing the god with a bag of grain as a shield, whilst wielding a blade whose tip was covered in a bottle cork. Meaning the god could, in a very loose interpretation of the term, serve both of his followers equally.

Gods, being gods, obviously had to live in places not easy to get to for mortals. Hence the wide and vast summit of Mount Karmorg being the most logical spot. The only problem was that farmers rarely trained hard enough to climb The Ten Thousand Steps, so it was usually only warriors who made it to the top to commune with Great Drom. Farmers tended to prefer if their deities visited them in the crop fields without the requirement to go for a lovely stroll up a mountain that took all day. In the view of farmers, if warriors wanted to waste their time climbing up thousands of steps, then more power to them. Crops had to be tended and that was more important than walking up a mountain to see a god.

Which was why, for several centuries, the only people who had even been up to the summit of Mount Karmorg were young men seeking the glory of battle and a few tips from their resident god of wheat and weapons.

So, when Topher Drunkenson, potentially last of his name, woke up one morning on the mountain summit, he had many questions. The first and foremost was how in Holy Drom's name could Topher get rid of this mother of all hangovers that was threatening to shatter his skull into tiny pieces?

Waking up with a hangover was not unusual for a man in Topher's line of work. That line being getting blindingly drunk as fast as possible, so you fell asleep quickly. However, he typically woke up of his own accord, which had not been the case this morning. No, this morning, something had been thrown with extreme force directly at his slumbering head because apparently gently shaking somebody awake was no longer common practice.

He reached up and gingerly touched the left side of his head, feeling a little painful bump forming.

"Well, that's just bloody brilliant," Topher said, opening his eyes slowly to minimise the pain of daylight.

Sitting up, he looked around the spot where his head had been resting and spotted an extremely unique-looking shoe. It bore a heavy wooden sole that looked like it would be well suited to creating lumps on the heads of sleeping men.

"Who throws a bloody shoe!" Topher declared, shifting around so that he could prop himself up on his elbows. "And why are my legs so cold?"

Looking down at the aforementioned appendages, Topher spotted the second most interesting thing of the morning. Both his legs were covered in a high and wide mound of white, fluffy snow. From the waist down Topher was encased in the stuff. At least he assumed that was what he was looking at. Snow and Derchripo were two words rarely used in the same sentence. The people of the island knew what snow was from stories, books, and the rare first-hand account of their sailors. But it was simply too hot in their little spot of the world for snow to happen, even up on the summit of Most Holy Karmorg.

"Oh, my Drom!" Topher swore. "I CAN'T FEEL MY LEGS!!!"

He tugged and pulled, moving around so that eventually he was on his stomach. Reaching forward, he began to drag himself out from beneath the snow. The chill, numb sensation seemingly remained behind with the fluffy flakes. In a matter of seconds, Topher had pulled himself free, the morning sunlight warming his legs enough so that he could feel them once more.

"It's a Drom blessed miracle," he said. "Now if only you'd do something about this bloody hangover."

Slowly, taking care not to throw too much energy into the movement, Topher stood up and looked around.

"What in the Seven Hells?" Topher said to

nobody in particular. "How am I on the summit of Mount Karmorg?"

The summit was nicer than he honestly expected it to be. There was a lovely little grove of trees standing off to the side of The Ten Thousandth Step, with a lovely little wooden bench nestled in amongst the trunks. A place for a well-earned rest after however long it took to get to the summit, Topher assumed. The summit itself was very flat and wide, so much so that Topher could easily picture somebody building a house up here. That was if anyone ever bothered carrying all the wood up. In the centre of the flat area was a lovely blue oval of light about the height of a tall man shimmering in the early morning sun. Then the mound of snow and the randomly abandoned…

"Hang on a bloody second," Topher said, immediately looking at the blue oval as it floated a few inches off the ground.

This was unlike anything he had ever seen in his entire life. It crackled with some sort of energy, little forks of lightning travelling around the edge of the oval while random ones sparked into the air or touched the ground. At the top of the portal there was a swirling tunnel of…something. Topher had never been one for words. After all the drinking he did, there was no point in learning fancy words because you just forgot them all after a good night of liquid revelry. He supposed, looking at the swirling tunnel, it was made up of either blue dust or magic. Following the tunnel up through the air, Topher was amazed to see that the oval before him had a much bigger brother taking up a sizeable portion of the sky.

"What in Drom's name is going on here?"

The thing in the sky could only be described as a maelstrom of magical energies. Thick blue and purple clouds swirled around a central spot, with lightning crackling through every few seconds like a storm threatening to break. If he moved his head slowly, Topher could just about trace the tunnel through the air and back to the top of the oval.

"I'm dreaming," he said. "This is a dream."

The sound of a sword being drawn from its sheath, the blade slicing through the air several times as the owner performed some elaborate moves, drew Topher's attention away from the shimmering oval of madness before him. He looked over his shoulder, then screamed and dove to the ground just as a sword tried to separate his head from his neck.

Scuttling like a misshapen crab, Topher tried to place the mound of snow between himself and his attacker.

"What is wrong with you!" he screamed from his frosty hiding spot.

"Me?" the sword-wielding maniac asked. "Demon, I did not climb Drom's Stairway to commune with The Great One, in order to seek guidance on how to close yonder giant swirling portal of doom in the sky, only to have a shapeshifter invade my homeland."

"Demon? Me? You think I'm a demon?"

The maniac pointed at the magical blue oval with his sword, then drew a line in the air so that the tip of his blade ended up in Topher's direction.

"For a man to climb The Ten Thousand Steps takes many days of preparation at the base of Mount Karmorg. During this time, they guard the first step so that none shall pass. I have slept there for three days and nights, readying myself for the trial of the climb. You cannot tell me you snuck past Erom the Mighty in that time. Ergo you arrived here by coming through that portal. Thus, demon!"

Topher frowned and tried really hard to think through his hangover fogged memories and figure out just how he had actually wound up at the summit. Covered in snow. Being woken up by a shoe. That had been thrown at his head. When nobody else was around. Beside a glowing portal of mystery and the bigger portal of misery in the sky.

He came up blank.

"First off," Topher said to Erom. "Women can be warriors too. So, it's a little sexist to suggest that only men can climb the steps."

Erom seemed to blush.

"Wha…ye…yes. Of course, they can. I wasn't saying otherwise. There aren't any around now, are there?" he asked, looking around the summit quickly with what Topher thought was a slightly fearful expression.

"Female warriors? No, there aren't at the minute. Secondly, Erom?"

"Yes?"

"No, that was the question. 'Erom'? As in, that's your name?"

"What of my name, demon?" Erom asked, turning to face the mound of snow once more, drawing a second sword from a sheath on his back and pointing both blades in Topher's direction.

"Would you cool it with that demon crap?" Topher said. "All I wanted to know was why your name was Erom when our god is Drom. It isn't something daft like your parents figured you'd be next in line for deity stuff just by using the next letter in the alphabet, was it?"

The momentary look of embarrassment on Erom's face was all the confirmation Topher needed. Before saying anything else, he buried his face in the snow and laughed as quietly as possible. What he did not expect to happen was the almost instant pain relief as the cold spread across his forehead. It was glorious. No wonder people on Derchripo suffered so badly from hangovers. Snow and ice had miraculous hangover healing properties, just none appeared on the island for people to figure this out.

Raising his head back out of the snow, Topher looked over at Erom.

"Look," he said. "I'm not a demon, okay? Yes, I have no idea how I woke up here this morning. Sure, last night isn't even a blur but just one hangover hidden memory that I will probably never recover. But I can tell you that I, Topher Drunkenson, am not a demon."

"Drunkenson?" Erom asked, lowering the tips of his blades ever so slightly.

"Yeah, Drunkenson. What? I took a pop at your daft made-up name so you're going to return the favour? Well let me shed some light for you there, buddy. All names are made up at some point. Only the popular ones survive."

"No, it's not that," Erom said. "I've heard tale of the family of Drunkenson. Powerful wizards from times gone. Brandishing magic that made even Mighty Drom fear them. Are you a wizard?"

"Well, I can make a drink disappear fairly quickly. But that's hardly magical." Topher said, shrugging his shoulders.

The warrior sheathed both swords and crossed his arms over a chest that Topher felt sure belonged on a dragon or some other huge muscular beast of legend. Frowning at the portal, Erom took a deep breath, which somehow made his chest look even bigger than before.

"Then what is this thing?" he asked. "Have you stepped through yet?"

"Stepped through?" Topher asked, standing bolt upright he arched an eyebrow at the ridiculous statement just uttered. "Into a magical doorway that seems to be connected to a scary copy up in the sky…after a night of drinking so heavy that I can't remember how I got to the top of a mountain? Of course, I did. Very first thing after waking up in fact."

"Fantastic! What did you see?"

"That was sarcasm, you bloody moron," Topher shouted, spreading his arms out wide. "Why would anybody do that?"

Erom looked from Topher to the portal and back again.

"To see what's on the other side," he said. "I thought that obvious?"

Topher looked around for something to throw at the warrior, spotted the shoe, and grabbed it from the ground. He took aim and was about to throw it when his survival instincts kicked in. Chances were, throwing a shoe at a man with two swords and a deep-rooted desire to use them would result in said swords being used against the thrower of the aforementioned shoe. Instead, Topher gently lobbed the shoe over at Erom in what he hoped would not be considered an attacking. It spiralled through the air, bouncing off the warrior's chest before falling to the ground like a fish.

"What's that?" Erom asked, looking down at the shoe.

"It's a Demon Shoe," Topher said, pointing at it. "Came through the portal."

"What makes it a demon?"

"It woke me up from drunken slumber, that's what."

Erom bent down and picked up the shoe, examining it closely and turning it over in his hands several times. Eventually he tossed the foot-covering object towards Topher, an action that caught the man a little by surprise. Instead of catching the shoe, Topher instinctively ducked and covered his head with his arms. It was not uncommon for people to want to cause him cranial harm.

Apparently, when enough drink was drunk, Topher had a tendency to be a little rude.

The shoe, unawares as to the many trials and tribulations Topher had faced in his life, sailed over his head, and went into the portal. As both men watched, the portal rippled as if somebody had just thrown a stone into a still pond. Each ripple ring was made from a different colour of the rainbow, glowing with some magical energy as it travelled along the surface of the portal before popping on the edge in a shower of sparks.

Topher, coming out from his protective position, looked over at Erom.

"Yeah," he said. "I am going to stick my head into that for the poops and giggles of it all."

"Oh good, I thought I was late."

Topher and Erom turned around to look at an elderly man sitting on the bench in the little tree grove. He wore what could only be described as a tattered brown robe that had seen days one would have hoped could be described as better. Reaching up with his hands, the man pulled down his hood to reveal a bald but beard-bearing head beneath. He stared at the two men with amber-coloured eyes that twinkled in the sunlight.

"It is so lovely down here," the new arrival said, looking up into the sky and around the summit. "I haven't been down in…well longer than I'd care to admit. Except for last night, of course."

Erom, without giving any indication that

he had lost his mind, suddenly dropped to his knees, bowing down in the direction of the new arrival.

"Oh, Great and Mighty Drom. Long have I dreamt of meeting you. Seeking your wisdom, receiving your blessing. To think that I, Erom of Lowplains, will be amongst your most chosen of chosen warriors is an honour you do not know," Erom said with his face nearly in the dirt.

Topher dusted down his clothes and looked over at Drom. Truth be told, he had expected something more impressive. The man before them looked like he had missed about seventy-five of the last meals in his life. There was no muscle or sense of power. His hands barely looked like they could crush an ant, let alone the boulders Drom was known for breaking just because he could. Topher was almost glad he could not remember climbing all the steps, because if this was the god he got to meet it would have been profoundly disappointing.

"Can you explain this?" Topher asked the god, gesturing from the snow to the portal and back again.

"Prostrate yourself," Erom hissed up at

him.

"I will in me hoop prostate myself. For all we know, he's the reason I woke up here covered in snow."

"Oh, I am," Drom said. "Don't you remember last night? We had some fun in the tavern."

"Are you telling me," Topher said, staring at Drom, slack jawed, "I went drinking with a deity last night and can't even recall?"

Drom nodded, reaching down to pick up two small stones from beside the left bench leg.

"Let me tell you a story," the god said. "And you, Erom. For my sake, sit up will you. That looks uncomfortable."

Erom did as instructed.

"Now, catch," Drom said, throwing one stone towards Erom and the other towards Topher.

Both men caught their stones and immediately felt magical effects kick in.

They were in Topher's memories. He knew this because everything looked so familiar and yet distinctly new all at the same time. It was how he felt most mornings after waking up and flashes of what had happened the night before burst through his mind. Looking around, Topher could not see Erom anywhere.

I'm here, the warrior's voice said from inside Topher's mind. *But I am without a body... how is that possible?*

"Magic," Topher said, rolling his eyes. "I've heard enough about it to know that there is always a stupid reason for something happening. Oh, look at that. I'm walking without thinking about it."

It was as if his body were not his own. The memory was playing out; Topher and Erom were just along for the ride. They were not actors in the story, more like audiences watching the play. All Topher was in control of was his eyes.

He looked around as his memory-body walked along the nighttime path from his little shack into the centre of Banaming. As villages went, it was a typical one. Homes, houses and huts laid out around the edge so that the more important buildings like storage, the main lodge and the three taverns had some protection from nefarious forces. Of course, of the three taverns, Topher was barred from entering two of them. You would think that a little thing like being   sick on the barmaids was to be an expected hazard of the job when it came to working in taverns, but apparently not. Which was why The Blue Dragon was not only Topher's favourite watering hole, but also the only one open to him. Thankfully Barbar, proprietary of the fabulous establishment, was wiser than your average barkeep. She figured the best spot for Topher to sit was at the one small table beside a window. His drinks were then brought to him, allowing him to easily puke out the window onto the rose bushes nobody really cared for.

The woman was nothing short of a genius.

Nobody was ever allowed to sit at his table either. Mostly because Barbar did not want to have to turn away a paying customer, but also because cleaning up puke was, in her view, most definitely not part of her job.

As Topher walked, or remembered walking, down the main path of the village, he was noticing a few things differently this time. The gift of hindsight was revealing a lot more than ever expected. Despite the fact he knew, and his memory was confirming, that this walk had taken place at night there were several flowers still in bloom. Almost like they had not gotten the memo about sunset. Along the path, there were strange scorch marks on the ground that Topher did not recall seeing during his original walk to the tavern. A discarded bucket sat beside a smartly dressed pig, which was definitely something Topher had never seen before. The animal looked down in shock at the shirt and trousers their portly form was bursting free from.

Something strange took place here, Erom's disembodied voice said. *The water from that puddle is flowing upwards into the bucket.*

I agree, Topher thought back. *But I can't remember this night at all.*

But we're in your memory.

I know that, but that doesn't mean I can remember it.

So basically, you got blind drunk tonight and don't actually recall anything from even before when you started drinking. You are a disaster of a man.

Topher ignored the insult and focused on the memory once more.

Memory-Topher shuffled along the small

path that led up to the front door of The Blue Dragon, pushed on it, then walked inside. Based purely on muscle memory, he turned left without looking at anything else in the tavern and strolled over to his table by the window.

Which was when things started to get interesting.

His table was usually nestled in the corner of the tavern, right beside a front-facing circular window for ease of stomach-content emptying. There was never a second chair and nor, at least to be best of his reckoning, a small tree growing out of the wooden floorboards. But even ignoring the sudden increase in interior plants, it was the fact his table was occupied by a hooded figure that really raised questions in Topher's mind.

"Eh, Barbar," he said, stopping to stare at the occupant at his table.

Isn't that Drom? He never comes down from the mountain, you must be truly special.

Topher tried to nod his head in agreement, then remembered he had no actual control over his body in this memory. All he could do was watch and listen.

"Please, sit," Drom said, pushing out an ornate wooden chair that had never been in the tavern before.

"Barbar?" Topher said again, while his legs seemingly drifted over to the new chair without waiting for him to decide on that course of action.

It was unusual for Barbar to not respond to the request of a customer, let alone ignore that same person twice in a row. He pulled back the chair and sat down across from the hooded figure.

Topher could not see anything of the person's face, the shadows from the hood obscuring everything in darkness. All he could see were two amber circles where the person's eyes should be.

"I haven't been to this part of the world in a lifetime," the hooded figure said. "Is it always like this?"

They made an expansive sweep with their left arm, indicating the rest of the tavern. Topher turned slightly in his seat and looked around at the oddly empty tavern. An extremely rare event since the tavern usually had at least one person drinking in it at any hour of the day. Barbar was also missing from her customary position behind the rosewood bar counter. Instead, for some unknown reason, there was a chicken walking across the surface of the bar.

It pecked at the crust of some bread, before glancing at Topher and letting out a squawk.

"I've never seen it like this," Topher said, turning back in his seat and seeing two mugs of foamy ale in front of him.

Mugs that had not been there seconds before.

"That's a neat trick," he said to the hooded figure.

Topher picked up the nearest mug, draining roughly half of it in one go, and immediately enjoyed the most perfect mix of tastes and flavours he had never experienced. As he put the mug down, Topher was amazed to see the mug magically refill.

"No, that's a neat trick," he said to the hooded figure.

"Imagine having a mug like that for the rest of your life," the hooded figure said. "All for helping out a stranger in a strange land."

"What's the favour?" Topher asked, taking another healthy glug of the magical drink, and watching with astonishment as it refilled again.

"Tomorrow somebody is going to try and close a door on me. I need it to remain open, for personal reasons."

"So, get a doorstop. I think Darvin at the end of the village makes them for a copper coin a piece."

"This is a special door," the hooded figure said. "It can only be closed in a very specific way. That being if somebody noble of spirit enters the door unintentionally."

Topher frowned; the mug of ale lifted halfway from the table to his mouth. This was certainly his first drink of the evening and, magical refills aside, he was certain that most of his thinking abilities remained in place.

"How can you walk through a door unintentionally? Isn't the whole point of entering a place via the door sort of…intentional?"

The hood shook from side to side.

"It is a specific wording of a magical compact made eons ago," the hooded figure said. "Each of these special doors has a different way of being closed and the one on Derchripo just so happens to have a strange rule to it. I imagine some warrior will no doubt show up, see the door, and walk through it. That's where you come in."

"Why me?"

"You're the seventh son of a seventh son, if I'm not mistaken," the hooded figure said, taking a small sip from their own mug of ale before placing it back down on the table. "In most places that means you are burdened with great magical purpose. On track to become a wizard, nonetheless. But here, on this island, that doesn't seem to be the case. The ley lines bend around the island and channel the magical energies you'd be able to channel elsewhere. But your lineage still makes you important. I can't see how, exactly, but there is something special about you. I'd say if the warrior happened to mistake you for a demon and slay you, that would make their spirit less noble."

Topher had heard the whole 'you could be a wizard' line numerous times in his life. Mainly when people tried to make fun of him for being the village drunk who earned money emptying out the communal outhouse buckets. But he had never truly dwelled on the fact he was the seventh son of a seventh son for the simple reason that it meant absolutely nothing to him.

Now, however, there was the possibility to have a never-ending supply of tasty ale in a lovely looking mug. All to just stop some warrior from going through some door they had no business going through. As Topher's dear departed father used to say, it was a no-brainer.

"Alright," he said. "But when do I get this most magical mug to keep? Wait, what was that bit about being a demon?"

"As long as that door remains open until sunset, a full twenty-four hours, then the mug is yours. I will hand it to you myself. All you need to do is make sure whoever climbs those Drom damned steps doesn't ruin my day."

"Steps? Wait…this door is at the top of Mount Karmorg? I'm not climbing those bloody steps. Warriors train for years before attempting to do that. They are stacked two men high each at some places, to test if the warrior can fly or walk on clouds or something. It would take me a month just to get ten steps up."

The hooded figure pushed back their chair and stood up slowly.

"Don't worry about that bit," they said. "The door is opening shortly, and I think you need a good night's rest."

They began to make circular motions with their left hand while pointing their right one at Topher, palm first. Little blue and green specks of light appeared in the air, drifting up from the ground. Looking down, Topher saw a circle of multi-coloured light form around his chair. He jumped to his feet, sending the ornate chair flying away from the table and crashing into the bar counter. The chicken squawked once more. Without saying another word, the hooded figure raised their right hand into the air and the circle of light grew more intense before the floor within it disappeared completely.

Topher blinked several times, staring at where the wood had been and where stones and grass now stood. He looked at the mug of ale, then up at the hooded figure.

"How strong is that stuff?" he asked.

"Strong enough that you'll have one Drom damned hangover in the morning," they said. "Sweet dreams."

With a final gesture the circle of light shot upwards, and Topher felt the contents of his stomach churn as around him the inside of The Blue Dragon disappeared. He was a few feet above the ground of what looked like summit Mount Karmorg before he dropped like a stone and landed in the dirt.

The last thing he saw before sleep took him was the hooded figure reaching through the magical ring and lifting the mug before both vanished from sight.

As memory ended, both Topher and Erom dropped the stones to the ground and returned to their bodies on the summit. They looked at each other.

"How do you not remember going for a drink with Drom?" Erom asked him. "I mean, most of us would kill any number of mythical beasts to get that chance. Yet you do it and then promptly forget."

Topher shrugged.

"I dunno. You heard it yourself. The booze was strong. I suppose that at least explains how I got up here without passing you on the steps. Confirming that, like I said before, I'm not a demon."

Erom nodded but placed on hand on the hilt of his left sword.

"That it does, but it raises other questions. Legends have it that wizards are not welcome on the shores of Derchripo. They tend to meddle in affairs that require no meddling. Getting people of diminutive height to steal wedding bands and drop them in fiery mountains for no discernible reason."

"Your vocabulary is pretty impressive," Topher said, hoping to derail Erom's thought process.

"I studied under Master Lore in the University. We had to read ancient tomes of knowledge while battling atop balance beams as part of our weekly exams. You pick up a few words between all the concussions. You also learn that in aeons gone by the warriors of Derchripo forced the last wizards off her fair shores so that her people could live meddle free."

Topher's hangover, seemingly having a mind of its own, decided that right then was the exact moment to get progressively worse. The throbbing in his head grew in intensity, to the point that focusing on any single thought took a tremendous effort of will. He raised his left hand, palm out, and made a calm gesture towards Erom.

"Look," Topher said. "Let's not be crazy here. We got shown some magical dreams using a mystical stone thrown at us by a god who people never see on a daily basis."

"DO NOT BESMIRCH THE HONOUR OF DROM!" Erom roared, drawing both his blades once more and twirling them around in his hands.

"Should people be able to do that?" Topher asked, indicating the swirling motions the warrior was making with his weapons.

Over on the bench beneath the trees, Drom leaned back and made himself comfortable. He crossed his hands and watched as events unfolded. Topher was not entirely sure, owing largely to how sore his head currently was, but it seemed as if the ground beneath the bench had changed from healthy grass to a strange blue and purple sand-like substance. Drom, apparently, had not noticed this transformation at all. But something about it was triggering a memory in Topher's brain; if only he had less hangover to worry about it might have allowed him to remember the memory.

A clanging of steel on steel snapped his attention back to Erom. The warrior had shifted his stance ever so slightly, both weapons held before him at the ready.

"Wizard," he said. "I'm going to send you through this blasted portal into whatever frozen hell is on the other side. Right here, in front of Mighty Drom!"

"Not exactly what I had in mind," Drom shouted over to them. "But it will do. Have at him."

Erom shouted a battle cry to the sky, then ran towards Topher with a look of murder in his eyes

"Drom above!" Topher screamed, running over to the big pile of snow and going around it so that Erom was on the other side.

As he approached the cool flakes, that were surviving exceedingly well given how long they had been lying on the ground, Topher's hangover did something none of his hangovers had ever done before.

It showed him things.

Around the summit, time slowed down. The magical energies streaming off the edge of the portal froze in thin air. Erom became a murderous statue. Drom, well it was hard to tell if anything had changed about Drom. Sitting was a non-action like thing to do. But for Topher, all time was moving normally. Which allowed him to see the seven ghostly figures standing around the mound of snow.

One figure he recognised instantly.

"Dad?" Topher said.

The ghostly father inclined his head, then smiled.

"I knew you'd figure this out eventually," his father said.

"Figure what out?"

"That you're a wizard, Topher."

"I feel that would have worked better had my name been 'Harry'." Topher said, frowning.

"This lad is useless," the ghost next to his father's spirit said. "This is what the seventh son of a seventh son gets you these days? How is he meant to be a Cold Mage?"

"A Cold Mage?" Topher asked.

He had been told tales of Cold Mages growing up. Powerful wizards who could do anything with cold stuff. In Derchripo it was a sure-fire way to generate amazing wealth. A nation that never knew about snow and had winters that were classed as 'slightly cooler summers' paid handsomely to men and women who could control the elements to make things cold. But the Cold Mages had been run off the island by a bunch of warriors. The stories went that one of the Cold Mages had sought to become a king, using magic to subjugate the population of the island. But Topher's father had said it had been the warriors who wanted the mages to use their powers so the warriors could become kings. When the Cold Mages refused, a lie was spread, one the people would believe, and all the Cold Mages were hunted down and killed or exiled.

But nobody had said that the stories had been anything more than that. There had definitely been no mention of Topher having magical powers.

He looked into the ghostly face of his father, then shook his head.

"I'm just about to die, that's all this is," Topher said. "There is no way I am a Cold Mage."

"You are one," said a ghost standing directly opposite from Topher. "For I was one. The portal, we closed it once before. Generations ago. It caused the ley lines to shift around the island. A worthy sacrifice, we felt. After all, having babies is just as sure a way to make more wizards as is exposure to magical energy lines that criss-cross the world. We just never factored in the people of Derchripo getting rid of us all. But now, the portal is opened once more. The lines on the other side have reconnected to the ones on the island. You can channel the energy of magic and cold."

Topher glanced over at Erom. The warrior had changed position slightly, his foot nearly touching the ground. Behind him Drom had moved as well, shifting and seemingly staring at Topher.

"That doesn't mean anything," Topher said to the ghosts. "I don't know magic."

"But you will," the spirits all said in unison.

Topher's head exploded with pain as his hangover disappeared, only to be replaced with what felt like centuries of arcane knowledge. Power coursed through every inch of his body with such strength he could feel it. Flexing his fingers, making fists a few times, Topher could sense the mound of snow before him. Not in the 'it is cold and nearby' meaning of the word, but rather he just 'knew' it was there.

Without thinking, Topher made a sweeping

gesture with his right hand and commanded the snow to move towards Erom.

Which it all promptly did.

A strong, cold wind blew and moved all the snow forward. As it rushed towards the warrior, Topher's mind exploded with a sense of clarity he had never known before. More importantly the hangover was entirely gone, removed from every corner of his brain. In its place there was knowledge of things mystical and magical. Information that Topher had never come across on his own. A gift from his ghostly family, no doubt. He understood ice and snow, cold and chill, on a level that most people barely understood their own feet.

As the snow reached Erom, Topher clenched his fist and commanded the fluffy white powder to freeze the warrior in place. The snow built up around Erom's legs, reaching up to his knees, then instantly turned into a large block of clear blue ice.

"Wait a minute," Drom said, leaning forward and pointing towards the two men. "What is the meaning of this? This isn't how it was meant to go. This was my sure-fire portal."

"What sorcery is this?" Erom asked, hacking at his ice-encased legs with his swords.

Large chunks of ice flew off into the air with each attack from the swords.

Topher watched the warrior try to free himself, then noticed that the summit of Mount Karmorg had changed ever so slightly. In the air were thin blue lines, drifting about on unfelt wind. As he looked at one it began to pulse, stopping when he turned his attention to another line which began to pulse.

"I can see cold," Topher said to himself. "Floating around like regular stuff."

Reaching out, Topher closed his fist and willed one of the lines towards him. It did so immediately, swirling around his hand like a ball of water. He knew it was cold but felt nothing. As he stared at it, entranced by the new abilities he had acquired, a glint of sunlight on metal caught his attention just in time to see that Erom had thrown a sword at his head.

On instinct Topher brought his arms up to deflect the weapon but channelled some energy into the little blue line around his hand. He willed it to form a shield. There was a rush of air, a little sprinkling of snow, and in his right hand the Cold Mage now held a large circular chunk of ice. The sword hit the ice shield tip first and got stuck.

Topher lowered the shield and stared at the sword.

"I could get used to this," he said.

"Do you see?" Erom asked, kicking his left leg free from the ice and continuing to hack at the right block. "I knew you had power and now you are plotting your ascension."

"Exactly," Drom shouted over. "Kill him, before he ruins everything. Throw him into the portal! Here, let me help you."

The god snapped his fingers, then pointed at Erom's blade. With a blinding flash, the warrior's weapon burst into flame. A roaring, hot shaft of red and yellow fire. Even standing apart from the warrior, Topher could feel the heat coming off the weapon.

"Well that certainly evened things up," he said, watching as Erom took one last swing at the ice and freed his leg.

"Now, you abomination," Erom said, twirling the fire sword around in his hand. "I will kill you before Mighty Drom and throw your vile corpse through the Doorway of the Gods, freeing these fair lands of your bloodline once and for all."

Topher had been threatened many times in his life. But there was something about having a warrior holding a flaming sword tell you he was going to wipe your bloodline from the world that really hammered home a fear unlike any other.

"Hold on a second," Topher said, looking at his hands. "Fire doesn't like water."

He pulled several of the blue power lines towards him, then funnelled them directly towards Erom's blade. As they moved, Topher imagined they were all jets of ice-cold water. Each line morphed mid-flight, pouring water out of thin air onto the fiery sword. Erom gripped the weapon firmly with two hands, bracing himself against the strength of the jets impacting the weapon. The warrior was pushed back several feet, while a cloud of mist formed around him as his blade's fire was put out.

After a minute Topher commanded the waters to stop and watched the mist clear, revealing Erom standing there with an unlit sword.

"Now," he said to the warrior. "Shall we talk about this like…"

Erom let out another of his battle-roars, the

sword bursting into flame once more. With the weapon held out to his left in both tree-trunk like arms, the warrior ran towards Topher.

"Oh Drom!" the Cold Mage swore.

He turned on his heel and began to run away from Erom. As the warrior passed by the other sword, he bent and dislodged it from Topher's ice shield. The second weapon decided that it wanted in on the fire action and also burst into flame.

Topher briefly missed the hangover he had woken up with only an hour earlier. It had not been trying to kill him with two flaming swords of death while a strange god watched from a little bench under some trees.

With nowhere to really run for cover, the Cold Mage decided to run around the portal. It, potentially, would prevent any weapons passing through it so that they could remove the life from a newly initiated Cold Mage. Then again, the portal was just a tear in reality occupying a space in time that allowed humans to see it.

Information Topher knew had just recently been inserted into his brain.

"Stand still, evil doer, so that I may smite thee," Erom said, thrusting at Topher through the portal with one of his flaming blades.

The weapon passed into the portal on Erom's side but, thankfully, did not come out on Topher's one. Meaning that if he could keep the portal between his frail body and the mound of muscles that made up the warrior, things would be okay. But Topher knew that was a stalling tactic at best. There was no chance that he could keep this up until Erom grew bored and went back to fighting other things.

A plan was needed. Potentially even a drastic one. Erom seemed like a nice enough sword-wielding maniac but, at the end of the day, living was a habit Topher really did not want to give up. If it came down to it, Topher was willing to make a very hard call.

Making another lap of the portal of protection, as Topher was now thinking of the magical doorway, he glanced over at Drom.

"Can't you get involved here?" the Cold Mage asked the god. "I mean it's your fault I'm here in the first place."

"Not entirely true," Drom replied. "I think your parents are the real reason you're here in the first place."

The god sat back and smiled.

Topher searched through his new magical memories for some spells that might be able to get him out of this situation. Several immediately came to mind, but most of them required time to cast. He was not entirely sure, but Topher felt that Erom was unlikely to give him a break from their battle so that a spell could be cast in which the warrior lost said battle.

The Cold Mage stopped running, turned around, and conjured two long shafts of ice in his hands. Brandishing the frosty points before him, Topher prepared to do battle with Erom.

The warrior stopped running and smiled.

"I see you've brought an icicle to a fire fight," Erom said, lunging towards Topher with both his flame swords coming in at wide angles.

Topher ducked forward, stepping just inside Erom's attack circle, then smashed both his ice sticks against the warrior's left foreman.

The sticks shattered into a thousand tiny pieces, while Erom's chest connected with Topher's nose and broke it.

"OH!" Topher roared, dropping to the ground, rolling away from the warrior.

Gingerly, he touched his nose and instantly regretted it as pain shot through his entire skull. The tips of his fingers came away with droplets of blood on them.

"Don't worry," Erom said, turning around. "You won't be alive much longer and then the pain will be a distant memory. Although not for you since I'm sure once you're dead you won't remember anything at all. FOR DROM!"

"Oh, this is good," Drom said from his observation bench. "A Cold Mage who doesn't know how to use cold offensively. Brilliant."

With blood trickling down his nostrils and over his top lip, Topher got to his feet and faced Erom. Maybe, just maybe, this was how it was always going to end for him. He had spent his life drinking and contributing nothing to the world. Now, after all this time, when it turned out he might just be special, a lunatic with twin flaming swords wanted to cut him down. What was the point in even trying to fight it any longer?

You utter moron, a voice in Topher's head said. *You have all the knowledge you could ever need. USE IT!*

Topher searched through the spells again and found two that might be useful. Raising his fists, the Cold Mage began to punch the air in front of him, pulling on the little magical lines to focus some energy. Each flung fist caused a little puff of frost to appear in the air and sent a small cone of ice flying towards Erom. The first one struck the warrior on his shoulder, leaving a nasty looking cut on the skin that immediately began to bleed. After that Erom used his blades to deflect or destroy the rest of the magical missiles, all the while walking with deadly purpose towards Topher.

Throwing every ounce of energy and strength he had into the air punches, Topher sent volley after volley of ice arrows towards the warrior. He slowly started to back away from the approaching, inevitable, doom.

Erom smiled, sending each missile off harmlessly into the air with a wave of his swords.

"Careful now," Drom shouted over. "Sustained magical usage has a tendency to tire a mortal out quicker than you would think."

The god was right. Topher already felt like he could easily drop to the ground and nap right there in the dirt. Of course, he knew if he did that Erom would make sure that dirt nap became a permanent thing. But there was nothing else to do. He could already feel his air punches getting weaker; the last two ice arrows had nearly melted in the air before even reaching Erom's fire swords.

Topher tripped over his own foot, dropping to a knee, and braced himself with his right hand in the ground. He aimed his left one at Erom and tried to conjure up a block of ice. The spell partially worked, but instead of being placed in front of the warrior, the large ice cube appeared directly behind him. Making it the least useful blocking item in the history of blocking items.

Sighing, Topher hung his head and waited for the fatal blow to come.

"Wise choice, wizard," Erom said, bringing both swords up high above his head and staring down with murder in his eyes.

Go on, the voice of his ancestors shouted in Topher's mind. *One last roll of the dice and you can drink until the end of next week.*

A spell, unsought, appeared in Topher's thoughts. It was not a particularly powerful spell compared to missiles made from ice. But it was also the best worst idea he had left open to him.

Falling onto his back, the Cold Mage brought up both his hands and summoned a strong spray of cool mist from the air around them. He focused on the spell, sending the jets forward so that both went straight up into Erom's face and blinded the warrior. Erom staggered backwards, dropping one of his fire swords so that he had a free hand to wave at the frozen mist hitting his face. Right as the warrior was about to hit the block of ice, Topher poured the last dredges of energy in his body to strengthen the power of the jets and force Erom back.

Then, just because the warrior had been doing it all along for no real sensible reason, Topher let out a roar.

"ROAR!" he shouted, feeling instantly foolish.

Erom, wildly swatting at the mist now with both hands, staggered back several steps and tripped over the large block of ice. He lost his footing, fell backwards, and went headfirst into the portal. Sliding along the surface of the ice, the warrior took mere seconds before every part of him had gone through the magical doorway. There was a shrill whistle, and the portal spun several times on the spot, drawing in dust and magical energies with each rotation before it vanished from sight completely.

Topher stopped channelling his frozen mists and looked at where the portal had been, greatly confused.

"FINALLY!" Drom bellowed, standing up from the bench and walking over to where Topher lay on the ground. "I guess it didn't matter which of your foolish souls went unwillingly into the portal. I had assumed it would need to be you, the mage, but it appears the warrior ticked all the right boxes as well. Never mind all that now; closed is closed, and I'm one step closer to godhood."

The penny slowly dropped in Topher's mind. He raised an accusatory finger at Drom and gave the god a long, hard, stare.

"You're not bloody Drom! You lied!"

The person with the amber-coloured eyes, formerly known as 'Drom', held up their hands and shrugged.

"In my defence," he said, grinning. "I never actually called myself 'Drom'. So that's on both of you. Nice job condemning your buddy to eternal torment, by the way."

"What?" Topher asked, getting up from the ground and dusting his clothes.

"The portal. It had to be closed by somebody of noble spirit who entered unwillingly. I do so love when prophecies are written like that. Utter nonsense that you'd only stumble on the right answer, literally in this case. But by sending him inside you've just ensured your warrior friend will suffer untold torment for eternity. As for you…"

The hooded figure held out their empty hands and made a tossing gesture, as if they were throwing something into the air. Mid-movement two daggers with blades as black as night appeared, landing hilt first into fake-Drom's hands.

Topher felt exhausted. If somebody suggested to him that sleeping for a week was an option he would have been dropping to the floor before the sentence had even been finished. But, it seemed, Fate had other ideas for how he should spend his day. As if fending off the attacks of a well-meaning warrior-idiot was not enough for a day's work. Now he had to deal with fake gods and magical daggers.

The Cold Mage looked up at the giant swirling maelstrom in the sky. Whether it was a trick of the light, or some new ability that had unlocked when his magical skills kicked in, Topher was unsure. Regardless, as he looked up at the pulsing magical sky-portal it seemed as if a man had just been spat out from the clouds.

A man brandishing two flaming swords.

"Erom?" Topher said, staring up at the falling figure.

"What?" the robed-one said, looking up at the warrior. "Impossible! Nothing gets out of there without tremendous work and power. Certainly not a mortal."

"WIZARD!" Erom roared from above them. "ALL IS FORGIVEN IF YOU STOP ME SAFELY!"

Topher closed his eyes and took a deep breath. He could sense time slow down around him, frozen as his magic kicked in. It gave him a chance to find some sort of spell that would work. But, above all else, Topher wanted a spell that could sort out two problems in one go.

Then, with the aid of his ancestors no doubt, the perfect magical solution presented itself.

The Dance.

Topher opened his eyes and felt the power of centuries coursing through his body as he drew on all the available energy in the air around him. He had no idea how he was doing it, but that did not matter. What mattered was The Dance.

As he began to move his hands in intricate circular motions, the Cold Mage felt his body lift off the ground on chilly winds. A sphere of cold currents formed around him, like a protective barrier. The winds were strong enough to push the hooded figure back a few feet. They held up the daggers but seemed to struggle to step towards Topher.

Turning his attention to Erom, Topher began to gesture with alternate circles towards the falling warrior. First his left hand, then his right. Waves of light blue energy shot forth from his fingers and raced towards the ground. With a wide waving gesture using both arms, Topher willed the thickest ice known to man into existence. It sprouted out of the lines of blue energy like mushrooms, growing upwards with every inch until a large frozen ramp was formed. Topher raised up his left hand, keeping the fingers together, and gestured towards Erom. At the end of the ramp a large curve formed, shooting straight into the sky, and sending out support beams of ice that embedded into the summit.

In seconds the largest ice structure Topher had ever seen was formed, ready to catch the warrior and bring him down to the ground safely. The Cold Mage kept powering magic into the ice slide so that it remained stable. As the spell continued Topher could 'sense' the structure as if it were his own arm. He felt a thud and knew that Erom had landed on the top.

"WooooHOOOOO!!!" the warrior shouted as he raced along the slide.

Topher waited until Erom was in the curve that had him at ground level before channelling more power into the slide and changing its shape. He added additional ice blocks to the end of the structure, creating a second ramp that continued past him and rose a foot into the air before ending suddenly. The end of the slide now faced the hooded figure. As Erom whizzed past Topher, the warrior waved.

"That's not Drom," Topher shouted from his floating sphere of cold currents at Erom.

"He is a fake."

"Understood!" the warrior replied as he slid by.

Hurtling towards the exit point, Erom lifted his knees so that the soles of his boots were facing forward. He flew off the last slab of ice, launching into the air, and sailed over the ground before slamming both his feet into the hooded figure's chest. The impact not only looked painful but sounded sore as well. Both boots struck with such force that the hooded figure was lifted off their feet and sent careening over the edge of the summit.

"NNOOOOOO!!!" fake-Drom screamed as they fell down to earth.

Erom dropped to the ground with a thud and lay on his back, looking up at the sky.

Topher ceased channelling magic and the sphere of cold surrounding him faded away. He stepped lightly down to the ground and walked over to the forlorn figure.

"We cool?" he asked.

Erom looked up at him with one eye closed.

"You're cool," the warrior said. "Some magic tricks you've learned there."

"They have come in handy today," he replied.

"Who was your man then if not Drom?"

"No idea," Topher said, shrugging. "He really wanted that portal to be closed. Turns out you and I were the only two who could close it correctly. Not sure if that's a good or bad thing, mind you. I guess leaving instructions in riddles isn't the best way to share information."

Erom shuffled up to rest on his elbows and looked around the summit of Mount Karmorg.

"You know," he said. "This place really isn't all that impressive when you get right down to it."

"Agreed. Fancy getting a drink?" Topher asked, extending his left hand.

"Sure," Erom said, grabbing the offered extremity and hauling himself up to his feet. "Just promise me you won't go trying to take over the island any time soon."

"I've just discovered I can make things cold on command.," Topher said, grinning. "I plan on opening a cold beer tavern that will be so famous people will come from all over Dechripo to get a frosty one."

"A frosty one?"

"That's what they will call 'chilled ale'.

Why would I want to be a ruler when I can give people cold drinks all day? I'll be rich without having to do any work."

Erom thought about this for a moment.

"You wouldn't happen to need somebody to guard your front door, would you?" he asked. "A place that popular is going to need protection from ne'er-do-wells."

"Let's talk terms," Topher said, smiling. "Over a frosty one."

The Righteous Old Guard

Damien Larkin

The Dead God's fire warms my face. Glancing up into the sky, I take heart from seeing his celestial throne approach its zenith. The time of action is nearly upon us. Soon, the heathens and unbelievers will pay the price for their blasphemy—steel and fire stand ready to scour them from this world.

Careful to keep my head low, I crawl closer to the jagged rocks in front of me. Aging bones creak with every movement, louder than the armour covering my torso. My withered hand grips one of the stones for balance; in my mind's eye, I remember a time when my flesh was youthful and unblemished. A long time ago now. Many years gone since I was a young man in service to the Dead God's will.

Peeking my head up, I gaze into the camp below, searching for the demon with the copper eyes. The thoughts of her revolt me, her very existence an affront to the pure and decent. I cannot spot her but note her many degenerate followers—men and women, all young and in the prime of their lives—sitting about laughing and sharing vats of wine. No care for the fields that need toiling, the farms that need tending, or the market stalls that require manning. They cavort carelessly, citizen and slave, noble and worker. The sight of their opulence enrages me.

"The time nears, Jonus," says Eppi.

I look over and meet her hard stare head-on. Ancient memories flow back, of countless times when we lay side by side, ready to launch an ambush. She is my oldest friend, an old woman now with many grandchildren, but today, we relive our youth. The Dead God wills it. We obey.

"Yes, sister," I say and clasp her shoulder.

She takes my hand in hers and squeezes.

A smile cracks across her tired face, but there is no joy in her eyes. Deep down, none of us wishes to be here—it is our people below, our kin. Destroying a heathen is much easier when they don't speak the same language or share the same blood.

"Have you seen him?" she asks.

Shame fills me, and I return my gaze below. Amongst the crowds of jubilant youths, I seek out Randl's face. A part of me hopes he has returned home or been tasked with foraging in the surrounding mountains. But I know that is not true. He will be down there, cavorting with the copper-eyed witch, suckling on her lies and betraying the ways of our ancestors.

"No," I say, and Eppi pats me once on the shoulder.

Above us, the Dead God's palace continues to near the top of the sky. I turn my attention to the accursed rift that tears the air open like a wound. The deviants worship the world above them, craving to find a way to reach the strange upside-down mountains dangling over us. Demons and abominations reside up there, the High-Priests tell us.

Here, where the rift is at its widest, is where

they believe they can ascend successfully. For three days, we have watched them. Volunteers drink themselves into oblivion and then climb the Sinner's Stone marking the epicentre of the rift. Only in this place will malevolent magic lift them from their feet and raise them into the sky; they laugh and wave while ascending until they disappear into the unknown. Here, in this place, we will purge them with hallowed flames and destroy the accursed rift once and for all.

"We should pray," Gammon, the High-Priest, says from behind me.

Without hesitation, we all comply and turn to face him. Heads bow low in honour of the Dead God. Hands rest on sword hilts or long-bows, the instruments of our conviction and tools to spread our religion's righteous word.

"Oh, most powerful master," Gammon beseeches. "You who shines your love upon our fields, who lights our fires at night, and who gives us warmth and sets our hearts ablaze. Eternal lord, sitting within your palace of flames, hear our words. Burn fear and temptation from our bodies. Scour us clean of filth and impurity. Strengthen our hands that we might strike down those who oppose you. You know us, most noble King. We have aged, but we are yours to command always. Guide us, your purification squads, that we might earn another victory in your name. Let it be done."

"Let it be done," we say as one.

Heart stirred and the righteousness of our task clear, I shove a weakling's doubt to the far corners of my mind. I unsheathe my half-sword and examine the sharpened blade; my hand wraps around the hilt, naturally finding the grooves from years of use. A rush of exhilaration flows through me as it did in my younger days. Back then, we were unstoppable—entire towns and villages purified in the Dead God's flames, heretics put to the sword and thrown onto burning piles. I yearn for the simplicity of those times when our enemies were outsiders, not our own people.

I slide out from behind the rocks and crawl carefully down a path leading to the bottom of the mountain and the edge of the unbelievers' camp. Long grass and rocky outcrops shield me from enemy eyes, although that doesn't concern me. In three days of observation, they haven't posted a single guard or lookout.

Pleasures of the flesh consume them; they eat, drink, sleep, and fuck without a care, all under our god's judgemental eye. That will be their undoing.

At the base of the mountain, I shelter behind another rocky outcrop. Behind me, Eppi, Gammon, and the rest of our team move into position. Two other squads slip down from different points opposite us to hem in the enemy. Rows of archers lie in wait above, ready to unleash a barrage of arrows when we attack. With luck, we'll overwhelm the more numerous degenerates before they even know what's happening.

A glance above shows the time of action nearly upon us. I tighten my grip on my half-sword while my heart pounds. Three men and three women all bask in the sun in front of me. By the brands on their faces, the men are slaves while the fine linen skirts of the women mark them as the daughters of merchants. They laugh with each other, holding hands, whispering into each other's ears. When one of the women kisses a slave on the lips, I become incensed. How dare she break the Dead God's law and cavort with such a creature? Today will forever be known as the day when decency and the rule of law struck back. We, the veterans, the elderly, the retired, the true servants of the city, will land a blow that will resonate for generations.

The Dead God's flaming palace reaches the highest point and a rush of energy bursts through my limbs. I feel my father's hands beating me as a child. I see heathen children mock the rags I wore to school. I hear the taunting words of a degenerate woman rejecting my advances before my eyes were opened to the Dead God's words. The burning anger within me explodes.

Snarling, I rush from my hiding spot and charge at the small group. I want to laugh at how quickly my aging bones still move and the fact that none of my targets have even spotted me. At the last minute, one of the women looks up. Her eyes widen when she sees my raised sword. She opens her mouth, but nothing comes out as an arrow plunges through her chest. The nearest slave turns in time to see me hack my blade down and bury it deep in his flesh.

Blood sprays my armour. Screams erupt. Arrows cleave through the air, cutting down groups of blasphemers. I yank my blade free and thrust it through the stomach of another slave; he raises his hands and unleashes a gurgling shriek. I twist my weapon and snap it out, allowing him to slump backwards, clutching at his wound. A swipe of my half-sword catches the other slave in the jaw. His blood spurts across the two stunned women, still sitting on the ground, frozen with fear.

I grab the closest one by her long blonde hair and yank her onto her knees. While her friend watches, I run the edge of my blade across her throat; a waterfall of crimson spills across her porcelain skin and flows onto her dress. I toss her away like a rag doll, her gurgles fading into the ever-growing din of battle.

The last heathen woman jumps to her feet, screaming, and turns to flee, but a stray arrow catches her in the thigh, and she crashes to the dust. She rolls over, her hands raised as I stalk closer. Begging for her life, she says she recognises me. Knows me as a kind and decent person. Someone who gives to the poor and teaches the young how to live good and modest lives. I turn my blade downwards, raise it high, and bury the steel right through her chest. She shrieks, then murmurs, her body shuddering as I twist and pull my weapon free.

All around me, the purification squads are sanctifying this area. Three heretics lie dead at Eppi's feet as she torches a make-shift tent; Gammon batters his club off a fallen slave-girl until her head explodes into a mush of brain and bone fragments. Bodies line the blood-slicked ground, arrows embedded deep in flesh. The wounded cry out for mercy, but they will find none here today. Smoke rises from the other two points of the camp, marking the progress of our other teams.

I push on and step towards a young shirtless boy crawling along the ground—a trail of blood from a wound on his back stains the dust. I boot him in the ribs, causing him to flip over. He yelps, his thin body shaking from the pain, his breathing laboured. Teary eyes fall upon me, and I recognise the lad as Justn, the baker's son. Like the others, his lips move, protesting the closeness of my blade to his chest, begging for his life.

"Why aren't you at home, boy?" I say, taking a step closer. "Why aren't you learning your father's trade or reading the holy scrolls?

Why aren't you in the temple or the communal fields?"

His mouth trembles, tears streaming down his cheeks; lies escape his lips, excuses for not doing his duty. I drive my sword into his flesh. His eyelids open wide as he screeches, and his hand grabs for my blade as if to pry it free. Fresh streams of crimson roll down his hands as he slices his fingers. I yank my half-sword out and plunge the blade into his heart.

The heretics are falling back now, trying to regroup, their numbers decimated by our savage attack. Arrows whistle on the breeze, cutting down those too slow to seek cover. Eppi and Gammon rush to my side, their weapons dripping with the blood of the fallen. Three more of our team gather, weapons drawn and ready to quench their thirst on the lifeblood of the degenerates.

Armed with lumps of furniture and broken glass bottles, two dozen of the enemy block our path of advance. They stand in an avenue of tents so the archers can't spot them. Behind them, a small crowd seeks to flee our wrath, running to the centre of the camp. I look over the heathens ahead, searching for my son's face but don't spot it. Terrified and drunken eyes gape back at me. None of them have armour on, their improvised weapons no match for sharpened steel.

Unleashing a roar, I raise my sword and charge. The sound of my voice causes three to drop their weapons, spin about and flee. With my allies at my side, we close the distance and crash into the enemy mass. I swipe, slash, and thrust. Chair legs and wooden clubs splinter when my blade chews through them. I shove a sun-kissed woman back and punch my sword through her navel. She stumbles, clutching at her wound, but before I can finish her, a boy with the same look as her smashes his cudgel across my arm.

My sword grip loosens as I shoulder him away. Pain tears up my arm. I grit my teeth to keep from screaming and wheel the blade around. The boy dodges and tries to hit me again, but I deflect the blow and shove him back. He narrowly defends against a thrust, small chunks of wood splitting from his weapon. Anger coursing through my veins, I swipe again. He blocks but exposes his leg, so I kick at his knee, causing him to lose his balance. I slam my blade down and crash it through his shoulder; he tumbles face first, and I stamp my boot onto his skull. The woman tries to throw herself onto the boy to shield him, so I smash my boot across her head too, until blood leaks from her ears and she lies unmoving.

Eppi stands to my right, her chest heaving as she cleaves through another victim. I swing my half-sword again and catch another heathen on the leg. He stumbles as Gammon cracks his head with his club; blood gushes across my face, urging me on.

Within seconds, the mob lies bleeding at our feet. We have yet to lose one of our own, yet our path lies carpeted with the corpses of our enemies. Even after such a short exertion, I gasp for air, my age revealing itself. No longer am I a youthful boy, swinging a sword with ease and cutting down heathen children without breaking a sweat. I suck in a deep lungful of air while Eppi slits the throat of a wounded slave boy. With the degenerates pacified, she snatches a chunk of wood from the broken pile of the dead and dips it in a nearby fire. She waves the flames across the tents beside us until they catch fire. Gammon mutters a prayer of thanks, and we push on.

We search the tents we pass as quickly as we can, seeking out any who try to hide from us. Several times, we drag wailing youths from their hiding places and shove them to their knees. We take turns purifying them, often cutting their throats, although Gammon prefers to smash their skulls open. The High-Priest mumbles prayers as we walk, invoking the Dead God's blessing for our holy works.

In the centre of the camp, the heathens make their last stand. They surround the Sinner's Stone, protecting it on all sides. Some of them have knives and swords, but most have armed themselves with whatever they could find. They stand defiant before us as the rest of the purification squads emerge from the sea of burning tents. Even though they outnumber us, they are no match; none have served the Dead God in cleansing this land of unbelievers. They know nothing of hardship or war, yet something still drives them, spurs them on. And then, I see her—the woman with the copper eyes.

Even in such a crowd, she stands out. A creature of immense beauty dressed all in black, her red lips curled into a perpetual smile, hair as dark as night, resting on her shoulders. For a moment, I sense her piercing gaze on me, sending a shiver of terror down my spine. Never before have I seen eyes like that, eyes that see past skin and pierce deep into the soul. In a single heartbeat, I sense she knows me. All my sins laid bare at her feet. Her lips don't move, but I can almost hear her voice within the recesses of my mind. She promises to wash it all away. Cleanse me of the guilt. Take away the screams of children burning on a fire that haunts me in my dreams.

"Stay strong, brother," Gammon says and grabs my sword arm. "Focus on the Dead God's burning love. Ignore the demon's temptations."

Scenes of death and destruction float before my eyes. I look upon the faces of my fellow citizens and, in them, see those who have fallen to my sword. Villages that existed for thousands of years disappeared as I carved a burning swath across this landmass. People whose names go unremembered cry out and beg even while I stab them. Smouldering corpses dangle from nooses, swaying in the light breeze. The guilt wells behind the floodgates and threatens to burst.

"Brother," Eppi hisses. "Jonus. You must resist. We are the righteous. We must serve. Resist the demon's temptations."

I look upon Eppi's face, but I still sense those copper eyes upon me, drilling deep inside my soul. Eppi spins about and snatches a torch. Tethered to the spot, unable to move, I watch as she slips her knife free and pushes it into the flames. She draws the heated metal and presses it hard onto the back of my left hand. The sizzling pain causes me to yelp, and I stumble back, shocked at the sensation of my burning flesh. I want to lash out and hit her, but my senses return. I am a soldier of the Dead God. I serve him with a burning heart in his purification squads. I belong to him. I am righteous.

As I turn to face the copper-eyed demon, Gammon and Eppi both slap me on the back. Those copper-eyes hold no power over me; the strength and purity of my convictions spur me on. I will do what it takes to scrub this land free of sinners and apostates, even if it means carving through my own people.

"For the Dead God," I say and lift my sword.

A cheer rings out from the purification squads. Weapons raised, we charge the heathen mobs. They tremble at our approach, but some push to the front, swords at the ready. Amongst them, my son, Randl. He stands off to my right, sword in hand, shouting at one of my comrades. I doubt if he saw me, but he knows I'm here. A son knows a father.

I crash into the enemy ranks with a ferocious roar. Steel sings as blades clang and clash against each other. I lunge at a woman armed with an axe, but she sidesteps. She swings the weapon at my head, but I block it and shove her back; a barb of pain eats into my flesh when the edge of a sword cuts into my arm. I jab and catch a heretic in the side before shifting my blade back to the woman. She dodges again and manages a glancing blow against my upper thigh. Snarling, I lunge again, this time catching the side of her face. The shock causes her to stumble and drop her guard. I bury my blade in her stomach, whip it out, and throw her to the ground, where she disappears under a tsunami of boots.

Another sword lashes out from the side, but my blade meets it. I swipe down and try to ram the tip of my sword into a heathen male's eye, but he resists. He curses my name, and I recognise him as the grandson of my neighbour, Luli. A fine young man, or so I always thought. He jabs at me, but his weapon only dents my shoulder armour. I manage to slash, and my blade eats into the muscle of his forearm; the sword tumbles from his grip and crashes to the dust. He screams something at me moments before I punch my weapon through his neck—a fountain of blood sprays out. His head lurches at an awkward angle. He slumps while someone behind him unleashes a heartbroken wail.

We have the heretics on the backfoot, our three groups pushing them closer and closer to the Sinner's Stone. The dead and dying mark our path. Like frightened animals, the enemy bunches in tighter, those armed with real weapons becoming fewer. Our advance has not come without cost. Although the archers have joined the fray, I spot less allied swords, axes, and clubs in my peripheral vision. Eppi still stands near me, hardening my resolve. We have fought together many times. Her presence spurs me on.

We unleash another war cry and advance again. I catch one heathen on the face, burying my sword deep into his skull. A woman behind him leaps past, her sword lunging; I deflect, but the force of her attack knocks me off balance. Stumbling, I manage to guard against another blow, but she swipes low and catches my unarmoured right leg. Agony rips up my limb but serves to feed into my anger.

Growling at her, I assault with an animal ferocity. She blocks every swipe and lunge, but her movements slow as she tires. She reacts too sluggishly, and I manage to grab her wrist, tug her in close, and run my blade through her torso. A small stream of blood dribbles from her lips; her mouth moves as if to say something, but no words come out. As the light fades from her eyes, I push her back towards her comrades. She hits the ground with a thud while the unarmed enemy in the back rows all screech in terror.

"Father!"

The word hits me like a blow to the stomach. Even over the sounds of battle, the screeches of the wounded, and the pleadings of the dying, I know that voice. Randl stands in front of me. His bare chest has splatters of blood on it, and fresh cuts line both his arms, but he waits with a bloodied sword in his hands. His blue eyes peer deep into mine. His chest heaves; he steps closer. My son. The degenerate heathen.

He opens his mouth to say something, but I lunge before he can speak. His eyes widen as my sword crashes against his; he forces me back but makes no attempt to go on the offensive. I slash at him, trying to take his head clean off. Again, he blocks but makes no move to retaliate.

"Father," he says as one of his comrade's collapses beside him. "I have no wish to fight you. Call this off. You have the power to stop this."

The Dead God's fiery wrath explodes within me. The pain of my aching wounds is seared from my brain by his explosive fury. I am wrath in human form. I will punish the sinners and right their wrongs.

Like a madman, I hurl myself at Randl. His sword swings in perfect time, deflecting from high, sweeping to block a lunge, even ramming his shoulder into me to drive me back. He does not strike at me. Coward.

"Father, please," he screams, tears rolling down his cheeks. "Please."

Flashes of him as a boy race in front of my eyes. I remember him as a toddler, barely able to walk, raising his hands for me to lift him. Wearing armour stained from a purification, I pick him up, and he giggles as he plays with my helmet. Another memory of training him with sword and shield by the river. He struggles with the weight of the weapon, but determination burns on his face. Every bruise he receives from me across his arms and legs, a badge of honour; he yearns to impress, to be like me.

I drive my sword at him again. Someone to his left tumbles and crashes into his knee. The action shifts him off balance. The tip of my blade cuts the side of his flesh, not a deep wound, but a wound, nonetheless. He cries out and lashes his sword. Power in this strike. Anger.

My weapon absorbs the blow. Cupping his left hand over his cut, he swings the blade again, fury replacing the concern that once danced in his eyes. He snarls and tries to take my head off, but I duck and lunge, the edge of my sword nicking his calf. His blade drops slightly. I slam into him and thrust at the right side of the body. Once again, my half-sword cuts through his skin, blood sprinkling from his minor gashes. His anger explodes. A grimness within me rejoices. How many enemies have I dispatched who lost their temper? The Dead God blesses the righteous who give in to the battle madness. He smites the blasphemers who are unworthy of his fiery protection.

Randl unleashes a roar and closes the distance between us. His sword moves with lightning speed, constantly trying to catch me off-guard, yet I take every strike, every thrust and cut. His arms tire, the speed of his movements diminishes. The death around him distracts. Too slow now to react.

When he raises his sword too high, I know I have him. Rather than meet the blow head-on, I hurl myself to the ground, roll once and come to a knee. His arm halfway across his body, he can't reach me in time. I lunge and drive my sword into his flesh, shoving it up past his ribcage and slicing through his organs. Randl blinks at me, stunned, the pain registering a split second later. His weapon falls from his grip as he tumbles to his knees. Blue eyes gaze at me, accusingly. His blinks become slower. I slip my sword out and rest the tip of the blade against his throat.

I remember holding him as a child, a tiny creature that I could nestle in one arm. His small hand wraps around my thumb for the first time, and I experience a father's love for a new-born. Countless games we used to play when I returned from campaigns flit across my eyes; long-forgotten lessons about our religion, city, and way of life come to mind. How I wished for so much better for my boy. I gave him a world scoured of evil acts just for him to turn his back on the truth.

"Father," he whispers, his face pale, his bloodied hand shaking.

I can see it in his eyes. He wants me to hold him like when he was a boy, to tell him everything will be fine and that I'll protect him. He doesn't want to die alone, not here, not in this place. The desire to reassure him nearly engulfs me, but the Dead God's will be done in all things. It is to him I owe allegiance and no other. I choose my words with care.

"I have no son."

On the last syllable, I run my sword through his neck. He twitches and gurgles, his hands flopping about at his sides. And then it is done. Another heretic exterminated in the name of righteousness.

When I rise to my feet, the heathens have been decimated. A handful of them fights on, driving the few of us left back with desperate ferocity. Standing in front of the Sinner's Stone, the copper-eyed demon observes the battle without a hint of concern. Her head moves as she follows the developments of the battle—no one guards her, the closest to her already locked in mortal combat. Their lines are reduced to small pockets of resistance. We can punch our way through and destroy the damned rift now.

Gammon meets my gaze and nods. With his free hand, he lifts the horn dangling from his belt to his lips and blasts it three times. The signal to launch the last phase of our operation. Concealed on the hill, a small team guards a cart of explosives. After three days of observation, Gammon swears he's worked out the exact amount of time needed for the explosives to detonate when it reaches the mouth of the rift.

By the Dead God's grace, we'll close that hateful rift forever and deny the demon her power.

Eppi stumbles to me, her left arm coated in red from a deep gash; her chest is heaving, and splatters of blood cover her face. She raises her sword. We both suck in lungfuls of air and charge the faltering enemy. Eppi hurls herself at two women armed with axes while I target the demon. She sees me coming but doesn't react. The foul copper-eyed abomination waits there, making no move to escape, her eyes burning deep into mine. I pull back my sword and lash out. Time seems to slow. She doesn't respond. My blade cleaves through the air, eager to tear into her flesh. A hair's distance away and the demon finally moves. With speed so quick I can barely comprehend it, she ducks, and my sword cuts through open air.

In an eyeblink, she's standing bolt upright again, her face emotionless, unafraid of being within striking distance of my weapon. I lunge, and again at the last possible moment, she swerves, avoiding my attack with ease. The fury within me builds again. This demon won't even give honourable combat. It taunts me with sorcery and black magic.

I slash and jab and push forward, aiming to pin her against the Sinner's Stone. The copper-eyed demon ducks, sidesteps, and bends at unnatural angles without so much as breaking a sweat. In all my life, I've never seen such speed. If she can move so fast, then why doesn't she try to attack me? At the way she veers between my swipes, she could easily close the distance and cut me down.

Eppi appears and places a hand on my left arm; I stop slashing at air and allow her to guide me a few steps back. The abomination remains standing on her spot, unfazed and staring right at me. A few paces away from her, and I glance around. Our purification squad has been victorious in purging the heretics. They lay sprawled across the blood-slicked dust, gashes across their limbs and heads. Some of our number are mixed with theirs. It saddens me to see so many comrades dead, but I take solace from the fact that they are feasting in the Dead God's fiery palace.

A rustle of activity pulls my attention to the right, and I see the wagon being dragged by some of the archers. A tarp lies draped over it, covering the crates of explosives we intend on using against the rift. The copper-eyed demon sees it too, but still, no flash of concern crosses her face. We surround her—axes, swords, knives, and clubs all drip with the blood of her followers. She looks us over, one at a time. Her only means of escape is clambering onto the Sinner's Stone and escaping back to her demon's lair above us. Her stoic demeanour offends me, so I bring up my sword and roar. The righteous howl back, and we charge, our weapons covering every angle she could escape from. We will dispatch her once and for all and mount her head as a warning to other apostates.

Except, she defies us. She spins and twists, blades and axes cutting through thin air. Her body contorts at impossible angles, slipping through gaps with perfect precision. She dances through the storm of sharpened weaponry, sometimes close enough that she could lean in and plant a kiss. No matter how fast we try to react, she moves with inhuman speed. Untouchable.

The demon bobs, dodges, and weaves until she is behind us, no longer hemmed in by the Sinner's Stone. She could flee, but she merely waits there. My limbs ache from exhaustion, the pain of my minor wounds leaking into the forefront of my thoughts. The Dead God's passion yearns for me to extinguish her, but how can I kill a creature that won't accept its fate and submit? The archers unleash a volley of arrows, but they slip past her or she takes steps to avoid them. She doesn't even glance in the direction of the arrows. Her eyes remain locked on us, an unwitting audience to her demonic power.

"Leave it," Gammon says "We will deal with her after. First, we must close the rift forever. The Dead God wills it. Let it be done."

"Let it be done," we echo.

When the cart reaches the side of the Sinner's Stone, I can taste victory. For all my life, I have looked upon the open wound in the sky, onto a strange world that cannot know our god's love. Scientists and scholars have wasted their lives trying to understand such an evil apparition. Even when we put them to the torch, some would not repent; they screeched lies that we should try to comprehend that which we do not know. To them, we shouted that we understand only what the Dead God wills us to. Today, we will put the matter to rest. Righteousness and holiness will return to our lands. Someday, when I am long deceased, the Dead God's message will spread to all the cities of this landmass. The only sadness I take from this is I will not be alive to purify those heathens and put them to the sword.

A savage howl rises up from the north of the camp. The archers release their arrows in that direction; I lift my sword high, and the purification squad rallies to me. We jog around the Sinner's Stone and see them—the rest of the demon's disciples. They must have been foraging for food in the surrounding hills. These ones have all donned armour and hold swords and axes; they look to the dead lining our feet and then to us. The copper-eyed demon makes no attempt to join them but stands idly by the Sinner's Stone, nothing more than an uncaring observer. I glance over at the wagon. Some of the archers stop hoisting it, but a wave of my hand keeps them at their task. At all costs, we must fulfil our mission. A nod at Gammon sends him racing to the wagon—he will ensure we succeed while the rest of us do what we must.

We rush the heathen onslaught, our swords and axes screaming out for their blood. The pain and tiredness evaporate from my body. This is the day; I feel it in my bones. This is the day when my life's work ends. I will take my place in the Dead God's palace and regale him with the stories of my deeds. He will smile at me when he sees the faces of the men, women, and children I have purified in his name. Friends, long since fallen, will embrace me. We shall celebrate until the end of times when the Dead God will scour the lands once and for all with sanctified fire.

Sharpened steel meets flesh with a wet slap and a screech. I yank my sword free and growl, searching for another target. A man with dark brown hair shrieks and swings an axe at my head; the blade misses most of my face, but the tip cuts through the cartilage of my nose. My eyes sting and water as I raise my sword. He swings again, hacking with undeniable fury, but his blows bring him no more satisfaction. I let him hammer away until he takes a two-handed grip and tries to strike again. I stab upwards and strike him through the throat. His eyes fall to mine, shocked; my blade skewers him, tearing through his throat. I kick his lifeless body aside, spitting on his corpse, and push on.

An elbow to my face sends me stumbling back. My vision blurs. I keep my sword at the ready, trying to disseminate the shapes of those around me as friend or foe. A figure lunges at me, and I manage to narrowly deflect. Squinting, I block another lunge but tumble to a knee after tripping over a corpse. My blade whips up to defend against a death blow. A youthful face screams at me and pushes down hard, trying to knock me backwards. Eppi bursts through the carnage, her sword slashing wildly. She carves through the back of the youth's unarmoured knee. When he tumbles to his knees she grabs his helmet, yanks his head back and runs her crimson-stained blade across his exposed neck. She extends a hand and hauls me up while the youth shudders and chokes on his blood.

These new opponents are more determined, their armour giving them an edge. Our numbers are fewer now. The Sinner's Stone lies at our back, the last of us defending it against the demon-followers' onslaught. Standing side by side with Eppi, I re-join the madness. My bloodied sword against an axe; I slam into another degenerate and knock him to the ground. Taking to a knee, I rip open his visor and bury my sword in his face. He releases a horrific scream as the tip plunges through cartilage and bone, and then falls forever silent. I spit on him and leap towards Eppi fending off someone twice her size.

A horn blast behind us signals Gammon's success. The enemy halts their attack and back-steps. I hear whistling and spy the copper-eyed demon making the sound; her blasphemous devotees pull back and reform, giving us a chance to band together. The dead litter the area between us. Most of them armoured youths, but several of our number lie with them. Good deaths, all. Good deaths to appease the Dead God.

I risk a glance back and spot the cart hovering off the ground, evil magic lifting it slowly into the air. The cart itself is packed with explosives—a single crate powerful enough to blow a hole in a city's wall. One hundred crates will blow a city block to pieces, incinerating every person and building in the area. We have the privilege of witnessing the destruction of the demonic rift before joining the Dead God in his fiery palace.

"Something's wrong," Eppi says. "Why isn't the demon ordering the attack? Why isn't she trying to stop us?"

I look across at the degenerates. Those with their visors up or who wear no helmets have their faces contorted in unbridled rage, mouths drawn into snarls, eyes squinting and burning through us. Their grips are tight on their weapons as they ready themselves. The enemy watches us, not the cart; they desire to fight and kill us, but the copper-eyed beast restrains them. She paces behind them, her gaze focused on the ascending cart.

Uncertainty tugs at the edges of my mind. I have seen the faces of the vanquished, looked deep into the eyes of heretics who knew their end had come. The demon should be trying to stop us—a flick of her wrist and her followers would charge us again. Why not finish the job?

I gaze up at the cart as it approaches the rift. Gammon spent days calculating the length of the fuse based on the weight of the cart and the speed that the foul magic lifted people up. If he miscalculated by a second or two, then our mission was for nought. I leave Eppi's side and backstep to Gammon while eyeing the demon. Gammon slaps a hand on my shoulder, his attention fixed on the cart.

"Trust me," he says. "This will work."

"Why isn't the demon attacking?" I say, the sensation we are missing something growing with every heartbeat.

Gammon mumbles something incoherent, too focused on our objective. Panic starts to overwhelm me. We're missing something. An enemy doesn't halt an attack to observe their own destruction. No one is that foolish. If she's quick enough to dodge my sword strikes, she should have the speed to intercept the cart in the first place.

I glance around at the bottom of the Sinner's Stone and spy four crates. We carried extra in case the enemy threatened to overwhelm us and we needed to blast ourselves to pieces to annihilate as many of them as possible. I rush to the crate and, with my sword, cut the fuse to a length of only a few seconds. Heaving, I lift the crate with my free hand and haul it back to our small group. Regardless of the outcome, the demon dies today. One of the archers hands me the flint and lighting stick he uses to add fire to his arrows; I take it and chip at the flint until the stick takes flame. A deafening bang nearly knocks me flat.

I catch myself and look up. The sky blazes with the Dead God's wrath. Flame rips across the rift, searing the wound closed; orange and red scour the demon's world from our pristine sky. A cascade of explosive fury works its way across the rift, wiping it clean and leaving an unbroken blue sky hanging above us for the first time in generations. A cheer rises and engulfs me; I am flooded with relief, the ache in my heart cleansed. When I turn about and spot the blasphemers cheering louder than us, ice rushes through my veins. The copper-eyed demon has a smile on her face, and she is looking right at me. In that moment, I know we have done her bidding.

"No!" I scream and pull the lighting stick to the fuse.

The heathens advance, screaming and laughing as they run. Gammon and the archers rush out to meet them; Eppi raises her weapon and prepares for our last stand. I will kill this demon. If it's the last thing I do, so be it.

The flame touches against the fuse. A hissing sound indicates we have seconds left. I drop my sword and grab the rope on the side of the crate two-handed. Using the last of my strength, I lift and spin to gather momentum. A sword punches through Eppi's chest. I grit my teeth to stop from screaming and spin harder. Gammon roars when an axe cleaves through his shoulder joint. I release the crate in the direction of the demon and unleash a howl; it spins through the air straight at her, and the explosion sends barbs of pain through my chest and face. Searing white light engulfs my eyes.

When I land, I know only pain. Every part of my body screams in agony. I force my eyes open and glance down at my battered chest. Shards of metal cover my torso, cutting through my armour, while small red streams leak from each wound. A larger chunk of twisted metal is buried deep in my thigh, and every bone in my left arm is obliterated from the way it sags. Struggling for breath, I prop myself up and glance around at the devastation.

The tents in the vicinity have all been demolished—they lie as crumpled, ruined sacks with flames licking at them. I am surrounded by scorched and broken bodies. I almost weep when I see Eppi's shattered and burnt face. My chest tightens as I gasp for air. I have to find the demon's corpse; I need to see her lifeless body before I join the Dead God. I imagine his hallowed call, the light of his palace kissing my face.

A shadow casts over me. Two copper eyes stare down. I want to scream, to screech, to curse her until the end of time, but invisible razors carve through my lungs. I reach for my knife, but my hand struggles to draw it. The demon takes to a knee, that perpetual smile plastered to her face, but those copper eyes hold no joy in them. I try again for the knife, but the pain numbs my fingers; the demon leans in close and slips the blade free for me. She wraps my hand around it and rests it on my chest. I want to plunge it deep into her face and carve out her eyes, but my strength has deserted me. I picture my friends calling out to me. We will be feasting soon.

"Thank you," the demon says in a soft, musical voice.

Her words astound and infuriate me. I pray to the Dead God to grant me strength one last time to do his bidding.

"I've longed to see the rift closed here. Already I can feel my power growing. You have served me well."

I scream, venting the air from my lungs despite the pain. I glare at my hand, willing it to move one more time; it shudders from the effort, but I cannot lift the blade.

"I . . . serve only . . . the Dead God."

"You worship a myth," she says.

I shake my head and snarl. I don't have the energy to stab her, but if I can prop myself up again, I may be able to sink my teeth into her neck. I struggle but can barely lift my head from the ground.

"There is no Dead God," she says while stroking my forehead. "Your people created a lie many generations ago to explain what you couldn't understand. Your god is a celestial body, no different than the many others that dot the night sky."

"No," I growl, unable to form any other word.

"Hush," she says and turns about.

She hauls something beside me. I turn my head and burst into tears at the burned and battered face of Randl. His lifeless eyes stare into mine; I want to recoil and run away, but my body refuses to obey. Tears stream down my face, mixing with the blood, forming pink droplets on the sandy ground.

"You can let go now," the demon whispers. "In your final moments, see if I'm wrong. Tell me when you see your god's face and hear the voices of your friends. Let go."

I close my eyes to hide Randl's face. My ears strain to hear words of welcome as my life slips away. Instead, the faces of the heathens I purified rush through my mind. I see them all so clearly—every death blow and last words thud through my skull. Finally, I see Randl as a child. The face he made when I killed him lingers when all the others fade. Copper eyes replace his own and glare at me.

She knows. She knows no one calls to me. Darkness envelopes, but those copper eyes remain steady.

The Dead God does not greet me.

Ocean Cloud

C. Marry Hultman

Rift, *tear, crack, break,* the words swam around in his head in a confused stream. Like the uncontrollable deluge of a waterfall.

Orr stared out the window at the immense split in the sky that hung over the stormy sea as an ominous portent of what might come. The bright, white light that emanated from the tear reflected in the dark waves and a steady trickle of water ran from it to intermingle with the sea below. He raised a worried eyebrow as he tapped the cold stone window frame with the giant golden ring permanently fused to his index finger.

"Explain it to me again, Captain Eräpuro," he said without turning around.

"Would that I could, Your Highness." Captain Eräpuro's nasally voice grated on Orr's spine. "As the kingdom woke, this had already appeared."

"You are telling me that this thing," Orr said as his tapping on the stone intensified, "simply came from nothing during the night?"

"My Lord," said the lilting voice of Captain Hahne. "The Watchers in the Southern Lighthouse tell of a deafening crack sometime during the night."

"And?" The tapping still escalated.

"Well," Hahne stammered. "We don't know."

"Your Highness," his aid Kettu stood next to him with parchment and quill in hand. "We are all as surprised as you are over these events."

"Fine." Orr turned in his chair and rolled closer to the stone table in the centre of the throne room. "Would any one of you like to explain what this beast is?"

Orr pulled a red wood walking cane from the back of his chair and tapped it against the table. A large body lay on the stone. A hulking mass of grey scales, protruding spikes simply dumped atop the royal dining table.

"It attacked one of the villages on the West Coast," Captain Hahne said as she walked closer to it.

"Just like the tear in the sky, it seems to have simply appeared last night," Eräpuro added as he picked at the tail of the thing.

It must be as long as the body and looked like a serpent with thick barbs in deadly rows on either side. At the end sat a thick ball that reminded Orr of a weight a blacksmith might use.

"It killed ten villagers and five of our soldiers before we could take it down," Hahne said and rapped her knuckles on the creature's head.

It looked like that of a lizard, but with a thick cap covering the skull proper, and it echoed as the knocks reverberated through the head.

"This roamed the West Coast last night?" Orr bit his lower lip. "That is this particular coast. It might as well have attacked the palace."

An awkward silence filled the throne room and the two captains, both dressed in red tunics and bronze breastplates, shared a worried glance. A velvety cape hung off their right shoulders as well. Orr observed them with disdain. They had not seen true battle in years, their uniforms more for show than function.

"I assume so, Your Highness," Eräpuro tried. "But…"

"What?" Orr raised his voice and both Hahne and Erapuro flinchedHis temper was infamous, and he had learned that he only needed to threaten to raise it for the people around him to react. A hint or a look was all he needed these days. He used to carry a hammer hidden in his doublet that he would slam into the walls, tables or even throw at his advisors, but the fines the council forced him to pay ended up costing him more than he felt it to be worth. Still, his aides were unsure if the silver object might not be hiding behind the delicately woven fabric he wore.

"You mean to tell me that a beast like this, that looks to be twice the size of a grown man, has wandered around undetected on this coast?" Orr rammed the carcass with his cane.

"Your Highness," Eräpuro pleaded. "We were unaware of its existence until it went to attack this morning."

"Perhaps it came from the tear." Hahne fell silent as soon as she spoke.

King Orr of Whisle, The Floating Kingdom, looked at her for a moment. He said nothing, only stroked his attempt at a beard with his gnarly claw-like fingers and furrowed his brow. Leaning back in his wheeled chair, he considered her words. To most the king might not cut an intimidating figure. He looked much younger than his sixty years, with unkempt sandy coloured hair that hung lifeless and oily in front of beady eyes. Everything about the king seemed ill-fitting, from his oversized doublet to the baggy trousers covering his twisted and withered legs.

"My dear Captain Hahne," he said through gritted teeth. "Are you suggesting that this, this thing, for lack of a better word, and the tear are connected?"

"Well…I," she squirmed as she tried to figure out an escape plan. "Not in so many words, Your Highness."

"Then what are you saying?" Orr pushed

himself closer to her, his bent hands gripping the wheels of his chair like a vice. He whacked the cane into her kneecap and she raised her leg, forcing her to balance on the other.

"Tell me, Captain." Orr's lips twisted into an evil grin. "What do you think this is?"

"Please, Your Highness." Hahne could not step back; it would be a taunt to the king and would result in more than a simple caning. "We have never seen such a creature before. It appeared the same morning as the tear came. We can see the water flow from the crack into the sea, why would it not be plausible that it emerged from that crack?"

Orr lowered the cane and then rolled backwards. Captain Hahne tentatively put down her leg and rubbed it with her hand. Eräpuro also backed away, not eager to get involved.

"I believe you are correct," Orr said and tapped his ring against the wooden armrest.

"Pardon me?" Hahne paused her movement for a moment.

"I believe that there is a link between this beast and the hole in our beloved sky." Orr smiled, but it looked more threatening than pleasant. "Send for Tuomainen and have her meet me in the great hall. Have her examine the specimen first so that she may give me a full report when I see her." He rolled the chair towards the great doors leading to the rest of the palace.

"When shall I tell her that you will see her?" the royal aid Kettu asked as she ran to open the doors. Her white robe fluttered around her, threatening to ensnare her legs.

"Do not tell her anything." Orr smirked. "I will be there when I have time." He looked over his shoulder. "Captains," he said and rolled out.

"Why is it always me?" Qat asked as he squeezed the snus between his fingers into a ball.

He placed it under his upper lip and felt the familiar burn as the poison entered his blood. The initial hit always felt best. The tiny shards of glass shredding his gums allowed the snus to work its magic. He tossed the cylindrical container to the man next to him in the boat, snorted and then spat a gob of brown mucus, aiming for the water but instead hitting the inside of the vessel. It lazily slid down towards the deck, leaving a brown trail behind.

"You are the best we have," Veek said as he dipped his own stained fingers into the snus. "The orders come from the very top."

"The King?" Qat looked at his partner.

"Maybe not quite that high up." Veek smiled, revealing his stained teeth.

A messenger had arrived at their little cottage on the outskirts of the capital; it was so far away that it was more or less on the outskirts of the fishing village Glumma as well. The messenger, who peered in through the bedroom window, interrupted their slumber and Veek took the note from the outstretched hand.

"Your services are needed," he'd said through a yawn.

Now they stood side by side in their boat, staring at a huge tear in the sky. With both their heads shaved and dressed only in short leather britches, they looked more like twins than lovers.

"Why does it always end up being me?" Qat bent down and picked up a long spear with a barb at the end.

"Because, dear," Veek replied, placing a

hand on Qat's hairy shoulder, "you are the best ahti in the Floating Kingdom."

"I was a fool to believe I could retire fully from these duties." Qat sighed.

"Whenever Whisle is threatened, you are called upon. It is an honour, really."

"I feel very honoured to be standing here staring at that pulsating crack in the sky." Qat hefted the spear in his right hand, feeling its weight and balance.

He closed his eyes, sensing the treated wood in his calloused hand. Willing it to become an extension of his own arm. The ahti were trained to use the power of the sea. To listen to her whispering voice in the distance, to read her every mood and be familiar with the beasts that dwelt within her.

Qat looked behind them to the raised shore, a plateau from whence soldiers and villagers had gathered to watch the spectacle. They seemed to know more than he about the tear in the sky. Someone claimed that they had seen beasts tumble into the water. Giant beings with horns protruding all over their bodies, like huge wingless dragons. Yet no one could prove it. So here he stood, getting ready to jump into the ocean, like he had so many times before. The scars on his old skin told the tale, like the tapestry hanging in the palace, of ancient battles with creatures and would-be conquerors. Qat flexed his toes, making sure the skin between them was still intact. Veek always scolded him for not caring for them enough, oiling them to keep the skin pliable and free from cracks, but at his age Qat could not be bothered. It was enough to care for the skin between his fingers.

"The message said to investigate the floor below to look for signs of beasts," Veek read from the communique they had received. "Engage and kill any of them you might encounter. Signed, Eräpuro."

"I hate that fucker." Qat spat another brown gob, this time hitting the surface. "If I die today, I am coming back from the Nether to kill the rank bastard."

"You say that every time."

I fucking hate this, King Orr thought as the sweat ran from the damp hair on the back of his head and then down his neck.

It soaked the thin linen shirt underneath

the doublet as he grabbed at the wheels and moved them forward. He grimaced as every movement of his twisted limbs tried to propel him forward as seamlessly as possible, causing him pain and anguish in the process. As if thousands of daggers cut into his sinewy body.

Kettu had long since learned that it was futile to try to assist the king; those who had tried were met with an uncontrollable rage. A tiny silver hammer stained with old blood hung from Orr's belt. It frequently cracked the masonry as well as skulls.

The creaking from the wooden chair forewarned staff and nobles that the king was approaching, and it gave them ample time to straighten up or shut their mouths before he entered a room, mostly in fear of a possible hammer flying at them.

Orr narrowed his eyes as he entered the grand ballroom that had now become a temporary morgue. Several nobles dressed in their finest garbs of blue and gold stood at attention yet bowed as he rolled across the blue tiles. Their eyes darted from his terrible visage to the table in the centre where an even more horrifying being rested.

Behind the beast stood a tall woman with short hair, dressed in white. Her face was so still and expressionless that one might believe it to be carved from marble. Her milky white skin only added to the illusion.

"Your Highness called for me?" Tuomainen asked in a stern voice. The icy voice, devoid of emotion matched her visage.

"I did," King Orr replied in a voice hoarse from the exertion of his laboured movement, yet wet from sweat running into his mouth.

"I assume it has something to do with this monstrosity on display on the altar." She cast her piercing blue eyes upon the scaly beast.

Her eyes moved to the king. She stared at him with an emotionless gaze. He had always hated it. Nothing he could do fazed her in the slightest. He suspected that she was the only being in the kingdom who did not fear him. Although on occasion, he thought he caught a glance of disdain from her. As if she looked down upon his withered frame and judged him for all that he was.

"I need you to tell me what it is," King Orr replied and wheeled around the table. His view of the tall, silver-haired woman was slightly

obscured by the mountainous form of the creature. "And then I want you to tell me if there
are more of them and how to defeat them."

Tuomainen placed a gloved hand above the
scales and closed her eyes. As the king came
closer to her, he could see her hair stood slightly on end, while the fibres of the white glove
pulled towards the body. Miniature sparkles
flashed, barely visible in the room flooded with
light from the grand windows lining the walls.

Orr looked at Kettu and then to the nobles,
still standing at attention along the walls. He
detested them as well. At least they feared him,
or his wrath. They would sooner slide a dagger between his ribs than bow their heads in
subjugation. The only reason he was still alive
was because there was no one else to take the
throne and forming a republic like the dogs in
the Westlands had done was not on the cards.

He remained in power only because he
had been strong enough to survive infancy; it
was not much of an existence, but he was still
the king.

Tuomainen jerked and gasped as the kinet-
ic link between her and the corpse broke. She
clasped her chest and leaned over the body.

"What is the verdict?" Orr said with disdain in his voice. He abhorred magic. The gods couldn't even grant him that to compensate him for his disabled body.

"It is not like anything I have ever seen before," Tuomainen replied and frowned. "To me, it appears to be some form of overgrown lizard. Like the ones we usually see among the archipelago in the southern seas."

"Could it have come from there?" Orr knocked on the scales again.

"I doubt it." Tuomainen repeated the king's action. "There is no island in that region that could house such a beast. It would have to eat a copious amount of food to grow to this size."

"Perhaps a magician conjured it from a smaller thing?" Kettu interjected.

"I sense no direct magic around it." Tuomainen ran her hand over it. "But there is residual power on its skin."

"Meaning?" Orr asked.

"That something indeed brought it here." She looked out one of the windows. The rift pulsated in the dark sky.

"From the tear?" Orr asked.

"It would seem so," Tuomainen whispered.

"That break in the sky is a portal of sorts that has brought this creature to us."

"But from where?" Orr grew concerned. "This is what we need to know, because we need to stop it. Also, how do we stop it?"

"It would appear that you were able to do so." Tuomainen grabbed the barbed spear sticking out from under one of the scales.

"This…thing." Kettu pointed to it. "It managed to kill ten soldiers before finally being put down. According to our reports, swords, axes and all manner of weapons simply bounced off the tough skin."

"Then I would say that we are in some trouble." Tuomainen let go of the spear.

"That is your answer?" Orr tapped the silver hammer on his belt. "That we are in trouble?"

"I fear the weapon needed to combat a horde of these monsters has not yet been invented." She walked a safe distance away from the king. "Your only solution is to seal the rift."

"And how do we do that?" It was Orr's turn to frown.

"Not sure." Tuomainen smiled.

SKY BREAKER

To most people the water would have been freezing cold. This time of year, Whisle always passed over the deepest part of the known oceans, and this meant cold water. Qat, whose skin was tougher and blood thicker than most races, could withstand the chill. His body moved in an almost dancelike fashion as he glided through the depths. He turned on his back and opened his eyes; a clear film covered them in order for him to see as well as on land. The glow from the rift bathed him in white light and he allowed the movement of the water to overtake him. Qat turned to explore the depth below him, allowing the eerie light from the rift to pierce the darkness. It illuminated the silver skin of a school of fish that darted from side to side, as if they were teasing him to come catch them. He straightened up and attempted to peer deeper, beyond the school. He thought he could see something reflected there, at the very edge of his vision. While slowly moving his webbed feet in circular motions, he remained suspended just below the surface, waiting to see if the shiny thing below would come closer. His right hand gripped the barbed spear as he held it at the ready.

Suddenly, the glistening object moved towards him. It grew in size and he sensed the ripples in the water as it propelled itself forward. His eyes narrowed as they strained to make out the bulky shape coming at him through the murkiness.

Qat gasped at the massive, hulking form that barrelled through the school of fish, scattering them to all sides. The thing coming at him opened its giant maw, revealing hideously pointed teeth made for shredding meat. Thick limbs with webbed claws at the end moved rhythmically, causing it to advance at a greater speed than Qat could have imagined. Deep set eyes under a massive brow reflected the light from above; like burning torches, they pierced the deep. At the end of the hulking head, scaly and green, a huge horn protruded. The beast had it trained on Qat, who grabbed his weapon with both hands.

It resembled a mix of a salamander and a tortoise, only several times larger and meaner. It seemed to have one purpose, and one purpose only. To gore him right through.

Qat closed his eyes and let his senses feel the movement of the water around him. He felt every living thing close by, the presence of the fear-stricken fish swimming in all directions, the cold current coming from the icebound southern isles, the warmth from the sun gently caressing the surface above, his own calm breathing, and the humongous beast hurling its massive body at him. Every fibre inside him screamed to get out of the way of the beast, but he remained, waiting for the right moment. He held out his hand and let his body somersault forward.

He opened his eyes mid-movement as the beast attacked empty water. Qat twisted his body in a spin and let the tip of the spear glide along the back of the beast. He expected a long gash to form, but the scales denied any kind of penetration and the weapon simply reverberated in his grip.

The beast turned to look at him. Then dove deeper again. Qat headed for the surface.

A crowd of villagers had gathered on the water's edge. Veek stood among them, having returned to shore after Qat dove in. They cheered as he broke through.

"Run," he cried as soon as his lungs filled with air.

They stood there, dumbfounded, as if his shout had not registered. Veek moved towards him, his hand outstretched to help him out of the water.

"No," Qat screamed. "Get back, run away."

It was too late. A cascade of water showered over the assembled crowd as the beast emerged from the icy depths. Its great maw enveloped Qat, jaws clenching around his midsection. Veek screamed as blood spluttered from his partner's mouth.

The creature landed on the shore. The rift in the sky pulsated as another being fell from it, similar to the one already in the water, but with huge horns protruding from its massive head. A mouth like the beak of a bird of prey snapped as it fell. Qat's mangled corpse fell on the grass. His eyes were wide open, but he did not register the scenes of carnage reflecting in them.

"Your Highness." The voice sounded like someone scraping stones against each other, so dry and gravely that the sound might ignite the very air around.

Orr turned his chair around, with great difficulty, to where the voice had come from and quickly placed a hand on his hammer, the only weapon he carried.

He had shooed away Kettu before rolling into his chambers. He had no interest in being around others at the moment. He felt feeble and inadequate. A king without the power or ability to save his own people. The Floating Kingdom had no true enemies for it seldom remained in one place, having a set route it followed year after year in concert with the seasons. So, when threats of this sort appeared out of nowhere the ruler needed to know what to do. But Orr felt at a loss. He had always felt that his brain compensated for his feeble body, but he could not figure out what to do about these mysterious beasts emerging from a rift in the sky.

Now he regretted getting rid of his aide for a few feet from his stood a dark towering figure. Dressed in a black robe, a hood casting its features in darkness, only two points of glowing copper light were visible in the shadow. The loose, hanging fabric hid the shape of the person standing before the king; even the hands were hidden inside the long sleeves.

A white cat moved from behind the figure. It pushed its head against what must have been the leg beneath the robe, then made a noise before it proceeded to scale the fabric.

"Who are you?" Orr's eyes narrowed as the cat came to rest around the shoulders of the figure, like a fur skin scarf.

"You know me, Your Highness." The deep voice echoed in his head.

"I am certain I do not." Orr slid the hammer from his belt.

"Even if there is reason for you to be wary," the voice said, "you need not resort to violence. In any case, you would not win."

"What do you want?" Orr's voice shook.

"I have come to collect a debt." The cat's eyes blinked sleepily.

"I am…." Orr felt perplexed. "What debt?"

"Do you not remember, Your Highness?" The voice seemed softer, more lilting. "Maybe this can brighten your memory."

The figure raised an arm to reveal a thin, bony hand. It was at first closed, but it slowly opened to reveal a coin. Orr cautiously rolled closer when, all of a sudden, the figure flicked the coin towards him. It spun in the air, and the king made ready to catch it, not wanting to look the fool and let it fall on the floor. The coin stopped in mid-air, continuing to spin before his eyes, only to float down and land in his lap.

Orr's heart sank as his gaze fell upon the round, golden piece of currency.

"Pick it up," the figure demanded.

With trembling fingers, Orr did as commanded. The side facing up bore the image of his father, King Lauri XI, one of the greatest rulers The Floating Kingdom had ever seen. These coins were no longer in circulation; they were still accepted as payment, but he had ordered them collected and melted down to mint new ones, ones with his face on them.

He knew this coin, knew the weight of it as he held it in the palm of his hand, his fingers too twisted to allow him to properly hold it up. With the help of the index finger on his left hand, he flipped over the coin. There was a mark embedded across the reverse side, right through the crest of his father. Like a tear running through it. Orr shivered.

"Do you remember now?" The voice grew harder again. Grating on his brain. "For I remember a young prince marking the symbol of his father and offering a coin in the Well of Souls in order to ascend the throne."

"That was simply a boyish wish," Orr spoke in a whisper.

"A boy who had enough of the torment of his brothers, the disdain of his powerful father. Tired of the disappointment in the eyes of the noble, the shame that consumed his mother and eventually took her life. A child who in the end, after praying to false gods at night, resorted to the strongest magic on the island. That of wishes."

It was true. His brothers had hounded him, beat him and tortured him for years. Called him names and made fun of his twisted excuse for a body. In some ways, he believed they had damaged it even more. A hatred, a crack had formed in his heart. One that grew bigger and bigger for every punch, kick, and name. It was true that one night he had rolled his chair into the forge in the courtyard, had taken a chisel and had marked a coin, but he had regretted it. Tried to forget it until his eldest brother Hristo had kicked his chair, with him in it, down the palace steps, just for a laugh. They had all laughed as he lay there writhing at the bottom, unable to get up. That was when he made his decision. That was when the tear in his heart widened beyond repair.

The very next day, he commandeered a horse and carriage to take him to the centre of Whisle, the most ancient place of The Floating Kingdom, where the Well of Souls sprang up from somewhere deep inside the bedrock. The elders claimed it was where life had begun, not only there, but the world as they knew it. They claimed that a wish attached to a token would inexorably be granted.

"I wish they all died." The voice crackled like burning logs in a hearth. "Those were the words you spoke that day. Do you not remember?"

"I do," Orr replied, his eyes still transfixed on the coin.

"There is magic so ancient in this world that only a few know of it," the voice continued. "Only those who were there at the dawn of time know the rules. A wish granted demands something in return. I was there to catch the coin when you dropped it in the Well. I have come to collect."

"What is it you want from me then?" Orr dropped the coin on his lap and looked at the robed figure. Tried to meet the fiery gaze of those copper points of light.

The cat stretched out, then climbed down from the shoulders of the figure, rubbed itself against the leg again, then leaped towards Orr. The king was taken aback as the creature landed on his lap. It circled around a couple of times, batted the coin across the room, then sat down, staring at him.

Its eyes were also copper.

"There is a portal in the sky." The voice bounced around the room.

"Yes," Orr replied. "Creatures spring from it."

"They do, indeed. They are not of this world but threaten it. They will wreak havoc on this land and eventually destroy it."

"Yes," was all that Orr could say. The relentless staring from the feline chilled him to his core.

"I want you to let it do so," the voice said.

"Why?"

"Because it needs to for this land to be reborn. Just like your father and brothers needed to die for you to take the throne, Whisle and the surrounding nations need to crumble for something new to take its place. A world more wondrous than you can imagine."

"What of the people? My people?"

"A worthy sacrifice for a noble cause." The voice became soft and seductive. "Believe me, Your Highness, this world will be a better place. A better place without those who look down upon you, who hate and fill it with intolerance for those who appear different."

"What do I need to do?" Orr sighed.

"Nothing," the voice replied. "Let it all unfold."

Captain Eräpuro stood on the widow's walk of the Southern Lighthouse and watched the four beasts that had emerged from the rift wreak havoc on the village and inhabitants below.

"Do nothing?" she said and shook her head.

"Those were the orders," Captain Hahne replied as she leaned against the railing.

"I think the king has finally lost his senses." Eräpuro bit her lip. "Whatever infection has riddled his body has finally reached his head."

"One can wonder if he was ever sane to begin with." Hahne pointed to a large bump on her head where the silver hammer had made an impact only a few days before. "So, we are supposed to stand here and watch the villages and cities burn and do nothing?"

"Those were the orders," Eräpuro replied.

Below the lighthouse, King Orr sat and watched the same events unfold. Kettu leaned on his chair with tears in her eyes. She had pleaded with him, but he had not moved. In the distance, he had seen the figure, an ever-present robed image, watching him from afar.

His heart ached for every home demolished, for every man, woman or child slaughtered by the things, and this was only the beginning. For the first time in his life, he did not sweat. He felt cold. His claw-like hand massaged his chest; the tear in his heart pulsated like the rift in the sky. A symbol of his connection to the vile destruction going on.

"What, by all the gods, is going on?" It was Tuomainen's voice coming from behind him.

He did not turn to face her.

"I had to come see this for myself," she

continued without waiting for a response. She came to stand in front of him. "You are allowing this to happen?"

Orr fingered his hammer. Tuomainen noticed the movement.

"Sorry, Your Highness," she spat.

"I am the king, and this is my decision." Orr did not look at her.

"What happened to your need to find out how to stop the creatures, to seal the rift?" Tuomainen asked.

"I changed my mind," Orr said curtly.

"So, the great King Orr, the defender of Whisle, the man who loves his people and kingdom, suddenly changed his mind and found it acceptable to have them all slaughtered?"

"It is more complex than that," Orr said, then changed his tone. "I do not have to answer to you. I do as I wish." He looked at her with distaste. Not so much at her gall to speak to him in that tone, but at his own actions.

"I care not for your reasons." Tuomainen leaned on the chair, coming close enough that he could see the details of the irises of her eyes. "I might not have cared for you as a person, or how you took the throne, but I always believed you could be a great ruler. Do you know why?"

"Why?" He tried to back away from her, but Kettu held the chair in place.

"Because I felt you genuinely cared." She sighed. "Your father was a great king, but he never showed it in his actions. All he ever did, every decision he ever made, was for the benefit of the nobility and church. You, every order I have heard you decree was for the people. Maybe because you hated the nobles, who in turn only spurned you. Whatever the reason, that was why I never left your side, and I thought we would defeat this threat together. You could have changed this."

She let go of her grip and straightened up.

"This is where I have had enough." She rounded the chair and vanished without another word.

Orr tried to call for her, but he could not find the strength in his voice to say her name. She was right. His hatred for those who had ridiculed him was in part because they did not believe he could rule the kingdom. He wanted to show them, and he tried. He did not need the approval or love of his father, brothers or the nobility. He could find it with his people. They were the ones to heal his heart and now he had betrayed them. He needed to make it right, and there was only one way to do so.

"Why are we here?" Eräpuro asked as she stood at the edge of The Well of Souls. "The kingdom is under attack, and we are staring at this old symbol of superstition."

"We are here to stop the attack," Orr replied.

"And how is that going to happen?" Hahne asked.

"A wish is the strongest power in the realm," Orr said. "This is our only option."

Eräpuro and Hahne looked at each other in abject confusion.

"Hand me your blade Captain," Orr said to Eräpuro, who did as he asked. "Every wish needs a token."

King Orr pulled the silver hammer from his belt and placed it in his lap, then took the knife and cut a line in his left palm. His fingers quivered at the pain, but he gritted his teeth at it. He smeared the hammer with his blood.

"Save my people," he said softly. "No matter the cost."

He felt a twinge in his chest. The tear in his heart getting smaller.

"We need to toss this into the Well," he told Hahne. "Push me closer and help me by holding my arm as I do it."

"Your Highness," Hahne said sceptically, but did as he asked.

She grabbed his hand as he gripped the hammer and together they tossed it into the air. Orr closed his eyes and waited for the splash, but nothing came. Once he opened them, he saw the robed figure standing at the edge of the Well, holding the hammer in its hand.

"Foolish king," the voice boomed. "A valiant effort, but a futile one."

"What is this?" Eräpuro said. "Who is that person?"

A white cat appeared on the figure's right shoulder, hissing at them. The copper points of light under the hood of the figure glowed intensely.

"Can you kill it?" Orr asked his captains.

"I hope so," Hahne said and drew her sword.

Eräpuro and Hahne advanced on the figure with all the swiftness of trained soldiers: swords raised and screaming out their war cries.

The robed figure quickly moved its left arm at Hahne, and she toppled backwards. A red gash marred her neck as she silently fell to the ground.

"Get the cat," Orr screamed to Eräpuro.

She dodged another attack from the figure, and a third. The cat jumped down to the ground and headed towards the king. The captain kicked at the robed figure, who did not move and instead took the force of the booted impact. It dropped the hammer at the edge of the Well.

Eräpuro turned after the cat as it leapt towards Orr. He still had her knife and swung it at the feline. The weapon itself did not connect, but Orr's arm caught the animal and forced it to the side, sending it toppling to the ground. Eräpuro changed direction and kicked the cat from behind with such force that she sent it several feet in the air. The animal tumbled in the air before landing on its feet, shaking its head in confusion.

The robed figure remained still, not going

for the hammer. Orr saw his chance. It was now or never, the point of no return. He had to do what all great leaders did.

He leaned forward in his chair and tumbled out of it. He hit the ground hard but forced himself to complete the roll. He felt the hammer against his body as they both fell into the Well.

The cold water welcomed him like an old lover. He could not swim. Had never learned to do so, his body too twisted to control. His eyes were open as he felt his body sink. The well was deeper than he had imagined, and he held his breath for as long as he could. He saw the hammer below him, heading towards a bright light.

Orr thought he could see a face down there. A radiant image of a face with beautiful, perfect features. A hand stretched out and grabbed the hammer. The one smeared with his blood, and his wish. The Well exploded with colour and Orr could no longer hold his breath. He let it all go.

The rift pulsated in the sky above The Floating Kingdom. It was healing. As water flooded his lungs, Orr felt his own rift mend. He had done right by his people, saved them.

On the grassy area around the Well of Souls, where the last bubbles of air floated to the surface, the cat with copper eyes climbed up on the lifeless body of Captain Eräpuro. The feline kneaded the chest of the corpse before sitting. The hooded figure moved close to it then looked towards the sky. In the distance the rift was visible, and they could see how it narrowed.

The cat squinted and began to purr. Playing on the sympathy of a pathetic king had proved easier than imagined. Another portal closed; another problem solved.

The cat relaxed, stretched out on the still warm corpse, and yawned.

BRING DOWN THE SKY

DAVID GREEN

Harbourside in the walled city of Bellon. Winter.

Lights danced across the black sky. Purples, oranges, reds, angry colours tinged with sickness. Rain poured from them; fat, stinging drops of putrid water, falling every day since the heavens tore themselves apart.

"Strange days we live in, friend."

Elodin pulled his eyes away from the maelstrom above, down to the gutter. A filthy beggar—how the man had so much dirt caked on him through the deluge, Elodin didn't know—sat before him, his worn, sodden cloak dripping with moisture, holding out a wooden bowl with nary enough coins in it to buy clean water at Harbourside's meanest tavern. A hacking cough ripped from the beggar's throat, one from deep inside his chest. Crimson bubbled on his lips, dripped down his chin.

"Aye." Elodin moved in close, placed his mouth near the man's ear, and tried to ignore the stench. "Think of this as a mercy."

He plunged his dagger into the beggar's chest, straight into his heart, up to the hilt. Pulling it out, he settled the corpse against the wall, wiping the blade on the cloak.

"I'll take this for payment, friend. May the afterlife treat you better," Elodin murmured, pocketing the dull coins with a grimace and a sour glance at the damaged sky. "Like it could get any worse."

"Elodin, I thought I told you to never show your fucking face in here again?"

The man in question spread his hands, wincing at the drops of rain making the floor of

The Broken Shackle slick and muddy. Though, he reckoned, enough filth flooded the floors already; a bit more would make little difference.

"Franklin, come on," he protested, fixing a disarming grin on his face. He hoped it was, at least. "I settled my debt. Even did an extra job for you on the side, gratis."

The meaty tavern owner scowled, his black pits for eyes shining with malice. "Take that shit-eating grin off your face before I wipe it off with my blade. You fucked my daughter, too, or had you forgotten?"

"Oh… that." Elodin *had* forgotten. This time, he fought to keep the grin from his lips. "Look, Franklin, I'm sorry, I am. Didn't know she was your daughter, did I? If I'd known, I'd have never—"

"Not good enough for you, is she?" he yelled, a purple vein bulging in his forehead.

The bar's patrons fell silent, wide eyes peering at the men. In the corner of his vision, shadows moved from the dark corners of the tavern. Franklin's heavies.

Great.

"Buy you a drink?" Elodin asked, raising his eyebrows and shrugging.

He didn't mind a fight, didn't really mind killing, but he found a lot of work in *The Broken Shackle,* folk with shady and not-so-illegal work on offer frequented there, and after he murdered the heavies, and Franklin too, he conceded, Elodin wouldn't be welcome.

Putting it mildly.

A rumble emitted from the innkeeper's throat. A laugh. Or what passed for one in Franklin's case.

"You can buy me a bottle, you old dog, and tell me the news from abroad." Elodin's muscles relaxed. "But if you so much as think about touching my girl again, I'll feed you to the pigs!"

A tap on his shoulder turned him around, smile fixed on his face. Elodin still wore the grin when the innkeeper's daughter, Sara, cracked him across the mouth with her palm then stormed off.

The crowd cheered louder than they had all evening.

"It doesn't count when she touches me, right?" Elodin asked, rubbing his stinging jaw. On reflection, he sighed. "Can't say I didn't deserve that."

"So, Franklin, anyone looking for work?"

After Sara had wiped the smile from his face, Elodin had boosted his spirits by drinking and winning a few pouchfuls of coin at dice, but not as much as he'd have liked. Wise to his tricks, the denizens of *The Broken Shackle* used the house die, not allowing him to pull out his lucky pair.

Loaded, of course.

Still, his luck smiled at him, slapping aside. Elodin's thoughts had wandered to the beggar whose life he'd ended, shame and guilt welling in the pits of stomach. He smothered them with more ale; he'd done the poor bastard a favour. Lung rot ate away at it, and Elodin had spared him from the true, bone-deep pain at the end of the disease, laying forgotten in some filthy gutter.

At least, that's what he told himself.

"Work? Times as they are?" Franklin growled, causing Elodin to blink, his thoughts clouding his senses. "Folk just want to drink, afeared of even looking up at the sky. Can't blame 'em, not left me tavern in weeks."

Elodin nodded, resigned, and slumped against the counter. He'd returned to Bellon for that very reason; people had given up. Holy men predicted that the end times loomed, and their followers believed them. Sickness and infection ruled the streets, crops spoiled, cities warred against their neighbours, and no-one, *no-one*, had use for a pick-pocket or assassin, leaving Elodin down-on-his-luck and broke.

If people had given up drinking and dicing, he'd have thrown himself from Gallimh's tallest tower before he even thought of coming back to Bellon.

"Not even a few rats in a cellar need killing? Come on, Franklin, I'm desperate."

The innkeeper chuckled. A sour sound like a cat hacking on a hairball. "There is something… a fellow, over by the back room. Came in a while ago. Asked about sell-swords and the like."

Elodin straightened. "Why didn't you say so before, man?"

"Well, don't quite like the look of him." Franklin swallowed, a frown thick on his craggy forehead. If Elodin didn't know better, he'd say fear ate away at the giant innkeeper's guts.

"Kept his hood up, spoke in this odd whisper. Don't turn around, but he's looking this way. Or at least I think he is. Fucking hood's still up, isn't it?"

Elodin drummed his fingers against the countertop, fingers sticking to it with all the ale spilled there. Money was tight, too tight to mention. He didn't want to tangle with anyone who gave Franklin pause—the scum and scoundrels frequenting *The Broken Shackle* didn't bear thinking about—but what he'd won at dicing, and lifted from the beggar, wouldn't last him days. Elodin nodded. The decision didn't require much thought, really.

"Think I'll go introduce myself. Bring over a couple of tankards, would you?"

"I'll send a girl," Franklin growled. "Cheeky bastard, what'd you think I am?"

Elodin moved away, hiding the grin on his face. Now he reckoned the man wouldn't kill him, he fancied he could tweak the innkeeper's nose a bit. A favourite pastime of his.

He weaved through the press of bodies in *The Broken Shackle*, drunkards yelling, laughing, dicing, and, in some cases, arguing and on the verge of blows. Nervous twangs of a guitar echoed from somewhere in the tavern, and Elodin laughed when he spied a spindly, red-haired youth of no more than eighteen summers clutching his instrument as a gaggle of spirited scoundrels screamed a myriad of song titles at him. Their eyes met, and Elodin reckoned the lad had pissed himself at least once already and would shit himself in the near future.

He soon found the room's corner, and the figure sitting alone, the inn's crowd steering clear of the hooded stranger on instinct. Or perhaps design. Elodin had seen magic, had witnessed the impossible, and wouldn't rule out the possibility that he dealt with a sorcerer or witch. He didn't mind; the person in the corner *wanted* something, and that put Elodin in the driving seat.

He hooked a stool from under the table with his foot and pulled it out, dropping onto it. Like clockwork, a harried looking serving girl slammed two ales down on the bench, the foamy liquid sloshing.

"Hear you need a job done?" Elodin smirked, taking a long pull from his tankard. "I'm your man."

The stranger inclined their head. Elodin

narrowed his eyes over the tankard, trying to get a good look under the hood without *looking* like he tried to. Amber eyes gleamed in the darkness when the firelight of the inn met them.

Elodin swallowed his ale with a gulp. He'd seen plenty of weirdness in his time, but a person with amber eyes? *First time for everything, so there is.*

"Strange days we're living in, friend," the stranger breathed. Their voice sounded male. Soft, airy, but male. Ice crept up Elodin's spine. The beggar he'd killed said the same words, not hours before. "I've travelled the world since the portals appeared. Did you know they assail everyone? Sea port cities. Lands locked with ice. Civilisations on the other side of the globe with technology you wouldn't believe, and people who you'd think stuck in the past. Everyone doomed if they remain open."

Elodin shrugged. He'd heard rumours of other lands, ones reached by months-long boat journeys only the crazy or desperate embarked on—and never returned from—but had no desire to see them. Bellon, and the other seven walled cities of Heltar, had more than enough fools, marks, and enemies to last him several lifetimes.

"So, we're all doomed. We're always doomed. Doomed from the lung rot—but we found plenty of medicine for those who can pay—or from the wastes between the cities— but we went and built the Chancellor's Roads and solved that little problem, didn't we?— and we're doomed again. Storms, acid from the sky. Eternal darkness. Like everything else, those who give into doom will perish, and the rest of us will find our opportunities and adapt. Life goes on, one way or another."

"What if I were to tell you there's no adapting to this? That you, Bellon, Heltar, *everything*, has months. Weeks, perhaps."

Elodin took a sip from his tankard. "I'd ask how you're so certain."

A short chuckle oozed from beneath the hood. "A fine question. You strike me as a man who respects directness, Elodin. I shall be frank with you."

His muscles bunched, like they did when he walked into an alley filled with shadows, or a room with armed villains who he knew meant him harm. "How do you know my name?"

An incline of the head. "I could lie to you,

tell you how your reputation precedes you, or how I asked Franklin over there to arrange a meeting. I shan't bore you. Elodin, I am not like you. Not the same as anyone you've ever met, or will. Those portals? I know them all too well, and I understand the carnage they'll unleash on these lands if they're not closed."

"How? You told me you won't lie, but you tell me nothing!" Elodin snarled, gripping the tabletop, teeth clenched.

"I come from a place beyond those portals. I've seen first-hand their design, their purpose. They cannot remain open, doing so means ruin. I know how to seal the tears in the sky, but, because of my nature, it isn't for me to do it. That's where you come in, and the rewards..."

"I've seen a lot when it comes to riches," Elodin grumbled, taking another pull from his tankard, but he couldn't hide the eager light in his eyes. "Keep talking, I'm listening."

The figure leaned back. "It's a simple job for one of your talents. I did myself a disservice before, and you. Your reputation *does* precede you, and I'm... aware... of your talents. The portals over Bellon need closing, and it's possible. There's an access point nearby. All you need to do is enter it, follow my instructions, and return for your reward."

"I'm no fool, stranger," Elodin growled, banging a fist on the table. "*Follow my instructions* could mean anything. Speak clearly or fuck off. I'll find work, I always do."

"Come now," the amber-eyed man purred, "there's no need for that. I need use of your sword, and your skills along with it. I daresay you'll find the task more difficult than murdering a poor bastard with lung rot in a filthy alley, but the reward… well. Saving the world, and the freedom that come with it, aren't for sniffing at."

Elodin slid a hand from the table, and under the folds of his cloak, gripping the hilt of one of his hidden daggers. "You followed me?"

Hissing laughter oozed out from the hood's black maw. "Oh, yes. I know *all* about you Elodin. You took your first life aged eight, murdering your killer of a father. Revenge for your mother, a noble gesture. Life on the streets suited you, made you strong, resourceful. Cold. A virtue, in your line of work. You've stolen to eat, thieved for pleasure. You've killed for pay, took lives for love and revenge, and done it so often, stained your soul so, so much. Darkness smothers its lightness now, so what's one more life? Well, that's what you tell yourself. But I can see, behind those hate-filled eyes of yours, that those words ring hollow. You've thought often of the beggar you put out of his misery this night. I'm with you, a mercy killing, but still, you wonder. Was there another way? You tire of all the death you've seeped your soul in, the blood on your hands that won't wash away, no matter how much you scrub. Am I wrong?"

The rest of *The Broken Shackle* ceased to exist. Darkness clouded the edges of Elodin's vision, framing the hooded stranger in its centre, his amber eyes peering from the gloom. His hand tightened on the dagger's hilt as the man's words washed over him, teasing memories and images of the corpses he'd left in his wake. His father, his best friend, numerous lovers. Priests, politicians, people who'd said the wrong thing at the wrong time. The beggar. Would he add this stranger to his red-stained ledger?

His fingers twitched, weariness washed through his limbs, and his hand fell from the hilt.

"You're not wrong," Elodin muttered, closing his eyes and downing his drink, losing himself for a moment as the ale flooded his mouth, rushed down his throat.

"There is another way," the stranger cooed. "Do this job for me. You'll never need work again. Never need to kill."

Elodin tapped his fingers on the ale-sodden table, one after the other, from little finger to index. This hadn't gone the way he'd expected, though, to be fair, not much had of late. He played the stranger's words over again in his head as he stared at the amber glinting in the darkness of his hood. One thing stood out. Magic.

He'd come across wizards, witches, fae, and all manner of creatures of the *other* before—sometimes for good, and just as many times for bad—and never enjoyed it. Magic felt like cheating. Elodin had skills, had honed his body and mind to work as one when fighting or sneaking, pushing his limbs to eke out a touch more speed, his muscles to exert that little more strength, his feet to pad that decibel quieter. He'd worked for it. Worked fucking hard.

Magicians… sure, they studied. They read their books, created the concoctions. But they were born with an advantage mortals just didn't, and would never, possess. And that didn't sit right with Elodin.

Still, a job was a job. And the stranger had it right. The blood Elodin had shed over the years weighed heavy on his soul, had turned it crimson. He knew, in his heart, he'd done the beggar a favour, sparing him from the lung rot devouring the rest of his organs; a slow, painful, and lonely death. But he couldn't stop turning it over in his mind.

Regret had forced its way into Elodin's conscience, and that led to hesitancy. He'd seen it in others. In his line of work, it only led one way: a path with death at the end of it.

His own.

"I've two rules when taking a job." Elodin nodded, grabbing the stranger's untouched ale and taking a sip. "I never work for someone who's name I don't know and face I haven't seen."

"A name," the voice came in a whispered hiss. Slow and pensive. "I had one of those once. Forgotten… but perhaps, one day, I'll wear it on my tongue again. People call me Wanderer. Will that do?"

Elodin nodded. "Better than nothing. And the rest."

"Well, that's not a problem for me."

Wanderer removed his hood, and Elodin gasped.

Apart from those amber-hued eyes, he appeared utterly unremarkable. Elodin had seen thousands of men wearing the same broad face, the same ordinary features. Wanderer resembled a farmer, a butcher, an innkeeper, a man playing dice. Elodin expected… *more*. Purple skin, scars, handsome on a scale beyond anything he'd seen, or just as ugly. Not this normal man smiling like he'd won a hamper on Estival Day. One who happened to have amber eyes, intimate details of Elodin's life, and a way to heal the sky.

Wanderer replaced his hood, hiding his genial features in the shadows once more, amber orbs shining.

"Do we have a deal?" he asked, Elodin's brain struggling to reconcile the voice he heard with the face he'd seen.

"I guess we do," he muttered, downing his

drink. In an evening where nothing else appeared real, at least the ale did.

"Then follow me." Wanderer swept to his feet, and headed for the streets.

With a clatter, Elodin let his tankard fall on the table, empty. He pushed himself up from his chair, unsteady in body and mind.

Elodin found Wanderer on the dark streets outside, cloak already sodden from the constant rainfall. The man didn't seem to mind. He stood with his head tilted upward, gazing at the maelstrom of colours swirling in the sky.

"Quite beautiful, really," Elodin murmured, standing alongside the man.

"No," Wanderer hissed, the venom dripping from the word surprising Elodin. It had appeared as if nothing phased the man, nothing could knock him off balance. "That thing, and everything to do with it, disgusts me. As it should you."

"Relax," Elodin murmured, staring down at him. Another detail about Wanderer's unassuming guise. He stood at an average height. "A joke, that's all."

"The rifts are nothing to laugh about, trust me," Wanderer spat.

"Trust you? Not bloody likely."

Wanderer sighed, as if he'd heard those exact words too many times to count. "Fine. Believe me, instead. The rifts must close; there's nothing *good* or *beautiful* about them."

Elodin shrugged, enjoying the fact that, for once, since sitting down with Wanderer, he held a small amount of power over him. "Did you just want to take the air, or did you have something to show me?"

Snarling, Wanderer turned on him, jabbing a finger in his face. "Don't get smart with me, boy. I've seen things you couldn't dream, done things that would make you *wish* you could curl up and die in a fucking gutter. Do *not* test my patience."

Hatred and frustration seeped from every word Wanderer spoke. They centred Elodin, righting his balance. They made the stranger feel more… human. *Threats. Those I can deal with.*

Cocking his head, Elodin offered Wanderer a wide smile. "You need me, remember. You'll do well to remember that, or you can find someone else to carry out your task."

"We both know that isn't going to happen, you'll take the job for the reasons we've discussed," Wanderer hissed, but he turned back to the sky, his soft voice even again. "Tell me, what do you fear?"

Elodin frowned. "Nothing."

A laugh from Wanderer. "Come now, we all fear something."

"Is that right?" Elodin crossed his arms across his chest. "Even you?"

"Even me," Wanderer answered, pointing to the sky. "I fear the rifts. I fear a prison, trapping my body and soul. My mind. Acknowledging your fears makes a man stronger, Elodin, and you'll need all your strength for the task at hand."

"Why do I have the feeling I'm going to regret crossing your path, Wanderer?" Elodin muttered, studying his boots.

He knew the answer, didn't have to consider it much. It often plagued his mind. On his long journeys, alone in the wilderness between the walled cities, he turned over the decisions he'd made in the past and vowed never to make the same ones again. He always did. Money. It always came back to that, or so he told himself, but he knew why he kept doing the work he did.

Elodin desired the thrill of the kill like a drug. The power of holding someone's life in the balance, of making the decision to end it, or grant more. He hated it afterwards, hated himself, but in the moment… nothing compared.

"Well?" Wanderer murmured, snapping Elodin from his thoughts.

He cleared his throat and viewed the pulsating sky once more. "Myself. I fear myself."

"As all men should," Wanderer breathed. "A wise thing to fear. Be mindful of it. Now, here's what you must do…"

Elodin raced through the night. His horse snorted as it ate up ground, galloping it once more after a brief trotting rest.

The sky continued to pulsate, but he'd almost grown used to it by now. *You can grow used to anything*, one of his old mentors used to say.

Before Elodin killed him.

He scowled, pushing away the same old

thoughts that had plagued him so much of late and scanned the blighted horizon. Deserted wastelands surrounded him. Withered, burned out trees, dry river banks, and scorched, brown grass. Only the truly desperate and depraved lived in the spaces between the walled cities now, and it had been that way for centuries. War had decimated the wilderness, as well as magic and plague.

And now the rifts in the sky. It's like fate wants us gone from the face of the earth, and we're too stubborn to allow it to scrub us away, no matter what it sends at us.

Wanderer had told him to journey into the wastelands, to Nomek Rock, the highest point on the route between Bellon and Shintak, the closest city. He knew it well, having made the journey too many times to count. Years before, when he turned his hand to honest work, he protected caravans travelling the route. After a few months, Elodin realised he could make more coin—and put himself at less risk—hijacking the merchant trains instead of fighting in their corner, and that was that.

His mount's hooves made the only sound in the wastelands. Not many travelled the routes anymore, and even less preyed on those brave enough to journey its broken and cracked roads. People slipped by in ones or twos, under cover of night, with as much speed as they could muster.

The split sky helped, Elodin conceded. Folk clung to the walled cities, even with the lung rot rife and money scarce, waiting for the end of days.

Elodin understood that. It wasn't for him—standing still never appealed, even when waiting struck him as the best option—but he couldn't begrudge people their feelings of despair. Speeding through the barren wilderness made him think the world had ended already.

Would that be so bad? The world with just me in it? Yes. Yes, it would. Can't think of anything worse.

Hunger gnawed in the pits of Elodin's stomach. He'd slow down soon and eat in his saddle and let his horse walk for a spell.

"Slow, my friend," he called. Easing back on the reins, Elodin leaned close to the horse's ear.

An object flew through the sky, passing just above his head. If he hadn't bent…

Wrapping his arms around the horse's neck, he clung to its body, and twisted.

An arrow came from the darkness, missing his shoulder by inches.

"Fuck!" he screamed, digging his heels into the mount's flanks. "Bandits!"

The sound of horses' hooves pounding across the barren plains exploded through the darkness. Bandits appeared from the gloom on both sides, loosing arrows. Elodin, low to his mount, teeth gritted, steered the beast with his knees but didn't need to urge it on.

The animal knew it had to flee.

Projectiles whizzed by, some thudding into the ground in Elodin's wake or in his path.

"Bring him down!"

Already tired from the sprint across the wastelands, his horse shuddered, sucking breath into tired lungs to power its failing limbs. Sweat on its neck lathered into foam.

"I've no coin," he yelled in response. "No goods! Leave me be!"

Elodin risked a glance. Five attackers. Not the worst odds he'd ever faced.

Do I turn and fight? Close the gap? Or do I—

His mount shrieked and crashed into the mud, an arrow sticking from its eye. Another slammed into its brain before it hit the ground.

Elodin jumped—he'd seen riders crushed by a horse before, been the cause of it countless times—and smashed into the muck, sliding across the rain-slick ground, the wind knocked from him.

Wincing, he twisted onto his knees, drawing his sword in a swift action, his sides protesting the movement.

His instincts screamed at him, and he dived to the side. An arrow whizzed by, disappearing into the darkness as the horsemen closed the gap.

From down in the mud, in the darkness, the pulsating maelstrom above framing them, the five riders on galloping beasts of pure muscle resembled moving mountains with gleaming swords in their hands.

Elodin almost shat himself.

The lead rider bore down on him. Sucking air into his lungs, Elodin held his sword out and dropped into a fighting stance, a trick he'd seen someone use in the same situation swimming to the forefront of his mind.

It hadn't worked then. Elodin had smashed the fellow to a pulp, his horse's hooves pounding the merchant guard into mush. But still, he had nothing else.

He had one chance, or these were the last seconds of his life.

"Fuck me," Elodin breathed as the ground vibrated, eyeing which hand the rider held his sword in.

The right.

Two yards before impact, Elodin slid to his side and dropped away from the sword, letting the horse brush past him. He swung, weapon in both arms lest the impact snap his limb in two, bringing the steel across the steed's fore and back legs.

Fiery blood spurted across his face, into his mouth, and he choked on it. Gagged.

The horse screamed. The mountain of flesh toppled, but Elodin couldn't wait.

He leaped at it, at the rider, sword above his head, and brought it slamming down, the blade severing the bandit's neck. His head hung on by a slither of sinew, lolling to the side, crimson pumping from the wound.

Still moving, Elodin jumped to safety. Another rider, reflexes too slow, the mount moving too fast, crashed into the screaming horse.

The sound of muscle slamming against muscle, and the splintering of bones, tore into the night.

Baring his teeth, Elodin raced forward and put another attacker to the sword, ending the man's screams as the horses crushed him to death, pinned as he was between two writhing animals.

"Two down," Elodin yelled, spinning around, blood-stained sword ready. "Who's next?"

The other riders reined their horses in, much to Elodin's relief. His heart hammered against his chest with such ferocity he thought it might burst through the bones. He'd gotten away with his trick and didn't fancy he could do it a second time, let alone thrice or more.

The bandits shared a glance, and the one closest to Elodin slipped out of his saddle and showed his palms.

"How about we talk, friend?"

"Friend?" Elodin spat. "Bit fucking late for that, no?"

"We just wanted to get your attention—"

"Shut your bloody trap." Elodin levelled his blade, pointing the tip at the rider. "I'm no easy mark, as I've proven, and I'm pressed for time. How about you let me pilfer those sorry bastards in the muck there, and lend me one of your horses, and we'll all be on our way. Counting our blessings, like."

The rider shrugged and removed his hood. The man wore an easy smile on his boyish face. "Sorry, Elodin. Can't let you do that, as much as I don't fancy fighting you. I know your reputation, and that manoeuvre with the horse was a damn fine one. So how about you listen instead?"

Elodin's muscles relaxed, his breathing slowed. Not because he felt at ease. No. Because he knew a fight approached. "How do you know my name?"

The other riders dismounted and approached the leader, flanking him.

Three against one's better than five. No question there.

"We take an interest in anyone Wanderer speaks with. Especially those he hires."

Pieces slid into place in Elodin's mind. Somehow, he'd been caught in the middle of trouble. An unwitting pawn, and not for the first time. Clearly, he had to pick a side. The option to walk away had long since disappeared over the blasted horizon.

These fellows tried to stick me with arrows. At least Wanderer talked to me. And he'll make me rich so I can leave this world behind me.

Elodin eyed the three men. The leader stood with his hands open; the other two reached for the pommels under their cloaks. Weights on the sides of Elodin's boots pressed against his calves.

"I'm a sell-sword. Work for the highest bidder, don't I?" Elodin pointed to his boots, then inched down into a crouch. "If we're talking, I'm going to take a load off. Killing takes it out of me, not as young as I used to be."

The leader took a slight step forward. "No issues with mercenaries, friend. A man has to earn a living, times as they are. We just take exception with who you're working for, and the job he's asked you to do."

Elodin laid his sword on the ground, shaking his head. The men took another step forward.

Good.

"Is that right?" he muttered. "Way I see it… you've no fucking right to interfere with my work. And I'm fucked if I'm explaining myself to you."

Elodin pulled the daggers free from his boots, throwing them underhand at the two flanking men. They slammed into the darkness of their hoods, sending them flying backwards, dead before they hit the ground.

He had no time to admire his handy work.

Grabbing his sword, Elodin rushed forward. The lone rider had drawn his blade with a snarl, anger blemishing that boyish face.

"You fool!" he hissed, stepping backward as he blocked a thrust. "You've no idea what's happening here."

Elodin bared his teeth. "What I know is you've made a terrible mistake, *friend*."

He pressed the attack, probing to take the measure of his foe. He'd survived so far when his fellows had perished, so he had to give the man some credit. He defended well, moving to intercept and parry with a strong arm, his eyes darting, looking for an opening.

Elodin wouldn't grant him one. He kept up the assault, feinting high, then swooping low, switching the paths of his attack.

His foe met them.

Sweat beaded on Elodin's forehead as their clash of steel rang out across the wastelands, their grunts of exertion punctuating the clangs of blade on blade.

The rider tried to surge forward, but Elodin doubled his attack, keeping him in place. In a place like the wastelands, with its uneven roads and potholes, footing could prove paramount.

Footing...

Elodin's eyes flicked beyond his enemy. The two bandits he'd stuck with daggers lay in a heap, just a few steps behind.

Let's see how this works.

"You don't really think you've a chance against me, do you?" Elodin bit out. Over the years, he'd found words could distract a fellow as much as a blade.

The rider didn't answer. His face grim. Eyes focused.

"I mean," Elodin continued, stepping back a touch. The bandit accepted the invitation and moved forward, his form eager. "I've killed four of you already."

Time to roll the dice.

Elodin stumbled. A gamble, but he suppressed a smile as he did. It had its desired effect.

The bandit, too eager, overcommitted, let his defence down and threw caution to the wind with a wild attack to press his advantage.

Elodin recovered, and the look of pure shock on his foe's face lent strength to his limbs. Holding his sword in both hands, he knocked back the attack, and turned defence into attack in the blink of an eye.

The rider shuffled backward as Elodin imbued his speed of attack with brute force, battering at the man's defences, forcing him back and back and back. Until…

The bandit's feet tangled with the corpse's legs sprawling in the muck. He crashed into the mud, limbs flailing.

Elodin slashed at the man's blade, knocking it far into the darkness, and skewered him straight through the guts, pinning him to the ground.

Breathing fast, he studied the dying bandit as the lights from the sky played across his boyish, agony-filled face.

"Why?" Elodin spat, shame, guilt, and rage

battling inside to come out on top. "I gave you the chance to run. Why fight me when you didn't stand a fucking chance?"

Blood trickled from the rider's mouth. "The portals… you can't close them… please…"

Elodin snarled and pulled his blade free. The rider's scream could have woken the wasteland's dead. "You're not bandits. Who are you? Can I expect more?"

The dying man coughed, blood spurting down his chin. He cradled his guts, his feet kicking. A vain effort to stop the pain. "No more… all that's left… Wanderer… please. Leave the rifts open. Please."

The man's whimpering stabbed at Elodin. Each groan of pain a dagger in his soul. He took in the scene, the dead men and horses, the rifts in the sky, and closed his eyes. The beggar's face bloomed in his mind, the look of betrayal lingering in his dead eyes.

"No," Elodin whispered, shaking his head. "I must close them. All this death… I can't do this anymore."

Raising his sword, Elodin screamed. A cry filled with decades of pain. Decades of shame. A howl filled with a lifetime of regret. The blade penetrated the man's chest, piercing his heart. Killing him instantly.

A man could take a week to die from a blade in the guts. An agonising death, alone in the wastelands.

Elodin could spare the fellow that.

Shuddering, he fell to his knees, limbs like water, and wept.

"I have to close the rifts," Elodin sobbed. "Don't you understand? All my life, I've delivered death and ill deeds. I need to believe, to prove, I can do something more. Healing the sky's my chance. Don't you fucking see that?"

The corpse didn't answer. None of them did. In the far distance, a beast howled, and the sky above continued to shimmer, a swirling bruise almost larger than the one staining Elodin's soul.

Nomek Rock loomed in the darkness, a hulking shadow blacker than the night standing tall on the horizon. A single, thick finger splitting the ground and reaching up into the pulsating sky.

Elodin slowed his horse as he approached,

the other tied to his nag's saddle coming to a steady trot, too. He'd pilfered the corpses and found nothing on them—no food, no coin, not even a memento or keepsake—but took a spare horse. He planned to gallop the rest of the way, in case more assassins came for him, and didn't fancy the idea of his mount collapsing before reaching Nomek Rock. Elodin had changed horses twice since and made good time.

The ruined road he travelled on smoothed out as he trotted and grew more narrow. Elodin had never been so close to the place before and had hoped to ride as close to the climb as possible. Sighing, he dismounted, and found a spot to tie his animals to. He wouldn't need them for what came next but wanted them fresh for the journey home.

A ruined archway stood before him, leading to steps that wound up to Nomek Rock proper. He studied the arch's material, frowning. The wars that turned the plains into a wasteland had destroyed much, consigned myriad customs and practices to darkness: a wealth of lost information, knowledge and history. Elodin fancied the construction of much of Nomek Rock found itself in this group; the archway gleamed, though brown dust marked the material in many spots. It wasn't stone or straw, but something else. It clanged when he rapped his knuckles against it, its hollow sound echoing in the gloom.

Elodin's frown deepened. He'd spied the place in the distance on his travels, and had reckoned it a tall mountain, or rock structure. This close, he saw that wasn't the case. The same material as the archway glinted under the sky's pulsating colours, and he saw silver steps winding around its circumference.

"A silo, they called it, many centuries ago. No one remembers. Ancient wars between nations destroyed anyone with the knowledge." Elodin spun, sword in his hand, then mouthed a silent curse. Wanderer stood by his horses, amber eyes shining from his hood's blackness. "That material you touch is called metal. Those who created it are long dead. After that, simple folk who crept out of the apocalypse prayed to it, thinking its tall point touched their gods. They weren't entirely wrong. Your wars wiped those folk away, too."

"Damn you, Wanderer," Elodin snarled, slamming his sword into its sheath, "I almost took your fucking head off."

A soft laugh hissed from the hood. "You can't kill me. No one can."

"I wondered if I'd find you here," Elodin replied, ignoring the ice weighing down his stomach. "Assassins came for me, you know?"

"Nothing you couldn't handle, clearly," Wanderer answered, joining him under the archway. He lowered his hood and gazed up at Nomek Rock's highest point. "You see how the rifts join there? At the tip? That's where you must go. There's a doorway that leads into the structure. Inside, you can enter the rift through a portal."

"Apocalypse," Eloding muttered. The rifts congregated and swirled with a frenzy at the place Wanderer had pointed out. "What is this word?"

"It is the end of things, and the beginning of something new, though the people who rise from the ashes are never as strong, as potent, as they once were." Wanderer's amber stare locked on Elodin's. It made his skin itch. "There have been many apocalypses since the world's birth. How mighty the people of this land stood before that first one. Now look at you all, scrambling in the gloom, scratching out your lives. Another apocalypse approaches."

"And so the portals must be closed." Elodin nodded. "No time like the present. What do I do inside?"

Wanderer's eyes narrowed. "It is different for everyone, so I cannot say. But I believe in you."

"Well, that's fucking reassuring," Elodin muttered, glancing at the thing Wanderer had called a silo. "Any more hints or…"

Wanderer had vanished, leaving Elodin alone with his horses and the smothering silence of Nomek Rock.

Filling his lungs with air, Elodin unsheathed his sword, the weight in his hand comforting him, and passed through the archway. A faint noise broke the silence.

Howling.

Wind blew through Nomek Rock's strange structure, causing the shining silver to whistle and screech.

The ice in Elodin's stomach spread to his chest.

The stairs clanged as Elodin stamped up them. The wind picked up, howling and whistling through the strange structure. The skies spun above him, a bruised maelstrom, pulsating and spinning with an urgent frenzy.

Of Wanderer, he saw no sign.

Midway up, he paused his climb and examined Nomek Rock. Stone appeared on the structure, but it had worn away so revealed the metal beneath it. Elodin wondered what manner of people could have created such a material, and why they tried to hide the stuff under rock. He took a moment to sweep his gaze across the silent wasteland. *What will stand if I fail and this apocalypse takes us all? Who will pick up the remains?*

Simple. He wouldn't fail. It struck him that Wanderer still hadn't told him what to *do* in the portal. Wanderer just told him to enter it. But Elodin had come this far, and wouldn't turn back.

He staggered as he reached the summit, the wind buffeting him, causing his cloak to stream. Elodin eyed the tip of Nomek Rock, where it touched the sky only feet above him, and gasped. Images swirled in the rifts.

No, not images… another place. A world in the sky! It shimmered beyond the many colours that shone through the portals and set Elodin's heart hammering.

It burned.

A lake of fire stretched out before him. It fell from the sky, the rain alight with flame. He reached out with a shaking hand, the rain from his world's sky peppering his skin. Elodin sniffed at it. The stench of rot and sulphur swam in his nostrils, and he nodded. The strange rain afflicting his land came from the portal.

He had to close it. Had to.

Lowering his gaze, he studied the side of Nomek Rock. A large wheel stuck out of the half-rock, half-metal door. Grabbing it with both hands, he twisted, grunting through gritted teeth as his muscles strained. The door refused until, with a screech, it creaked open.

Elodin peered into the darkness, then entered the silo.

Red lights lit the room. The colour of blood on water.

Elodin blinked in the gloom, pausing as his

eyes grew used to the low light. Listening. A hum tickled the edges of his hearing, a whirr and buzz unlike anything he'd come across before.

"Hello?" he called, his voice bouncing around inside the metal shell of the silo.

Blinking lights caught his attention, materialising from the crimson haze. They appeared on some kind of metal desk built into the far wall. Glancing around, Elodin noticed nothing else. No bodies. No portal.

Frowning, he crossed over to the lights, his feet making the floor rattle. A doorway shrouded in darkness loomed beside the metal desk, but he ignored it for now. Words flickered on the metal desk, beside the lights. Words in white on a dirty green background in his language.

'Zero Hour: Evacuate All Personnel. Countdown to Launch of Response Ballistics: 00.00'

He understood the strange writing, but the words had no meaning to him. Elodin reached out, scrubbing his fingers against the words. They continued to flicker, brighter now after he wiped away the thick dust covering them.

Turning, his eyes took in more of the room. A chair with wheels attached to its legs stood abandoned by another wall. Large white writing covered it.

'Nuclear Silo Station Nevada 004'

"Silo," Elodin muttered, pulling his cloak tighter around him against a sudden chill. He didn't understand the other words, but the first one, nuclear, put a chill in his bones. "Guess Wanderer wasn't lying about that. What is this place?"

Letting his eyes cross the room again, a shimmering blue light through the far doorway grabbed his attention.

The portal. Must be.

Drawing his sword, Elodin crept towards it. The illumination grew brighter as he approached. Engrossed by it, he stumbled as he crossed the threshold.

Glancing at his feet, Elodin scuttled backward, his stomach lurching.

"What happened here?"

A charred skeleton lay across the doorway, clinging to the darkness between the warring blue light of the portal and the red room. Scrubbing a hand across his mouth, Elodin knelt. The empty sockets stared into his soul, the skeleton's wide grin mocking him. It held a secret, some clue as to what the silo was, what Elodin's future held, but it would keep it to itself for eternity.

Elodin stood, and brought his boot down hard on the skull, crushing it until it became dust.

"Let's get this over with."

A small set of stairs lay behind the bones, leading up to a pulsating blue tear of light. A slither of colour in the darkness. Elodin approached it, each step he took on the metal echoing, until he stood before it, his face reflected in the shimmering light.

He held out a single shaking finger and touched the portal. It passed through, the chill of cold water kissing his skin.

Painless.

Filling his lungs with air, Elodin stepped through, and his world turned black.

The darkness turned grey and, out of it, a colourless shape emerged.

Elodin moved towards it, weightless and

heavy of limb all at once, his footsteps making no sound.

The grey vista had no features, no form. The ground and sky, if Elodin could call them that, merged together, a monotone horizon of which distance proved impossible to judge. The impossible view stretched off past the ink-blot shape before him and, when he glanced over his shoulder, behind.

Of the portal, he saw no sign.

Elodin's fingers twitched, and he moved to draw his sword.

Nothing hung by his side.

Still, he kept moving. The dark stain grew as he approached, and formed into something he recognised. A table, with an empty chair in front of it. Like in a tavern.

A hooded figure sat behind it, an ignored tankard to the side.

"Wanderer?" Elodin whispered, standing by the chair. The figure didn't move. Didn't so much as look up.

"What is this place?" Elodin demanded, his words flat in the dead air.

The figure continued to stare at the table top. Elodin slammed his hands on it. The tankard didn't rattle. Didn't even shake. "Who are you?"

Snarling, Elodin grabbed the figure's hood and flung it backward. Shock widened his eyes. Ice trickled down his spine. His limbs lost their strength. Falling into the empty chair, Elodin stared, jaw slack.

It wasn't Wanderer.

Elodin sat across from himself.

"Why are you here?" he asked his doppelganger.

"You're asking the wrong questions," it answered, its voice thin and cracked.

Elodin, his skin itching like it begged for him to scratch it off so it could escape this grey place, studied his match. The differences swam to the surface.

The portal-Elodin's eyes appeared to swallow the light around them. No white existed there, just black pits. Its greasy hair stuck to its scalp, and faint red lines ran across pale skin stretched across a gaunt skull.

It. Yes, it. This isn't a person. Not a twin. An it. An abomination.

"You're me, aren't you?" Elodin whispered, tearing his eyes away from the figure.

"My dark soul made flesh."

"Right you are," it nodded, lips twisted into a cruel smile.

The grey background flickered; flashes of Elodin's life appeared, showing the lives he'd taken. The light dying in so many eyes. His father. The beggar in the gutter and the riders who'd waylaid him in the wastelands. Countless more.

Run.

Elodin's limbs urged him to listen to the voice inside. He had nowhere to go, no portal to escape through, but his body begged him to flee just the same. Across from him sat the worst of himself, the depraved dark corners of his mind staring back at him, the thing he feared most.

Himself.

Wanderer's words made sense to him now.

'Tell me, what do you fear?'

'Myself. I fear myself.'

'As all men should.'

"He knew," Elodin spat between gritted teeth. "That bastard *knew* what I'd find here!"

"You placed your faith in the wrong person," his shade answered, cocking its head, black eyes mocking. "Not the first time."

Betrayals from Elodin's life flashed against the grey surface, ones he'd committed himself or had suffered. Too many to count.

Placing his hands on the table, Elodin cursed his lack of weapon, even if he doubted it would do much in this place. He asked another question instead. What else could he do?

"So, what happens now?"

The black-eyed devil grinned. "You close the portal, of course."

"So, he didn't lie about that? Wanderer, I mean? The sky must be healed?"

The grin turned into laughter. It echoed around the grey void, the background flickering to show images of Elodin and Wanderer back in the walled city and outside the silo, the stranger's amber eyes glowing in the murk.

"Does it matter? You're not leaving this place."

It all clicked into place. Wanderer promised Elodin he wouldn't need to kill again if he did this, but how could anyone be so sure? Said he'd never work again, too. Elodin replayed the conversation with Wanderer in his head… he'd never mentioned money. Just rewards and freedom.

"You see, now," his doppelganger croaked. "Good. This rift needs death, Elodin. A multitude of it, bleeding into the void. And you carry so much. The weight of every soul you've ever taken bears you down. They scream for release, for absolution, and you know well that you wail for it too. Don't you? And don't bother lying… I *am* you."

The air around the table shimmered. Elodin's sword materialised, the blade glistening in the half light. He laid his palm on the blade. The metal cooled his flesh.

"Will closing the rift stop another apocalypse?" he asked, his hand sliding up to the pommel.

"Does it matter?"

"I hate you," Elodin hissed, fingers wrapping around the hilt.

"You don't," the shade smiled. "You fear me. You always have, and there's only one way to be rid of me."

The grey void shifted. The table disappeared. Elodin found himself on his feet, sword in hand, chair gone. A world drained of form and colour stretched around him: an endless expanse of regret. The blade weighed his arm down.

"I can't do this," he whispered as the horizon flickered again, showing him the face of every soul he robbed.

Elodin closed his eyes. He didn't need reminding. He remembered them all.

"No more death at your hand," came a whisper in his ear. His doppelganger lurked behind him. A spectre on his shoulder. "Isn't that what you want?"

"Yes."

"Let me help you."

A chill ran through Elodin's body as his shade stepped into the same space he occupied. The sword spun in his hands, the blade's point aimed at his body.

The images continued to flicker. Elodin took a moment to watch the last few faces, the lives he'd taken only hours and days before, and bowed his head.

"Forgive me."

He fell on his blade, shock widening his eyes as steel passed through his gut. He slid to the floor, grunting as the sword's hilt hit his abdomen. Crimson pooled beneath him, and brought colour to the grey world.

Black entered the edges of Elodin's vision as he shuddered on the blade, coughing out blood. Before him, Wanderer appeared, hooded and cloaked, amber eyes glowing from the gloom.

"You've done well," he whispered, "and you've got what you deserved."

"Are you really here?" Elodin slurred, his tongue thick.

"No," Wandered replied. "You die alone."

Elodin collapsed on the floor, his limbs weak, feeling gone in his legs. Those amber eyes vanished as he slid into oblivion.

From below the silo, Wanderer watched as the sky turned black. Whole once more. The constant rain, acidic and spoiled from the rifts, ended, though the smell of rot in the air would take years to clear. If it ever would.

He smiled. *Another down.*

He studied Nomek Rock and thought back on those who'd made it. *They thought themselves gods. No, more than that. But look who still stands.*

Clicking his fingers, Wanderer stepped into the shadows and vanished. He had more places to visit, more work to do.

The portals *would* close, and he'd have his reckoning. The entire world would.

STORMCHILD

LEE C. CONLEY

The sails cracked in the howling wind. Waves broke into an icy spray as the prow fell down the crest of another foaming swell. The spray stung his face, but it was a sense that made him feel alive. Lighting flashed in a leaden sky that threatened rain.

"Secure that line!" The nearby bosun's voice, hoarse from screaming over the howling wind.

The water seemed black, and the sea heaved. Dark swells loomed all around. The wind whipped the water, making waves that broke into white-crested peaks. The roiling sky fought its eternal battle against the tumultuous depths with savage ferocity.

Ulfgar stared out from the prow, shielding his face from the biting wind and spray as he squinted at the sails ahead.

"We've got them," shouted Lars from beside him, clamping his hand on his hat to stop it blowing away.

He glanced beyond Lars, over the storm-wracked sea. The Kira, a ninety-gun leviathan, surged through the churning waves, merely a stone's throw from his own flagship. Its crimson sails bulged, straining against the swell.

Behind them was arrayed the rest of their fleet; at his command, those ships would fall upon the enemy, and the Noraph would be torn to pieces.

The enemy ships floundered in the storm, disorganised, unprepared. He would turn the dark seas to a crimson froth with their filthy blood. He looked over to the open deck below him. His marines stood on the deck in ranks, their muskets slung at their shoulders. He turned to his first officer. Lars watched the nearing sails of the Noraph fleet through his eyeglass. The crew were making ready, scurrying back and forth securing lines and hauling ammunition and powder. Sailors were loading the deck guns and piling shot, whilst overhead his full sails snapped and cracked in the cold gusting wind.

"Prepare yourselves," he roared down to the crew, his voice battling against the gale. "This day we fight!"

The whole ship roared the battle-cry in unison. Ulfgar turned back to Lars and returned his grin. "It is too late for them now, the fools. Signal the fleet to full sail. We will attack in good order. Let them see their death approaching."

His ships tore into the enemy fleet in two long columns, like wolves let loose amongst a flock. With his sabre drawn, Ulfgar pointed at his chosen prey, the nearest ship, a fat hulled frigate. The wheel-man guided the ship in at his command. The prow of his ship swung around, bringing the shining muzzles of a full broadside worth of cannon onto the side of the enemy vessel.

"Fire!"

There was a terrible jolt and a thundering concussion as the cannons of the upper deck erupted with gouts of flame. He watched the gun crews immediately ramming more powder charge and wadding into the iron muzzles before they became wreathed in an obscuring cloud of acrid white smoke. The timbers of the Noraph ship exploded as shot punched into its wooden belly. Splinters flew and men screamed into the howling wind. Its forward mast splintered and snapped. It toppled like a felled tree, dragging the tattered sail as it fell away into the sea. Another volley erupted, only visible from the muzzle flashes through the smoke. The heavy thirty pounders roared from the lower gun deck, followed quickly by a volley from the middle deck and the upper deck in unison. Through the smoke, he saw the devastating damage that two full broadsides had wrought on the enemy. The ship listed and would sink quickly. Few ships could stand long against the StormChild. His flagship was one-hundred and twenty-eight guns of pure fury—a maelstrom of fire and lead. A ship that was feared on all the oceans of the world. They had no chance. Men screamed and fought the churning water as it stole them into its depths. Ulfgar's marines fired volleys from the gunwale, firing into the water as they sailed through the wreckage, slaughtering any within range—a small mercy from the icy clutches of those dark unforgiving seas.

He glanced at the Kira; his second ship of the line was engaged with an enemy ship. She pulled in close, and there was a flash of cannon before lines and grappling hooks flew to lash her to her prey.

"Jules is already looking for prizes," shouted Lars over the wind. Ulfgar grinned. His brother was an ambitious lad, but Ulfgar must give him his dues—he commanded the Kira like a man many years at sea. He took out a silver watch on a chain and checked the time before placing it back in his pocket.

He saw the black jackets of Kira's marines spill over the rails and board the stricken ship. Muskets cracked with small billows of smoke. He could make out the glint of bayonets and a sword held aloft by one of her officers as he led his boarding party. The Kira's warriors slaughtered their way across the smaller ship's deck. He looked around at the chaos of battle. He watched Noraph ships colliding as their disorganised crews panicked, grappling hooks flying to bind the attackers to their prey. There would be prizes this day. He saw volleys sweeping the open decks before soldiers piled over the rails to storm the enemy ship. Cannons flashed and shot whizzed back and forth between the ships with plumes of smoke. Swords and hatchets rose and fell. Sprays of crimson flew as men hacked at each other furiously. Over it all, the wind howled at the slaughter; this was truly a day for wolves. There would be no escape for these weakling foes.

An eerie ripple of light and colour flashed through the water, purples and reds, but somehow also green in hue. He started at a deafening crack of thunder which rolled overhead, louder than any he had heard in his life. At first, he thought it was cannon but this was no roar of powder. The sea heaved unnaturally. Lightning flashed. Ulfgar stared up into the sky, awestruck. A flash of red lit the deck. *It was red! Red Lightning!* Like forks of fiery blood rending through the clouds. Then it flashed again. The sky split with an awful cracking and tearing. Some sort of thing appeared high above him—some sort of rift—it rippled with terrible colour akin to those flashing through the depths below him. It looked like the Northern Aurora, the sky fires of the gods, but this was different. This was altogether more terrifying to behold. An immense and eldritch thing of power like nothing any human eye had seen before, the very sight of it clutched at his heart with a cold grip of iron.

The fighting lulled. Sailors and soldiers stood motionless, watching the sky, rapt by the same awe which froze him to where he now stood. A blinding red flash caused him to shield his eyes. He heard the screams of men and women, competing with an explosion of timber. The unnatural red lightning had struck one of the enemy ships. It immediately burst into a flaming wreckage which began to slip beneath the waves. The flash seemed to linger as if seared into Ulfgar's vision; it was as if he had stared into a fire for too long. The arcs of lightning seemed frozen, failing to dissipate with their usual flash, instead splitting the sky and disappearing beneath the waves to emit a strange, ruddy glow from the depths.

What remained of the burning ship finally disappeared, claimed entirely by the sea, leaving flaming flotsam and charred bodies which seemed to be getting sucked towards the frozen glowing arc of lightning. It throbbed with a malignant crimson.

Ulfgar felt his jaw hanging slack as he stared dumbstruck. *What sorcery was this?* Another blinding flash struck the roiling empty ocean somewhere out on the nearby sea. Again, the strange forks of lightning lingered, not dissipating, like trees of terrible colour branching down from the heavens. The strange rift rippled overhead, filling the sky. It felt ominous, malignant.

Ulfgar snapped his attention back to his surroundings and surveyed the ships entangled before him. Of the distracted soldiers, some stood bayonet to bayonet with their foes; most stood frozen by the incredible sight.

This distraction is our chance to finish them. This is the god's work. He flicked a glance at the burning wreckage where a ship had once been. *The gods struck down the enemy! Our gods!*

"Fight!" he bellowed. "Kill them all!" He slapped his horn-man from his reverie. "Blow the horn, man. We fight!"

Raising the twisted black horn to his lips,

the horn-man blew. The deep braying note blasted out over the windswept sea. Ulfgar watched as his men lurched into motion. He watched sabres that had been raised and then frozen overhead finally crash down. He saw bayonets thrust over rails and punch through Noraph flesh. The sporadic crack of musket fire rippled over the battle once more, joined by the crushing explosions of cannonade broadsides. The chaos of bloodshed and slaughter erupted, all bathed in the eerie glow of the frozen lightning and the ominous rift overhead.

"The gods are with us! Fight!" he bellowed to his warriors, as the prow of his ship once again angled to board a smaller Noraph warship.

The ship, hopelessly outgunned, began to turn to escape the withering fusillade of StormChild's batteries. Ulfgar watched the ship swing about. He thought to give the order to turn in pursuit, to keep them locked within his full broadside.

"Sir?" asked Lars, awaiting the presumed order to turn.

A flickering at the stern of the enemy ship caught his eye. Three glinting lanterns winked at him from the rear of its command deck. *The signal lamps!*

"You there," he snapped at a nearby marine. "Give me your rifle."

"Sir," he nodded, his reply accompanied with a frown of confusion.

"Is it loaded?"

"Aye, sir," said the marine as he relinquished his weapon.

Ulfgar thumbed back the flint hammer with practised ease. Raising the weapon to his shoulder, he took aim.

The rifle flashed with a hissing *crack* and erupted with a gout of white smoke.

"You've fired one of those before," commented Lars with an awed grin.

"Aye," replied Ulfgar as he handed the marine back his weapon with a nod. Through the clearing smoke he saw only two flickering lights remained. The centre lamp had shattered, spilling burning oil.

"Excellent shot, sir," applauded Lars.

They watched the fire spread and take hold through the gaps in the roiling smoke. The enemy bridge crew noticed too late. Ulfgar saw them as they began to panic and shout. The flames slowly took hold. As the gunwale and stern rails charred to embers there were flashes as the other lamps ignited, spilling liquid fire over the stern.

"Where in the gods did you learn to do that, sir?"

Ulfgar watched with a set jaw as the flames danced across the enemy ship's hull, engulfing the rear of the ship. "Trained with the infantry when I was a lad."

"Didn't know that."

"I was young once too, Lars." Ulfgar's hand found the watch again in his pocket.

"Poor devils," said Lars, all excitement suddenly leached from his voice as he watched the burning ship.

"Aye," said Ulfgar, turning away and setting a grim face. "Keep her clear," he called to the helmsman. He pushed away thoughts of burning sailors and snapped out a telescopic eye-glass to survey the enemy ships ahead. "Move to engage the frigate," he said as he snapped the telescope shut.

"Very good, sir," acknowledged Lars as he tore his gaze away from the stricken flaming ship. "Damn good shot," Ulfgar heard him murmur.

He had to suppress a grin. *I would never have made that in another hundred shots.* He chuckled to himself and wished Jules had seen it. His younger brother would no doubt be suitably impressed. He cast a sidelong glance at the Kira; the ship it was engaged with had struck its colours. *Good lad.*

Something strange and unsettling caught his eye. A glowing light seemed to rise from the depths. Another rift-like tear opened beneath the surface, spilling its lambent glow into the murk. It was captivating. Then his heart froze. For a moment it looked as something huge and dark blocked the glowing light. A dark flowing oily thing disgorging from the submerged rift, erupting forth like a jelly squeezed and birthed through too small a hole.

Had he imagined it, some trick of wave and light? He stared at the dark shape. Then it pulsed and flinched, spreading out. Something broke the surface, like humps of a colossal whale, glistening and grey. *What is that thing?* Dwarfing his flagship, it seemed huge—like an island emerging from the depths. A foul stench pervaded his nostrils, like bile and rotting fish.

"Is that oil?" said Lars, from beside him.

Ulfgar stared a moment, lost for words. "I have never seen anything like it… In all my years…"

The mass shuddered and slipped beneath the surface, causing mighty ripples that became waves. There was a surge. He saw the dark shadow glide beneath his keel. The first rolling wave struck their hull, jolting them as if the seas were suddenly wracked by a mighty storm. Some nearby ships collided and smashed together. A smaller ship's deck was completely swamped.

With a huge rush, the sea exploded outward. A hulking black bulk erupted and slowly rose above the waves from the midst of the battle. Ships caught by its emergence shattered like kindling or were dragged beneath the waves in the surge. Ulfgar stared, petrified in paralysing horror. It was a thing of glistening black blubber, a gargantuan sprawl of fin and claw. The leviathan rose from the waves, almost in slow motion, towering above the highest masts of the entangled fleets.

This was a monster, so unimaginable and terrible he feared for his sanity just to gaze upon it. A hulking leviathan of the blackest depths, something out of the darkest mythic legends. Even the oldest sailor's most far-fetched tale could not conjure up this… this horror. Such things couldn't truly exist, yet there it loomed. He couldn't believe what his eyes showed him. It was as if, in that moment, all he knew was madness, as if all he knew was a joke, as if reality could not coincide with the existence of such a thing, for surely it could only exist in nightmares.

A luminous eye, at least he thought it looked to be an eye, surveyed the ships arrayed before it. Torrents of water cascaded down from its oily hide, falling like a squall onto all who looked up at it.

Then it fell.

It slammed down onto a ship, obliterating the vessel beneath its immense bulk in an instant. Ulfgar watched, stunned, as the bulk rose up once more to loom over another ship. *No…the Kira.*

He cried out an impotent warning. "No!" he screamed, but his words were stolen by the wind and crash of waves. He could only watch helplessly as a nightmare maw opened amidst the oily blubber. A throat ringed with teeth and fangs, like the mouth of a giant lamprey. "Jules," screamed Ulfgar, reaching out his hand as if to somehow save his brother's ship.

The thing ripped into the Kira's hull, a leathery coil wrapping the foremast and constricting like a squirming snake, snapping timbers. The mouth tore through the hull, incising and thrashing. The Kira broke in two like a rotten splinter. "No," Ulfgar roared.

"Sir, we must do something," said Lars, the panic plain in his voice.

"Open fire!" yelled Ulfgar. He snapped his head to Lars "Signal every ship, open fire." His voice dripped with vehemence. "*Kill* it!"

The StormChild's cannons thundered, belching plumes of white smoke along its port side. For the moment the enemy was forgotten as all ships, friend and foe alike, began to release a fusillade of withering lead shot into the thing's hide. Ships broke off from their vicious boarding actions and swung round to engage the nightmare colossus, cannons flaring.

The eruption of cannons only seemed to anger the thing. It raised a bulky claw and smashed through the deck of the nearest ship with indifference.

Ulfgar watched the wreck of the Kira slip beneath the waves. "Jules," wailed Ulfgar. His heart lurched at the sight, at the thought of his dear little brother's fate. No man could survive those frothing waters.

Another full broadside thundered from the StormChild's guns. Ulfgar's ears rang. He could see men's mouths moving but there were no words to be heard. The thing seemed to flinch as his cannons struck home and turned its regard upon them. To his horror, the thing surged towards them. The bulbous bulk of what Ulfgar took to be its head briefly submerged. The luminous eye, visible beneath a rolling wave that marked its approach, seemed to be locked on them, on him, on his very soul.

'Ready a full broadside! Every cannon we have, on my mark,' snapped Ulfgar as he watched the nightmare approaching. He pulled his sabre from its sheath and ran his eyes along its blade. *I will die with a sword in my hand, damn it.* He heard the gun officers shouting his order.

It rose up off their side. Streams of water fell from its back as it slowly ascended to tower over the StormChild.

"Wait for it," he bellowed, raising his sword over his head. His words were echoed by his officers below and accented with low calls of, 'steady.'

The great yellow eye blinked and regarded the ship with an indifferent malice. Ulfgar could have sworn it looked right at him. With a sucking wet sound, its gigantic maw opened up, revealing rows and rows of savage triangular fangs. A gut lurching stink washed over them; the smell of rotten fish and bile intensified, making Ulfgar's gorge rise. Lars vomited beside him.

'Fire,' screamed Ulfgar, slashing his sabre towards the thing.

The ship rocked back at the kick of a whole volley, turning his ship's side into a pall of thick, blinding acrid white smoke. Shot punched through blubber with eruptions of viscous black oil and slime. Teeth shattered and splintered. The eye widened, spasming, and then it snapped shut. The thing seemed to flinch back as the cannons struck home. Its stinking mouth unleashed an ear-shattering shriek.

'Reload,' bellowed the officers of the gun

crews.

The StormChild limped towards the shadow of hills that framed the quiet bay. The hearth fires of a small fishing town huddled the shoreline, releasing a thin haze over the bay. Smaller boats could be seen crowding the small harbour, their masts still and calm. Ulfgar regarded his wounded ship and sighed. Her rear mast had been un-rigged, and what remained of its splintered stump had been sawed back. Half a dozen ships trailed in their wake, the remnants of his broken fleet. It had been a rare fight. The leviathan… that monster had sunk four of his ships, and several Noraph, before another huge broadside had driven it back to the depths. Men had been driven to snivelling wrecks at just the sight of it; he had a brig full of madmen who had once been good sailors.

Ulfgar stood at the prow, turning the silver watch in his hands. Jules had left it in his cabin when he had last come aboard; it was his brother's—a parting gift from their father on receiving his commission and leaving home for sea. Its silver lid was stamped with their family seal.

He had one the same somewhere in his cabin. He had meant to return it to him when he next saw him. But now he never would. Ever since the battle he had carried it, a token of luck now, a reminder of home, a reminder of young Jules.

His younger brother was gone. They had always been close. Jules had looked up to him. He had eagerly followed him into service to the empire. The Kira had been his first command, and his last. Ulfgar fought back a tear as he remembered his last words to their mother. "Look after him," she had said. She passed away since, joining their father in another place. Ulfgar had failed her. Jules was gone.

They had searched the wreckage and flotsam. They had pulled some sailors from the water, desperate half-drowned survivors, but Jules had not been among them. He squeezed his eyes shut as a tear escaped to roll down his cheek.

Footsteps approached behind. He cuffed the tear away and took a deep breath to steady his reserve.

"Sir," spoke Lars' voice. "Orders?"

Ulfgar regarded the bay and the port town. "Bring her in. We'll drop anchor in the bay and go ashore in the launches."

"Very good, sir."

A fire burned high from the beacon of a stone lighthouse which nestled on a stone-piled breakwater. It was that light which had guided them through the choppy waters. The storm had settled but the sky was still leaden, and the sea still dark and angry. The Noraph fleet was all but destroyed. He had seen two ships flee, but the others had all found a home beneath the waves. Those poor devils had taken the brunt of its wrath. They were already defeated, prizes had been taken, and then it had come. The leviathan had erupted in their midst, smashing and rending all asunder. It seemed to have birthed from those strange lights, slithering from the depths of the abyss to breach the surface in its primordial fury. It had smashed ships to splinters, both imperial and Noraph alike. What in the gods had that murderous beast been?

As the StormChild drew level with the grey stone tower, Ulfgar spied a lone figure. Stood on the seaward rocks at the tower's base, a cloaked figure watched them. Ulfgar could see it was an old man; the long grey beard was all he could make out. The old man's face was wreathed in shadow beneath his hood. Ulfgar offered the man a casual nod and a two-finger salute. The motionless figure returned a slow nod and continued to watch the imperial ships limp in to make anchor in the calm grey bay.

Launches made their way to shore; provisions were to be purchased and repairs arranged. A crowd of curious locals had gathered on the town's harbour wall. Ulfgar did not know this place. The storm had thrown him off course, but he reckoned by his charts this must be the Armarth isles, and this harbour likely a place known as Fellshore. The charts of this region were not as accurate as those of empire waters. Well, he guessed he would find out when they came ashore.

The men welcomed some firm ground beneath their feet and a little time ashore while the work crews attended repairs. The foreboding sense of dread and shock seemed to sigh in relief at the safety of dry land. The thing could not haunt them here. Sailors could sleep on dry land, there were taverns, all out of reach, or so they all hoped, of that lurking monstrosity. A thing they all knew was real and still haunted the unknown depths somewhere out there.

All told their tale to the local townsfolk and fishermen. This place did indeed turn out to be Fellshore, a far-flung and remote port on the very frontiers of the empire's reach. The empire traded with the free ports in these distant waters where the folk were a strange mix of seafaring peoples, but friendly enough.

The StormChild sat at anchor, surrounded by the tattered remnants of the fleet, and would remain until the repairs were complete and his ships seaworthy. Ulfgar spent most of his time aboard the StormChild, and each day that passed, he would see the lighthouse keeper standing watching them. Sometimes it felt like the man was watching him, and at those times he would offer a wave. The lighthouse keeper often gave no reply, just standing there, a watching sentinel.

"Who is that man?" asked Ulfgar.

"Who, sir?" replied Lars.

"Him," said Ulfgar with a gesture towards the lighthouse. "Our watching friend there. He watches us." He paused. "Watches us like a cliff hawk… like a damn warden at a prison."

"Sir?" replied Lars, turning from his supervision of the busy work crews. Seeing the man, Lars continued, "Yes, he's a strange one isn't he. Always seems to be there. I've heard about him actually. The locals on the docks say he's watched the lighthouse for years, say that he keeps himself to himself. Apparently, he's a storyteller, keeps the local legends and the like."

"Must be a sailor then."

"Yes, quite," laughed Lars. His face darkened a little. "Well, word got about… about that thing out there—the monster. Well, the dock foreman reckoned to me, if anyone round here knew anything about something like that, it would be him."

"The men are talking about it on shore?"

"Sailors talk, sir."

Ulfgar frowned and slowly nodded. He didn't know if he liked the idea of such rumours spreading. He should have put out an order, told them all to keep their mouths shut. *What's the point, though? The talk would be all over the fleet and the docks. There's no containing it now. Damn. How in the gods will I ever explain this to the admiralty? They will never believe it.* "Aye Lars, that they do," was his only reply.

He put the thought aside, his eyes finding the lighthouse. There he still stood, ever watching. Then Ulfgar saw him turn and disappear into a door.

"Must have known we were talking about him," commented Lars before turning his attention to the work crews.

Ulfgar didn't respond to the quip, his brow creased in thought.

"Lars, ready a longboat," he said.

The oars dipped and rose from the surf dripping, the oarsmen pulling in unison. The launch rocked heavily in the windswept water.

"You think he knows something?" asked Lars, holding his hat in the bracing wind.

"Aye, I do," replied Ulfgar, holding himself steady in the rocking boat. "That old hawk might just know what that thing was out there. He might know an old story. Something."

Waves broke against the granite grey breaker on which the lighthouse perched. The boat bumped against the little stone dock on the lee-side of the tower. Ulfgar's boot trudged onto the wet stone, and he clambered up to the door at the base of the tower. Lars clambered up behind him, still clutching on to his hat.

A battered wooden door was set into the base of the stone tower. The door creaked open as Ulfgar raised his hand to knock. He froze. As he came face to face with the cloaked man. The lighthouse keeper's hood covered his eyes, and the lower part of the face that was visible was cracked with ancient lines and wrinkles. The pair regarded each other.

The man's wizened mouth cracked a smile, revealing yellowed teeth. "Ah, you have come. I thought you might." He shouldered his way past and hobbled to cast his gaze over the waves of the cloud-covered seas.

Ulfgar followed.

The man stood a while watching the waves break, then he spoke. "Oh seas… not seas, but expanses fraught with tears."

"What?" asked Ulfgar, casting a bemused look at Lars.

"I know what haunts your dreams, friend," said the old man, turning to Ulfgar and clutching at his arm with skeletal hands. Ulfgar glanced down at the man's hand, thin pale skin stretched over bone, made all the paler by the deep blue of his uniform's jacket to which the old man clung. "It took something. I can see it in your eyes, captain. You paid your toll to the seas. A heavy price."

Ulfgar had no reply. He tried to harden his expression but his eyes betrayed his grief. He saw Jules' face in his mind, the memory of the final time he had spoken with him. Ulfgar raised his eyes to the man's face.

"I have seen many strange things," continued the old man in a voice of rasping paper, "but there is a look in the eye I know all too well. There's something else." Stood this close, Ulfgar could make out the man's darkened face beneath the hood, piercing eyes studying him from the shadow. *Those eyes… how strange.* "You saw it, didn't you?" said the man, after a pause.

"I don't know what I saw," admitted Ulfgar.

"But you saw something. I know you saw the very air tear, the very sky crack. Look," he pointed high into the sky. "It's there still, a terrible thing that has rent the sky. I have never seen one so big like that." Ulfgar followed the man's finger and true, the strange aurora-like lights still burned the heavens beyond the clouds.

"What is it?" breathed Ulfgar.

"Who knows? They say the rifts are tears between heaven and earth, or between hell…"

"How do you know this? Who are you?"

"How do I know?" the old man repeated his words. He seemed to chew them with his mouth before replying. "Because I've seen things, too. These are not the first rifts to open. It has been many years, but these came sooner than I would have thought." He raised his face back to the sky. "And this is worse than I have seen before. It's too soon."

Ulfgar was transfixed by the man's strange eyes, like none he had seen before. As the old man raised his face to stare into the heavens, light spilt over his features. *Those eyes.*

"What did you see?" asked the old man. He turned his head to meet Ulfgar's regard, pinning his gaze with those strange amber eyes. They were like copper, like two small bright coins, his pupils dark in their centre.

"It came from the sea, lights and colours. The sky split just like you said, but so did the sea. Colours shining from beneath the waves, and then something terrible came, something colossal… some nameless thing." The old man's grip tightened as he spoke. Ulfgar continued, "It was something that could smash a ship to kindling. It rose high in the sky, yet still sank beneath the waves and surged through the depths." It felt good to finally give voice to what he had seen. When they had talked about it on the ship, no man had described it. They had all seen it. None could bring themselves to give words to the thing, perhaps fearing speaking of it would summon it back.

"It was a monster," broke in Lars, speaking from behind. "A huge… *thing*. It took everything we threw at it, and shrugged it off as if it were nothing."

Ulfgar nodded in agreement. "It was dark and wet, and blubbery. Some terrible leviathan from the depths. It did that," said Ulfgar, gesturing to his fleet anchored in the bay behind them. "It smashed our fleet to splinters."

"From the depths," repeated the old man, "or from the rifts… from the underworld, from another place."

"It was some demon of the sea," whispered Ulfgar.

"It was exactly that, Captain," nodded the old man. "A thing that should not be." He turned back to the seas. "Things must be getting worse if the tears are cracking the seas."

"I saw it appear like lightning beneath the waves," confirmed Ulfgar.

"By the gods," muttered the old man.

"What is it? How do we stop it?"

"Stop the rifts?" He shrugged. "You must destroy it, captain. You must seek the thing that emerged, hunt it, and send it back from where it came, send it back to hell."

"Captain…" hissed Lars. "Ulfgar… This is madness. You can't be serious…"

Ulfgar silenced him with a firm gesture, not tearing his gaze from the old man's face. Those strange copper eyes, eyes of almost luminous amber, bored into him. Those eyes, so intense, almost cat-like. He had truly never seen their like.

"Only then can the rifts be sealed,' continued the old man. 'How will become known in time, but first anything that emerges must be sent back to oblivion if there is to be any hope."

Ulfgar grunted.

"Perhaps your price was too high, Captain? Yes, perhaps the fates were cruel, but you are owed a vengeance. Perhaps only you have what is needed to see it done. Claim your vengeance. But you must do it; if you do not, then more rifts will come, more horrors will come forth, and this world will eventually be lost to a nightmare."

"Captain, the admiralty will never allow it," insisted Lars.

"They have not seen it, boy," spat the old man, with a gesture to the seas. "They don't know… but you know." He turned to Ulfgar. "You saw it. So go kill it, send it back. It is our only hope. Your only hope of vengeance."

"But how?"

"You survived it once, you must face it again. Only you understand, captain. Take that mighty ship of yours and see it done."

"Captain, I do insist. We should go. This man is clearly mad… if you beg my pardon."

The old man grinned at the young officer's words. He threw Ulfgar a piercing look. "Kill it, lads. The world needs men of valour like you. You must not fail."

Captain Ulfgar stared at the sea. He had lost track of how much time he had been standing there. His hair had grown long and had become streaked with grey. His beard had grown and become unkempt. His heavy coat wrapped about him, his hat pulled low over his eyes, he stood watching the endless swell and roll of the sea. Sometimes the wind would whip the swells so they crested into small waves crowned with white spray. Gulls wheeled overhead. The distant roar of waves crashed against the jagged ribbon of iron-grey cliffs on their landward side. The sky brooded, a rolling leaden carpet of grey clouds. The sky seemed to match his thoughts. He took out Jules' old watch from his pocket and checked the time. He closed it and looked down at the watch, turning it over in his hands before slipping it back into his coat pocket.

He returned his gaze to the sea and absently ran his fingertips over the ridge of the old scar across his palm. The scar of a promise made, an oath. An oath of vengeance.

"Oh sea, not seas, but expanses fraught with tears," he muttered, repeating that strange old man's words from long ago. They had stuck with him; he often thought of what that strange old man with the unearthly eyes had said. *And the old watcher had been so right.* He saw that now. The sea was indeed a cruel mistress.

The ship rocked gently, and behind him, the calls of sailors at work provided a background noise he hardly seemed to hear. Yet those crashing waves and the call of the gulls seemed forefront in his thoughts. He heard footsteps approaching.

"The Wave Eater has nearly finished the re-supply, sir," reported Lars.

"Very good," replied Ulfgar without turning.

Lars seemed to hesitate. "Captain Averland asks on a response to the dispatch."

"The dispatch…" replied Ulfgar distantly. "No, I've not had a chance to read it yet."

"He said it was urgent." He hesitated. "From the Admiralty."

"Aye, I suspect I know what they want."

"New orders, sir?"

Ulfgar grunted sourly. "Most likely," he replied dismissively. "Any more reports on the missing merchant convoy?"

"Well, yes actually," admitted Lars. Ulfgar

turned to regard his first officer. Lars kept himself clean shaven, though his face had grown lined and he looked tired. *I have been pushing the men a bit hard of late… but we are so close. I can feel it.* "We have a confirmed sighting, seems to be the most recent, last sighted off the Claw Isles."

"That's not far."

"Less than twenty leagues. They were due to make port here a week past. A passing schooner sighted them near the isles just before a storm blew in. The ship is presumed wrecked off the isles. They are some treacherous waters, I hear."

"Hmm." Ulfgar scratched at his wiry beard. "Rifts?"

"Indeed, they have been sighted in these waters recently."

Ulfgar nodded thoughtfully. *It's out there; I can feel it.* He looked Lars in the eye. "That's where the beast is lurking."

"We've heard nothing but rumour for months—"

"That's where it is," cut in Ulfgar. "As soon as the last provisions are aboard, chart a course for the Claw Isles."

"Of course, but Captain… uh… the dispatch? Captain Averland is awaiting your response." *He knows what it says, or at least suspects.*

Ulfgar grimaced. "I'll see to it now," he snapped. He had not meant to use that tone of annoyance, yet it came.

"I will return to my duties."

"Yes, yes," waved Ulfgar dismissively.

Ulfgar took a last lingering glance out at the grey sea and then made his way to his cabin. He threw his hat down on his desk and eyed the sealed parchment that rested there. He suspected he knew what that dispatch contained. Looking for any excuse to put off reading the damned thing, he picked up his log book and leafed through the entries, reading the odd one here and there.

March 20th
We proceed south from Fellshore. No sightings of the fleeing remnants of the Noraph. We seem to be skirting a storm but the seas remain calm. May it stay that way.

April 12th

The thing still glows in the sky. It is best observed at night. It reminds me of the auroras of the far north, but less fleeting. This thing burns like a fire across the heavens—quite beautiful really, but something about it is sinister. It's unsettling.

April 25th
More flotsam, more wreckage. We pulled a single survivor from the water. He was half-dead and completely mad. He rambled about sea monsters before succumbing to what the surgeon claims is exposure. He fell dead in the surgeon's arms. He was committed to the sea that claimed him. We seem to be on the right course, though. Jules will be avenged.

At the mention of Jules, he sighed and flicked further on to later entries.

November 30th
We've been at sea for weeks since our last call to a port. Still no sign. No contact with the Noraph, no sign of our elusive prey. There has been little to no wind. We are becalmed, it seems, and the fleet drifts. I did see whales

today though, four of them. They were big. I found myself envying those surging tails; we could do with that—they need no sails, no wind. Majestic beasts.

December 18th
We are heading back North East. We should sight land somewhere around Cape Arkis soon. I aim to make port at Sarsan. I hope there have been some sightings of the creature or some rumour. I will send a report from the imperial consulate there and report our status. The Noraph seem to be in disarray in these waters, their presence is scant, yet still they lurk here and there. Only today, we sighted two ships fleeing east from us. After we smashed their fleet last spring, they have yet to recover. We broke them, well... that thing broke them, but it was an imperial victory nonetheless. I intend to report a continued threat, however. I also intend to continue my hunt of the creature, and to do so I will continue my orders to patrol the South Sea and engage the enemy where we find them. I will chase it to the darkest of seas.

He flicked through several pages. Weeks

upon weeks of entries. Weeks, months, even years had passed. *Had it really been that long? Have I really lost years to pursuing this beast?* He noticed the entries were becoming less thorough in recent months. He seemed to have gone days or weeks at a time sometimes without writing in it at all. He had certainly become preoccupied of late. He read one of the newer entries, only a few weeks old.

July 19th
There has been discontent amongst the crew. Some of the men have been disciplined. It seems some of them have taken to calling me Mad Ulfgar behind my back and sadly not with affection. Lieutenant Lars tells me that there has been talk across the fleet. Do they really think me mad? I will continue to proceed west; there have been reports of missing ships in the area.

Ulfgar sighed and closed the log book. Even his men were beginning to think him a madman. He saw them whispering behind his back as he passed. *How could they not understand? They saw that thing; they alone should understand we must destroy it. They are afraid of it though…* He glanced down at the dispatch sitting on his desk, the crimson wax stamp of the Admiralty glaring at him. Ulfgar already knew what it would say. What else could it be? He picked it up and broke the seal.

For the eyes of Captain C. Ulfgar,
Posted (Commodore Second Class) in command of the Seventeenth squadron of His Imperial Majesty's Navy.

You are ordered to cease operations immediately and return to Porth docks to report to the admiralty post haste. Captain Averland of HIMS Wave Eater has been ordered to provide escort and is forthwith attached to the seventeenth under your command until his escort duty is complete. Do not delay; the Seventeenth is overdue by several months, and although your dutiful diligence in patrolling the South Sea has been noted, you are now required to report and receive new orders.

Lord Admiral W. Typhon,
of His Imperial Majesty's Navy

"Dutiful diligence…" muttered Ulfgar with a scowl. *They mock me.* "Damn it," he cursed, hammering his fist and tossing the parchment back onto his desk. *I knew it.* They were recalling him. He knew he had no choice this time. He had pushed his orders to the limit and he should have reported back a year ago. *Has it really been that long?* he thought with a glance at the logbook. If he did not return this time, they would declare him renegade and hunt him down. They could possibly court-martial him either way, but then again perhaps not; he was a hero of the empire, he who battled the leviathan and lived, the vanquisher of the Noraph fleet. He no doubt had medals awaiting him on his return. His scowl returned. *They have even sent that lapdog Averland to bring me home, too. He is just waiting for a command like mine.* He took out the pocket watch and spoke to it. "You will be avenged, brother. I will not rest until I have my vengeance, I promise."

He surveyed the charts spread over his desk. He followed the scattering of pencil markings showing wrecked ships they had come across, rumours of lost vessels, and outbreaks of the rift phenomena. Officially they would be reported as losses to the Noraph enemy. But he suspected otherwise. There was a pattern to it though, a trail. He had followed that monstrous thing for thousands of leagues back and forth across the South Sea. He had hunted it obsessively, following rumours of sea monsters wherever he made port.

Ulfgar located their current position and traced a finger north to the Claw Isles. There were several nearby markings, missing ships and locations of other strange incidents; several were localised within fifty leagues of the little group of islands. He considered the charts thoughtfully. *It must be there. Oh, how long I have hunted you. Is this where you have made your lair? Finally*... He glanced at the folded dispatch. He was being forced to return to port. He really had no choice and Ulfgar knew it. He peered closely at the Claw Isles. It was not far off his return course. *One last shot.*

He strode back up onto the bridge of the StormChild and adjusted his hat.

"Lars?"

"Yes, sir."

"Send word to Averland. Tell him we make

sail for Porth docks with haste. Tell him we are duty-bound to investigate the disappearance of a convoy of merchantmen last sighted off the Claw Isles as it is just off the course home. Assure him we will discover their fate as we return to port and will not linger longer than necessary. Tell him to form up with the rest of the squadron, and that I have received orders for him to attach himself to the squadron under my command until we reach port. Oh, and thank him for his escort."

"Very good sir, anything else?"

Ulfgar threw a glance at his officer. "Yes, set a course for the Claw Isles."

The dark shapes of the Claw Isles rose up from the sea to make silhouettes against the horizon. The Isles protruded from the sea like twisted claws grasping at the low hanging wisps of cloud.

"Signal the fleet. Prepare for action. Load all guns and have the crews ready on alert."

A junior officer nodded and departed. Ulfgar watched the signalman waving his orders to the other ships with a pair of small flags, and a fresh array of signal flags were hoisted up onto the main mast alongside the imperial colours. The ships slowly formed up around the StormChild.

"Do you think it's here?" asked Lars as he surveyed the cluster of islands with his eyeglass.

"Something happened to that convoy," replied Ulfgar with his eyes on the surrounding seas.

"Could have been the Noraph, or pirates. It could have been a storm; these isles are marked as treacherous on the charts…"

"Or it could be the beast," frowned Ulfgar. "What does your gut tell you?"

"I… I'm not sure, sir."

"It's out there. I can feel it." He took out his watch and checked the time.

"What's the plan then Captain?" asked Lars, straightening and banishing the doubt from his face.

"We approach with caution, staying in formation. We sweep these waters for wreckage or any sign of the convoy. If it's here, it will come, but it will find us waiting instead of lumbering traders." He turned with a sly grin. "And these ships have teeth it just might remember."

The squadron combed the waters around the isles before heading in closer. The light was fading, turning the sky into a stunning vista of deep purples and burnt oranges. Strange lights flickered in the water as they drew closer. Ulfgar realised they were rifts, splitting open and slowly disappearing into nothing. As they drew close to one of the larger isles—more a huge blasted rock with a twisted spire of slick stone jutting from the waves—the lookouts began shouting and pointing.

"Wreckage, sir," reported Lars. Ulfgar raised his eye-glass. There amongst the surf bobbed barrels caught in nets and splintered timbers entangled in floating lengths of torn sail. Then he spied the skeletal timber frame of a ship's hull that had been driven against the rocks and was lodged there by the crashing waves. *Looks like we've found the convoy.* He scanned the nearby rocks for any signs of survivors, but there was nothing but cold unforgiving stone and foaming hopeless sea.

The squadron crept silently between the islands. It seemed eerily quiet and still. No birds wheeled overhead, no sign of life to be seen anywhere. Just the roiling sea and the crash of waves, which seemed accented by the strange lack of anything else. All hands aboard seemed to hold their breath, perhaps in anticipation and readiness, or perhaps each of them fearing to bring life to this still dead place, for fear that life would be noticed by something terrible. *They feel it too. It's here, watching.* The sailors silently watched the strange glowing lights of tiny short-lived rifts appearing and fading in the waters around them, twinkling like stars beneath the waves, their strange lambent lights glowing to life and dying in the murk. Ulfgar watched on, bewildered as he spotted an old shoe drifting out of one rift, only to be swallowed up again by another one. It was eerily calm.

Then, as he knew it would, it came.

Without warning, one of the frigates let loose a volley with a crash of fire and white smoke. Ulfgar saw tentacles had uncoiled around the ship and assailed it from all sides. *The Wave Eater... Averland...* The probing gelatinous prongs flinched away from the cannon's sudden spite, and retreated beneath the waves.

"It's upon us," roared Ulfgar in manic excitement. "It's here!" He turned to his crew on the deck below. "This day we fight! Ready yourselves and fight like devils! Sound the horn!" The horn-man blew a long braying note that echoed out though the dusk sky.

A dull rumbling came in reply, building into a roaring thunder that seemed to come from all around. With an eruption of water, the frigate was smashed onto its side, its cannons silent as men screamed and fell into the water. The luminous yellow eye rose menacingly from the darkening sea to glare down on Averland's stricken ship that had dared to defy it. That same terrible eye that had haunted Ulfgar's dreams all these years. Its horrifying regard then seemed to swing towards him.

"Kill it," screamed Ulfgar, his mouth twisting with hate and foaming spittle. "Give it everything we have."

The amassed cannons of Ulfgar's fleet let fly, screaming death and fire and smoke. Cannon shot punched through the oily black blubber, and even as the monstrous thing rose up to tower above the highest mast, it quivered and flinched with every massive volley. The waters of the Claw Isles suddenly became enveloped in an acrid fog of powder smoke yet, above it all, the leviathan towered with its single terrible eye. The StormChild's cannons roared in a savage broadside, the ship rocking sideways with the ferocity of the combined fury. "Reload," shouted the gunnery officers in unison.

Ulfgar clutched his brother's pocket watch in one hand and waved his sabre in the other. He watched the leviathan swing its gaze from him to focus on another ship which had strayed close to it. The determined little ship poured cannon fire into the beast's bulk until a massive claw ripped its belly out and it began to sink with horrifying speed. With a blood-curdling roar, a monstrous mouth yawned wide and descended as the leviathan lunged down into the sinking ship to tear it to pieces.

Tentacles slithered from the sea and wrapped another ship behind him. Still the cannons roared and, with such concentrated fire, terrible gaping wounds began to show on the leviathan's form, opening its stinking bowels to spill fetid dark viscous slime into the sea. Ships cracked and split. All around him, cannons thundered and men screamed. It seemed like all the ships were fighting their own private battles with many separate foes, but there was just one—just one titanic foe capable of entangling many assailants at once with a gluttonous array of limbs and appendages.

Thick tentacles slid from the water and seized the StormChild, sliding over the decks and wrapping the hull several times. One clutched at a mast and snapped it like a twig, the rigging and sails tumbling down as the mast collapsed like a felled tree. Lightning flashed overhead and with it came the flash of rifts, almost as if the rifts were just another weapon the leviathan wielded.

Ulfgar screamed and hacked at the nearest tentacle. His sabre sliced through the dark jellied blubber and spilt stinking dark green slime over the wooden boards of his ship. The air seemed to still around him. He turned. The giant eye rose up over the side of the gunwale. It was right there staring straight down at him. He screamed and ran at it, plunging his blade into its hateful regard. The creature shrieked and recoiled, its unearthly screech deafening him. He saw a flash and the ship shuddered. A point-blank broadside exploded into the creature's abdomen. Tentacles exploded and the entire gigantic mass of the thing shuddered and seemed to pull away.

Ulfgar bellowed a laugh. "Ha, taste the flaming fury of the StormChild, you bastard. I will have my vengeance!"

Another flash.

Not cannon fire though, this was different. A great rift sheared through the sea and sky, a vertical cleft which tore down from the clouds and plunged into the sea directly ahead. It was the widest he had ever seen, like a deep fissure in a cliff-face.

The ship groaned and timbers buckled as the leviathan's writhing gelatinous tentacles recovered and constricted once more.

"You will not have me, beast," roared Ulfgar and he grabbed the spinning wheel of his ship and held it to sail true directly into the rift. "Fire," bellowed Ulfgar. "Fire everything we have!" Cannons boomed and cracked, his gun crews spewing a fusillade of fire into the bowels of the creature that enwreathed his beloved ship. The rift looked like fire, the fire that flows over the embers of a log in a hearth. Men screamed as tentacles whipped about. A poorly loaded cannon exploded, sending bodies and flames raining over the deck. The deck of the StormChild became a hellish landscape of flame, blood and horror. He watched a man plucked screaming from his feet and flung far over the side of the ship by a tentacle that seemed to be a living malicious thing all of itself.

He felt the mighty impact as something hammered into him, as if he had slammed into a wall of stone. Suddenly, he was sprawling through the air. A flailing tentacle had whipped up from the grey waters and hurled him away. He was falling, the water rushing up to meet him.

He crashed into the icy sea with an impact that drove all the air from his lungs. The water constricted his chest and stole his breath. He struggled beneath the waves, his lungs burning. Panic set in and he fought and clawed his way to the surface. The breath he took on reaching the surface was explosive. Ulfgar coughed and spluttered and dragged in another deep breath. He swam to a nearby piece of wreckage, a timber spar which trailed a length of ghostly white sail in the water. Ulfgar clung to it desperately in the choppy waters and turned to find his ship.

The StormChild was enveloped by a black writhing mass. Ulfgar watched the bulk of the leviathan rise, its amorphous head lifting to chew upon her hull. He saw a luminous eye, and a clawed limb rearing up to seize the ship's hull. His eyes were fixed on the strange circular mouth sawing and twisting away at her timbers. An impossible mass of tentacles writhed and squirmed, and thewed muscular limbs protruded from a colossal mass just out of view beneath the waves, its claws slamming and swiping into her side and spearing sailors with needle-like talons. The thing meant to snap his ship in two with claw and tentacle, just as it had done to so many others, as it had done to Jules' ship, the Kira. StormChild surged into the rift, her prow disappearing into the fiery horizon. He watched the fire rip through StormChild's sails and rigging. The leviathan weathered the flames even as they singed and charred its squirming bulk; such was its fury at the ship. His beautiful ship, the domination of the sea, was ablaze and soon to be little more than a wreck.

With a percussive *boom,* a massive explosion ripped through its hull. *The powder magazine.* The huge fireball enveloped the ship and erupted in a mighty explosion. The prow disappeared into the rift and both the beast and the tumultuous flaming fissure took the brunt of the blast, sending a strange quiver through the strange breach. The rift seemed to devour the explosion and it began to expand and twist, and beyond its horizon, Ulfgar glimpsed something strange. He saw darkness, yet there was something there. Some glimmering ghost of another place. Another world, an alien landscape. He floated amongst the wreckage, his face illuminated in fire, and he was transfixed.

A shock wave blasted out from the expanding rift. The colours distorted, it seemed to flicker in and out of existence as if struggling to maintain its lambent presence. The leviathan shrieked an unearthly howl, parts of it sucked into the rift. It struggled to free itself but would not release the StormChild, and the flaming ship inexorably surged into the maw of the rift and with it the leviathan. With an earth-shattering thunder, the rift surged outward into a great sphere of golden light. It stretched out a mile or more to the horizon in every direction, and both high into the sky and reaching into the untold depths below. It quivered a moment. Then all was light and thunder. The world imploded with a blinding flash of light.

He found himself falling once more. The wind whistled through his hair. At first, he thought he had been thrown high into the sky, but he realised the sea was just gone. He saw a great sphere of nothingness had replaced the glowing sphere the rift had made. The water was gone; it had disappeared with that flash of light. A huge expanse of nothing yawned beneath him. In the distance, a great wall of water quivered at the limits of the sphere, an unmoving wall of ocean, not yet realising there was no longer any water within the spherical emptiness to hold it at bay. A mile or two below, the seabed was revealed, like a stretching desert of sand and rock littered with old shipwrecks that had not seen the sky in centuries. He found himself high above that suddenly dry land below and plummeting towards it. Creatures fell with him, marine life that had only moments before been swimming through their marine home now twisted in the air, falling with him.

He saw fish tumbling and even a helpless whale slowly spiralling down. He saw the remains of his ship spinning away into nothingness, still enveloped by what was left of the leviathan. Most of the ship had been destroyed in the explosion, and it rained down in large pieces. Both the leviathan and the front prow had been sliced away with a clean cut where they had been caught within the rift before it had collapsed. The bulk of the leviathan was still impossibly huge; it must have been greater still but much of it was simply no longer there. Ulfgar guessed it must have been thousands of metres long but it mattered not now. Now everything tumbled to its doom.

He laughed. His eyes fixed on the flopping lifeless carcass of the leviathan. They all raced towards the bedrock below. The wall of water that surrounded them for a mile began to shudder in the distance and, finally realising there was a space to fill, it crashed into the empty expanse like a mighty waterfall. The thunder and crash of the roaring waves filled his ears as the frothing torrents raced to reclaim their stolen domain.

He screamed his defiance to the gods and

the falling leviathan. The thing was dead, slain by his hand.

The remains of the leviathan impacted the bedrock and burst into a splatter of rotten black jelly, the wrecked pieces of the StormChild in its clutches splintered with it. He hurtled behind it all, the angry wall of sea rushing to envelop him. He twisted in the air, preparing his body to dash upon the rocks amongst the carcasses of the impossible horror and his beloved ship.

It did not take me. I am the master of my own fate. "Jules…" he muttered. "I will see you soon, old boy." His laugh became a manic cackle as he plummeted to his oblivion.

SOMETHING WONDROUS

H.L. TINSLEY

Tuesday was generally a good day for the inmates at Warterscut. It was the day they got to go out. Granted, dredging the canals around the alkali factories was unlikely to be most people's idea of a good time. But other people didn't spend eighteen hours a day every day in a cramped cell with one bucket and three other men.

There wasn't much in the way of scenery to enjoy, a clustered vista of looming chimney stacks and furnaces blowing plumes of unending smog skyward. Now and again, a carriage would rumble past, the occupants viewing the inmates from behind velvet drapes as they clutched handkerchiefs to their noses. Occasionally one of the new motorcars might thrum past at a lick, but not that often.

Each week the men would assemble in the yard and sign the roster, volunteering their time in service of the city. The wagons left early in the morning, carrying the unpaid workforce under heavily armed escort. If you behaved, you got a sandwich at noon. Any man who tried to use the dredging as an excuse to run would get one pistol shot in the back and another in the leg, just for good measure.

There were three things everyone liked about the work. First off, you got to spend eight hours outside, which was more than you got the rest of the week. Second, you were allowed to use the bush. Two guards would stand on either side of it as the inmates took their turn to go behind and drop to a squat. For any of the men dwelling in Warterscut at His Majesty's pleasure, it was their only solitary shit of the week.

The third thing was the part everyone liked best. The inmates called it scum gold. To a man with nothing, almost anything can look like treasure and there was always something interesting floating in the mire. One week you might get a dead bird, another it could be an old boot. Once they got one with the foot still in it.

Yes, Tuesday was a good day.

Or, it was for everyone except the poor bastard assigned to laundry duty.

Instead, they got to spend the evening washing sweat-and canal-soaked overalls in vats of hot water steeped with chemicals so acrid you could kiss your nostril hairs goodbye. The guards were supposed to assign prison duties according to the rota. In reality, the decision mostly hinged on how much they happened to dislike you that particular week.

Hence, Camellia Larkin had kept his head as low as possible for the past six days. At this point, he could tell which of the inmates approached just by the shape of their feet. Sitting in the canteen, Camellia saw a pair halt in front of him. Grey socks, one half of the right shoelace missing, a slight odour of burnt toast.

"Alright, Cam?" The feet spoke.

"Not bad, Daff."

Daffodil Stanley was in for three counts of

robbery, two counts of causing actual bodily harm with a croquet mallet, and one of driving a Hansom carriage through an arcade. All of which were, impressively, achieved on the same day.

"Got a favour to ask." That was prison talk for '*I need something doing, and you're going to do it.*'

Cam might have been new to the gang, but he wasn't new to the life. With a third of a sentence still left to serve, it was never advisable to refuse a polite request. Daffodil's feet coughed. Cam looked up and met his eyes. "What do you need?"

"Lavender's got a new boy up on the fifth floor. Seems he's not cut out for the job. We need you to go and give him his notice." Daffodil didn't elaborate on what the lad's role in Lavender's enterprise might be, or what it was he had done to prove himself unsuited to it.

Shit.

"Always happy to help." Cam rose from the bench. "Which cell?"

Once suitably furnished with appropriate directions, Camellia walked the flights of stairs, passing by several of the finest lodgings public taxes could buy on his way.

On the third floor, someone threw the contents of a bucket between the bars of their cell. Cam drew short, narrowly avoiding a drenching. Without turning, he side-eyed the perpetrator still holding the can.

"Oh, fuck." The inmate dropped his gaze. "I didn't mean it, Cam, swear to God. I thought you was a screw. You know I'd never - not to one of Marian's boys. You know that, don't you?" His legs were shaking. "Go on, it never even touched you. We're alright, aren't we?"

A cold silence lingered. Cam let him sweat for a couple of seconds. He didn't relish doing it, but being a part of the Botany Boys came with expectations. Lavender Marian demanded each of his employees command a certain level of respect amongst the inmates and wouldn't like it if one of them let an insult slip by unchallenged. Turning, Cam crooked his finger towards the prisoner. The man hesitated. Rolling his eyes, Cam repeated the gesture. Tentatively stepping forward, the inmate made another attempt to apologise. Grasping the loose material of his shirt as he came within reach, Cam dragged him forward until his face hit the bars with enough of a crunch to see justice satisfied.

Four doors along, he arrived at the residence of Marian's latest recruit. Word had doubtless reached the boy already that Camellia was on his way. Termination was a short but definitive process. Nobody liked getting their ear bitten off, but rules were rules. Cam hoped the lad would have the sense to take it with a bit of dignity. Squealers didn't last long in Warterscut. He turned into the cell, expecting to see the boy waiting for him.

What he found was something different entirely.

"What the hell?"

The boy was in the room alright. He was five feet up in the air, spinning like a pendulum on a string. Only there was no string. At least not that could be seen. The kid wasn't so much hanging as he was floating. His eyes were open but didn't seem to be looking at anything. Abandoning any plans for ear-biting, Cam dove forward and took hold of the boy's feet. "Come on." he tugged so hard he felt the lad's trousers begin to slip. Even the entire weight of his body wasn't enough to bring the inmate down. "Fuck."

Racing back out onto the walkway, Cam leant over the railings and yelled out. It was still the mid-dinner rush, so the unit was virtually empty. Just his luck that this was the one time none of the screws were around to do anything.

The door of the next cell opened, and a head popped out, followed by a plume of sweet-scented smoke. "Camellia? What you doing up here?"

Forget-Me-Not was a frequent visitor to the floor. It was the best place to get good weed. Reaching out, Cam grabbed him by the arm and pulled him out onto the walkway. "What's wrong with you?" Horror replacing irritation, Forget-Me-Not's eyes widened. "What the fuck?" Mirroring the actions Camellia had already taken, he ran to pull the boy down.

"I already tried that." Cam looked up at the floating inmate. His heart hammered against his chest. What was he looking at? How was any of it happening? There had to be an explanation. It was a trick of some sort. That was it. "How the fuck did he get up there?"

Without any logical explanation for what

they were seeing, Forget-Me-Not seemingly decided he must not be seeing anything at all. He began pacing up and down the cell, fingers shakily running through his hair as he muttered something about getting a 'bad batch'.

Cam didn't know what to do about the boy, or even if he was still alive.

But he did know raving like a mad man was the last thing Forget-Me-Not should be doing. Ranting brought the guards. That brought the doctor, and that got you nothing but pain. Darting deeper into the cell, Cam pressed his hands to Forget-Me-Not's mouth and pushed him against the brick wall. "Pull yourself together. We need to figure out a way to get him down."

Forget-Me-Not's pallor was as pale as driven snow, eyes widening like saucers. Cam saw something in his face change, an expression of panic transforming into one of abject horror. Glancing back, he saw what his companion was looking at and felt something like a blow to the gut. It seemed to happen in slow motion, the boy tilting as though on an axis. His whole body moved in tandem, limbs fluid from left to right until he was upside down. Somehow Cam knew what was going to happen even before it did yet could not move to try and stop it. Sure enough, after a moment of floating in his new position, the young inmate plummeted, skull meeting with the concrete floor and his body buckling like an old accordion. Someone was screaming.

It took Camellia a few seconds to realise it was him. Prison life often led a man to see things he wished he hadn't - the sort of stuff that made your mouth drier and your trousers wetter. That he could deal with; this was different.

Anyone else might have thought they imagined such a thing, but Cam would swear blind as the lad crashed down, he saw the flicker of a smile on his face. He didn't have time to do much else other than scream. He didn't even get the chance to move out of the way before Forget-Me-Not doused his shoes with vomit.

The cell door swung open, and a guard stood surveying the brain matter on the floor. "What the fuck did you two do?"

Camellia reached up, touching his forehead with one hand. Already the lump below his hairline was coming up lovely. His right eye was swollen shut. There was a creaking from the bunk below, followed by the groan of a man whose ribs had recently been introduced to several prison-issue batons. Beatings were standard. Camellia had survived many. This one, however, was unlikely to be the end of their troubles. Neither he nor Forget-Me-Not had bothered explaining what they had seen to the guards. What was the point? Nobody would have believed it anyway.

Cam rolled onto his side, wincing as he did. "You alright, Franklin?"

Beneath him, Forget-Me-Not shifted. "Think I've got a couple of broken ones."

"Keep that to yourself. Any of the hacks hear and you'll be down the infirmary with that mad fucker." It said a lot about Doctor Porter that most of the inmates would rather suffer mangled limbs and broken bones than endure the agony of a visit to the prison sanatorium.

Forget-Me-Not was no doubt in pain. For some reason, the man never seemed to stand up to a hiding as well as the rest of the gang. The guards knew this, so concentrated their efforts where it would be most worthwhile.

Forget-Me-Not didn't speak to him again for the rest of the night. Across the room, Lavender and Daffodil slept soundly. No doubt they would have words in the morning.

Camellia sank back on his pillow and tried in vain to get the image of the floating inmate out of his head. It was as though his mind were stuck on a loop, repeating the same half-second. Instead, he lay there all night, replaying that crooked smile over and over until the first timid beams of sun stroked the side of his face, bringing Tuesday with them.

They also brought the wrath of Lavender Marion.

Cam rolled over to find his boss eyeballing him, legs swung over the side of the top bunk on the opposite side of the cell.

"Quite the mug you've got there." Marion had the look of a bulldog, with pock-marked cheeks that hung half an inch lower than the rest of his face. The loose skin around his neck moved with the words. "What have you got to say for yourself?"

Cam sat up. "Look, Lav, the boy wasn't

my fault." He quickly added, "And it wasn't Franklin's either."

Lifting one finger, Lavender brought silence down upon the cell. The other boys were still asleep. Either that or they were being smart and pretending to be.

Marion leaned forward. "You know, when I heard you were getting transferred here, I was happy. I thought, 'what a nice surprise'. All the boys back together again. But you've forgotten the rules. *You* fix problems. You don't bring problems to us."

The first lesson to learn when it came to being part of the crew was you never spoke when Lavender was talking. Cam kept his mouth shut because he might have been going mad, but he was far from stupid.

"I'm starting to suspect you might not be enjoying the work anymore." Lavender's lip curled into a sneer. "Perhaps you're getting a bit too big for your boots."

Now, this was a tricky one. As much as you didn't want to open your mouth while Lavender was talking, sometimes he expected an answer. The problem was you could never tell if he had finished or not. A bell rang out from down the hall.

"Guards are coming in a minute, so we'll discuss this later." Lavender Marion jumped from his perch. The impact of his landing roused Daff, who wasn't great in the mornings or, for that matter, any other time of day. Before Cam had the chance to draw any conclusions as to what that conversation might entail, one of the guards appeared, rattling a stick along the iron bars before coming to a stop. The cell door swung open.

"Up and at 'em, boys. Morely, Hill, get down for breakfast. You're dredging today." The guards were the only ones who ever referred to them by their last names. "Riggs, Larkin." His eyes narrowed. "Laundry duty."

Camellia took the long route down to the laundry room, detouring to stop by the cell he had visited the night previously. The body of the floating inmate was long gone. Governor Andrews would have seen to it before the blood dried. Now there was a man who never got his hands dirty. Rumour had it the man was a germaphobe. Most of the inmates had never even seen him, and those that had couldn't describe him as anything other than 'tidy'.

Standing in the exact place where the lad's skull had caved against the floor, Cam tried once again to come up with some explanation for what he thought he saw. There was nothing to mark the cell as peculiar – aside from perhaps a vague scent of something foul.

Crouching, Cam touched one hand to the floor. He had no idea what he expected it to feel like, but it felt like a floor ought to, cold and unyielding. In the end, it seemed that what was below his feet and above his head was plain old concrete. And that whatever Cam thought he saw, he was mistaken. By the time he got down to the sub-floor to report for laundry duties, Forget-Me-Not had already been and gone.

"Taken him t'infirmary," Mackey explained when Cam questioned it.

The old man bent over a wooden cart piled high with overalls. Mackey was a lifer and spent more time in the laundry room than anywhere else. Some figured it was because he was too old for working the canals. Anyone who knew him well knew it was just because he liked it there. The old-timer preferred his own company. Forty years of baking salt-cake in the factories came to an abrupt end when a bottle of sulphuric acid exploded and hit him in the face. Eight months of hard living without an income had led poor Mackey to a criminal career that lasted four days, resulting in one dead foreman. It turned out he wasn't very good at not getting caught, which hardly made it seem worth it.

"Why the fuck didn't you stop them?"

Mackey spat at the floor. "Busy."

With that, he pushed the cart to the other side of the room. It was too late to do anything for Franklin now. Maybe he'd get lucky. Sometimes Doctor Porter would go down to the canals with the inmates, leaving the orderlies in charge of the ward. Mackey reappeared with a box of detergent. Cam took it, pouring the contents into one of the vats of water and ignoring the immediate burning sensation the smell brought.

"You've been here a while, Mac," Cam started. "Ever seen anything weird happening?"

Mackey grunted. "What sort of weird?"

"Any sort of weird."

"I try not to notice things, and you shouldn't either." Bent over his washtubs, Mackey hauled the first load of dirty clothes into the water. With over three hundred men in residence at Warterscut, laundry was an endless and unappealing vocation that mostly involved trying not to think about what sort of stains you were looking at.

"Mackey." One of the guards appeared in the doorway, a bundle of clothes in his arms. Most of the prison officers were out with the dredging gang, leaving behind a skeleton crew of six or seven to man those left behind. Holding out the soiled garments, the guard made a face. "Stinks like the underside of a ball bag in here."

Stopping short, Cam felt an uneasy sensation. "Those the dead kid's?"

"They were, now they're prison-issues again."

Abandoning his vat, Cam walked across and offered to take the bundle. Not caring much one way or another who took them, the guard turned on his heel. Cam looked down at the clothes - grey shirt, grey trousers, white t-shirt that was well on its way. Taking them to the sorting bench, he rifled through the pockets. They were empty. Not that he expected anything different. Personal items were prohibited. Anything the boy may have secreted in his clothes would have been found and taken to the governor. The truth was, Cam didn't even know what he was looking for – drugs, maybe. The sort that made you float in mid-air and turn yourself upside down, he supposed.

Garments still in his arms, Cam turned to the wash tub. Steam curled around the edges of the room, creeping like vines towards the ground. The smell of the powder churning in the water seemed even more overpowering than usual. Almost like the steam was trying to choke anyone that came too close.

"Fuckin' hell, seen dead men move faster than you." Mackey took the clothes before Cam could stop him. He threw them in. Then, just as quickly, the old boy went in after them.

Cam didn't have time to wonder why he'd done it. From the way Mackey reacted, it seemed as though it wasn't until the split second before he hit the scalding water that he even knew he was doing anything at all. The older man broke the surface, strangling out a scream as he clawed at the burning skin. Cam raced to the side of the tub, which was big enough for several men to have occupied comfortably. Stomach pressed against the sides, he reached out, arms straining. "Grab my hand! Grab my hand!"

Mackey's face was already peeling away.

Cam tried to extend his reach without falling in himself. "Take it!"

Mac didn't seem to be hearing anything. He was turning red, like a lobster boiling in a saucepan. The smell of blistering skin began to overpower the stink of soiled clothing, and Cam realised he wasn't coming out of his own accord.

"Shit, shit, shit." Leaning in, Cam drove his arm into the water and fished around for any part of Mackey he could grab that wouldn't come off in his hand. Gritting his teeth against the pain of the heat, he finally got hold of a bit of shirt. "Guard!"

Dragging Mackey, who seemed to be in a state of shock to the edge of the tub, Cam tried in vain to pull him out. He was dead weight. "Guard!"

The officers never came when you called.

They heard you shout and turned up in their own good time. Cam shook his head, gritted his teeth, and called out the only word in Warterscut that ever got their attention.

"DOCTOR!"

That brought the guard who brought the dead boy's overalls running back.

Clamping one hand over his mouth, he winced. "What the fuck is that smell…?" His eyes widened, taking in the sight of Camellia with one arm in the water, Mackey's head banging against the side as he bobbed up and down, unconscious.

"Help me." Cam's arm felt like it was cooking down to the bone.

Between the two of them, they managed to pull Mackey out. Cam collapsed against the floor. Almost immediately, he realised he couldn't breathe. His lungs felt too big for his chest, pressing against his rib cage, yet somehow not able to pull in enough oxygen. He couldn't tell if Mackey was dead or alive. Blood pumping around his veins, Cam heard the guard blow the whistle alerting his counterparts in other parts of the unit to the commotion.

By the time assistance arrived, Cam was unconscious - and blissfully unaware of the fact that the next time he woke, he'd find himself in the ominous company of Doctor Porter.

Warterscut Prison had been standing for one hundred and twenty-four years. It was far enough outside its neighbouring city for the citizens to sleep peacefully at night yet close enough that they could rely on it for a steady supply of cheap and dispensable labour.

For several decades, Warterscut supplied men to work the roadside, digging out the earth to lay sewer pipes, horse shit littering the streets flickering against their faces, churned up by the spinning wheels of each carriage that went past. Some inmates got to bust their bones in the many factories and foundries, hauling heavy loads like pack mules. These days the only work they did was the dredging. Still, it meant for a little over a century, Warterscut had been witness to many a battered body, broken bone, and gaping wound.

In most prisons, the highest forms of currency were weed, wine, and tobacco.

In Warterscut, it was aspirin. Bandages came at a premium too. The high cost of medical supplies could be wholly attributed to the presence of Doctor Cornelius Porter.

Head of the infirmary, he could spin a broken thumb into a three-week stay wherein your thumb would be healed by day two, and the rest of the time would be spent isolated for any number of imagined infections. All the while subject to the good doctor's unique brand of experimental therapy.

"Larkin Riggs." Doctor Porter was there to greet him as Cam stirred. "Camellia, they call you, correct? Pretty, like the flower. Not often I get two of your lot in on the same day."

Head pounding, Cam groaned. The ticking of a clock on the wall sounded like the thundering roar of a stampeding horde. Rolling his head, Cam looked across the hospital beds for a glimpse of Forget-Me-Not. Mackey was lying, still unconscious, in one. The rest were empty. "Franklin?"

"Franklin Wells?"

Cam nodded.

"Forget-Me-Not?"

Cam nodded again.

"Moved on."

Cam's eyes shot open. "What does that mean?"

Doctor Porter ignored the question, pressing one hand to the wound on Cam's arm without warning. When Cam recoiled in pain, the doctor nodded as if that told him something anyone with eyeballs couldn't have guessed. There was a word for men like Porter, and it wasn't healer. Craning his neck, Cam tried to ascertain whether Mackey was asleep, unconscious, or dead. The doctor turned his head to follow the line of his gaze. He said nothing, merely gesturing for one of the orderlies to attend to the other patient.

"Now then." He turned back to Camellia and pulled a thin metal implement from his coat. "Shall we begin assessment?"

Cam wasn't a medical man but. like most, he found many of the trials undertaken during Porter's assessments to be both unnecessary and performed with an unnatural avidity that twisted the stomach. The doctor leant forward and pinched the burnt skin on his arm, nodding when Camellia once more cried out.

"Hmm, good." Porter placed Cam's arm back against the bed and turned away. Across the room, an orderly was placing instruments in a drawer. Frowning, the doctor hurried over. "No, those must be faced up."

Relieved to have a moment of respite, Cam fell back against the pillow and looked up at the ceiling. There was a damp patch right above his head. Not so much it would drip down upon him, but enough to offer a lingering threat of it. He narrowed his eyes. Not water. Nor was it blood. No, this was a thick and black, tar-like substance. Cam twisted his head, eyes narrowing as he tried to determine what manner of thing it might be.

Before he could draw any conclusion, the barred windows rattled, and the ground shook. The glow of light from outside shot beams of yellow across the walls. Camellia clung to the bed frame. Several orderlies fell, scattered to the floor.

"What in the hell was that?" One of the guards staggered in, holding both hands to his head. Cam had no idea. He didn't know what had caused the blast.

An intelligent person might have guessed it came from the factories. Accidents weren't uncommon. But the nearest factory was several miles away. More than that, as the waves of impact washed through the walls of Warterscut, the air rang with the distinct sound of distant voices - voices speaking in a language beyond words.

Protocol dictated, in the event of an accident, the dredgers would return to the prison to be confined in their cells until the guards could restore order. By the time they arrived back from the canals, Porter and the orderlies had taken their equipment up to the yard.

What remained of the guards focused their efforts on securing more dangerous inmates than those in the infirmary. Left with nobody but Mackey for company, Camellia rolled from the bed and stood. Light danced in his eyes. High above them, a glow danced between the bars of the small windows. From down there, it appeared as though the world outside were aflame. Cam walked over to Mackey's bed. The still-unconscious man was bandaged head to toe, like one of the mummies on display in the city museum. Cam had seen one once, long before his life had gone down the pan. He might have been on a date, but he couldn't for the life of him remember the girl's name, only that she was too good for him.

There was a yell from down the corridor, a guard calling out for more supplies. Cam glanced down at the trays of gauze and tape. He could have taken them. He could have hurried outside to find Daffodil and the others, helping to stick them back together again.

But the fact was Cam had never really liked them that much, never liked the way they did business. Or the way they would have him clean up the mess they made when things went south. The kid, for example. Camellia pictured the moment the inmate's neck snapped. A shudder rolled down his spine as if to assure him it was still in one piece.

There was something vile about Warterscut, always had been.

But Cam had long supposed that was the doing of the residents more than anything otherworldly. Nobody in their right mind would think otherwise. Yet pushing the cabinet across the floor with his one good arm, bringing it to rest below the window, Cam knew deep down what he would see beyond the bars even before he reached up on the tips of his toes.

Outside, the world had caved in on itself.

Inside the yard, inmates and wardens turned on each other. Prisoners, clothes still slick and wet from the canals, ran amok around the gravelled pen where they took their exercise. The guards pointed their rifles at them and screamed for order. Above all that, the sky now ripped asunder blasted forth such an ungodly siren as ever heard. It blew like a fanfare to madness. Cam tightened his hands around the bars, gritting his teeth against the vibration of it, the shuddering pulse of each wave of sound rearranging his insides.

So, this was the way the world would end.

Watching the chaos unfurling, Cam caught sight of a familiar face.

Lavender Marion roared at the rift, defiant in the face of a power far greater than he. But it was not Lavender that Cam was watching. Forget-Me-Not, face bruised like forgotten fruit, limped across the yard.

"Franklin!" Cam's voice fell upon deaf

ears. "Franklin!"

"He can't hear you." A voice sounded from behind him.

Turning, Camellia shrank back at the sight of Doctor Porter, his white coat spattered with blood and dirty water. "What did you do to him?"

For a moment, the doctor seemed confused by the question. Then, to Camellia's surprise, he strode across the infirmary, tooka perch on the edge of a bed, and drew his hands up to meet his face. "I have done nothing, achieved nothing. My time is up. I have failed. Now they will come to take back what is theirs."

"What are they?"

Porter glanced up. "The wardens."

Momentarily ignoring the disorder outside, Cam got down from the cupboard and stood facing Porter. Side-stepping to the left, he reached across and took hold of a discarded bottle. Smashing it against the wall and holding it aloft, the jagged edges gave him confidence the doctor could not do to Cam whatever it was he had done to Forget-Me-Not without risking his own life. The way Porter looked at him drained it in an instant. The doctor's face rippled like something beneath it was trying to break free from a flesh cage. Porter steeled against it. The contortions stopped, and the skin settled.

"What the fuck are you?" Camellia wasn't ashamed to admit he was afraid. Nor that his trousers were wetter than they had been moments ago. "What the fuck are the wardens?"

Porter shook his head. "Not your wardens. *Hers*." Before he could speak another word, the viscous black substance that clung to the ceiling dropped.

It wrapped about his head, the doctor falling to his knees. Cam watched as Porter tugged in vain, trying to break free of the substance bound to his face, covering him down to the waist. Despite the fear, Camellia dropped the bottle and ran to Porter. The doctor lay on the ground, body convulsing and throwing out each limb in turn. Cam tried to pry the stuff from his nostrils, attempting to rip holes through it to allow the doctor to breathe. It was impenetrable, yielding like soft butter in his fingers yet toughening like a hide the moment he tried to break through it. Porter fell back. Dead. Gone.

Whatever he had been, he was no longer.

And just as quickly, the tar-like substance became liquid once more.

"What the hell are you doing, Riggs?" The voice pulled Camellia from his trance-like state. Looking up, he saw a guard, rifle in hand, staring at the pair of them.

A moment later, another appeared. "What's going on here?"

Realisation dawning on his face, the first levelled his barrel. "He's killed the doctor; the bastard's gone and killed the bloody doctor."

Cam shook his head. "No, I didn't." The first shot, a warning shot, hit the wall. "I swear! It wasn't me. None of this is me; this whole place has gone mad."

The second guard twitched, fingers loosely running over the trigger as though he were deciding whether it was worth shooting one prisoner as nearly three hundred more ran amok amongst the cells and halls. Gesturing to the door behind him, he kept his gun trained on Cam's chest. "Get on your feet." Eyes sliding to his colleague, the guard grunted. "We'll take him with us, secure Andrews, get what's left of the others out through the south wing gate."

Hands held up in surrender, Cam stood.

"What about Mackey?"

They didn't seem to understand the question. "What about him?"

"You can't just leave him like that."

The two guards exchanged glances. The first looked towards Mackey's bed, face creasing in confusion. Cam felt a pit in his stomach. Somehow he knew before he even turned around that Mackey's bed was empty.

When he did look, the knot tightened. Mackey's bed wasn't just empty – the blankets lay undisturbed, corners tight against the mattress, as though nobody had been in it at all. Not for the first time that day, Camellia wondered if perhaps he was losing his mind.

Or worse, maybe he was dead. He had died, been judged for his sins, and was being punished. Maybe Lavender got him in the night. It wouldn't be any less than he deserved. Perhaps there had been a great fire, and now they were all getting what they deserved.

The guards, seemingly growing tired of waiting for Cam to make up his mind, focused their rifles back towards him. "Move it, now."

Away from the infirmary, Cam and his escorts moved slowly through the corridors, the two guards working in tandem to check each cell they passed. All were empty. It seemed the few inmates left behind when the others began their day of labour had since gone to join in the rioting. Shots rang out, rifle fire and whistles blew so loud the sound could penetrate the thick walls. Up ahead, Cam spotted the head guard instructing his subordinates to clear a path to the governor's office. But procedures set in place to gain control in a jailbreak did not cut the same muster when dealing with an apparent apocalypse. His orders went ignored and, after a moment, he too disappeared into the winding corridors. Soon, Cam realised he and his two guards were the only people left in the building.

The governor's office was on a well-secured floor. Arriving at the door, they stood for a moment as the first guard searched for his keys. Cam noticed the way his hands were trembling.

"Hurry up." The second guard was no longer pretending this was an escort mission – it was his way out, an escape. Cam wanted that too. He wanted to be free of the walls that seemed to groan and heave as though the building itself were breathing.

The key jammed in the lock. Cursing, the guard struggled against it, tugging away as if the door was trying to swallow the key up rather than turn the lock.

"Move out of the way, let me…" His colleague's words were cut short. Eyes bulging, the guard grappled for something to anchor himself as his feet left the floor. "Help me…"

Before Cam could reach for him, the second guard too began to rise towards the ceiling.

"Please, please…" No more than two words tripped from his lips before whatever strange force enveloped them hauled both men with great speed upwards.

Of course, whatever it was had not accounted for the presence of the hard ceiling. Their spines snapped, bodies dropped to the floor as though discarded. Sick with fear, Cam waited to see if it would take him too. But it did not. Frozen with his back against the door, he saw nothing, heard nothing. Cam felt something, though. He could have sworn it felt as though something leaned in closer, sniffing him, getting a sense for what he was, and then dismissing him. It vanished, like a ripple in the air, searching through the building.

Barely able to make sense of anything, Camellia turned and tried the key. Unlike the guards, he found no resistance in the lock. Turning it, Cam swung open the door and, for the first time, stepped into the office of Governor Andrews.

"Close the door behind you." Governor Andrews sat in a plush chair. His hands were placed calmly on the desk, palms flat against the firm oak. Camellia moved forward, doing as instructed. Andrews leaned back, bringing his fingers up to press them beneath his chin. He eyed the inmate for a moment before nodding towards the east wall. "Care for a drink?"

Cam moved slowly, sidestepping around the nicely decorated office. Bookshelves heaved with what looked to be ancient tomes. Beneath the window, an impressive leather-bound ledger sat, encased in glass. He stopped, glanced down at the writing - if you could call it that. Governor Andrews let his head tip to one side as if he were coming to a decision. After a few seconds, he stood, the neatly pressed lines of his suit jacket remaining as crisp and tidy as ever they were. "I'll pour, shall I?"

With that, the governor emerged from behind the desk.

Cam staggered back, heart racing. The top half of Andrews moved as one might expect, but his feet did not touch the floor. With each step, a small black cloud appeared beneath the soles of his shoes. Andrews cast a knowing smile. "No need to recoil. I'm just a man – no different to you." He let his hand come to rest on the glass case. "Mine is a borrowed power, on loan for a short time." The governor sighed and then straightened his shoulders.

Slowly, he walked over to a mahogany cabinet and retrieved two glasses and a decanter of port. On returning to his desk, he poured them each a measure and touched one finger to a photograph in a silver filigree frame. "Have you ever had a wife, Larkin?"

Cam shook his head, unable to make words.

"Here, look." Andrews turned the frame. "Did you ever see anything as lovely?"

Even in his fear and confusion, Cam could admit that he had not.

Mrs. Andrews was quite the loveliest thing

ever captured in sepia tones. Even in the muted brown tones of the photograph, he could see the pale delicacy of her skin. He saw the way her hair tumbled around her neck, how the flecks of amber in her eyes shone like the dying embers of the last star in the morning. She was more than beautiful.

Ethereal. Enchanting. Fascinating.

"Sit," the governor requested.

Compelled to do as instructed, Cam felt the padded seat rush up to greet him as if his legs had no other choice but to bend on command.

Andrews took a sip of his drink. "Do you know what it is to be married to a creature of infinite nature? Something that existed long before we crawled from the ooze, and shall remain long after we are dust?" He considered the glass in his hand. The governor frowned before continuing. "What manner of being would cage such a thing? Build it a prison of despair?" He shook his head. "No, I will not believe what they say of her."

"What who says?" Camellia finally found his voice.

Andrew's brow darkened. "The jury of knowing things." The way he spoke suggested that this was a perfectly normal conversation and that Camellia would, of course, completely understand what Andrews meant by that.

Instead, Cam felt he had stepped through a looking glass into a world turned upside down. There was the ringing of another rifle shot outside. Taking the second glass, Camellia downed the liquid in one. "Your wife is the one doing all of this?"

Andrews slammed his glass on the desk.

Cam felt a shiver roll down his spine on seeing the anger in the governor's eyes.

"She does not do it on purpose. That is what *they* cannot see. Now she is leaking into the world because I cannot withstand her gifts anymore."

A dark realisation washed over Cam. "She uses you, doesn't she? You call her a wife, but it's more than that. Why? What does she use you for?"

Governor Andrews stood, clasping both hands behind his back. "Nothing I would not do joyfully."

"What does it do? The book? Is your wife a book?" Even as he said it, Cam realised how stupid that sounded. As if a woman could be a book.

"She is everything." Andrews smiled. "But, if you wish for a more concise answer, no, she is not a book. If you went to my home, you would find her sitting there now just as perfectly and serenely as you see in that picture. Fact is, she has not moved for over forty years. She is kindness, you see, as much as chaos. She has no wish to drain this world of life, any more than she did any of the others left in her wake."

Treading lightly on his carpet of rolling clouds, he came to a stop. The glass case containing the book glinted against the burnt orange light. "Years ago, she escaped through the rift, and ever since I have held it shut in place. I am merely a mortal vessel. But I cannot do so any longer."

Unable to take anymore, Cam felt the tears rolling down his cheeks. He felt broken and humbled at the knowledge of such things existing, far beyond the measure of all his understanding. "So, she is something immortal, escaped from a prison beyond the world, only to encage herself here of her own volition? Why? Why would anyone do this?"

Andrews seemed surprised at such a question. "Because a cage built from love is far preferable to a cage built of fear."

Behind him through the window, Cam saw the pulsing rift tearing the sky in two. It seemed to be growing larger. Andrews looked mournful. If Cam didn't know better, he would have said that the further apart the rift tore, the louder he heard the governor's heart breaking.

"They will come for her soon," he lamented. "A human body is not built to sustain the barrier between worlds for this long." Andrews sighed. "Mine is breaking. The tiny drop of power she gifted me has waned. That is why the sky opens."

"How do we close it?" Until that moment, Cam had not asked for fear there might not be a way. But something inside him began to stir, a sense of something finally coming to rest in his mind. Andrews might have been driven mad by the power coursing through his veins, but it was the madness of a man in love – not a man who wished to end the world.

A man in love will try to keep the world alive.

"There is a way – but I have run out of time." Andrews pressed one finger to a button on the side, a mechanism springing into action. The wooden base of the cabinet collapsed down, revealing an intricate network of brass cogs grinding and whirling against each other. "Look closely at the book, tell me what you see."

Rising from the chair, Cam walked across the room and peered through the glass. The symbols on the page seemed to turn and twist about, trying to arrange themselves on the page. They never settled for more than a moment. Cam stared at it, watching the cogs work yet not complete their cycle. "There's a piece missing. The dredging." He nodded slowly. "That's what they were looking for out there."

"The machine must be complete for the translation to work," Andrews explained. "Once it has completed a full cycle, a name will appear on the page, and when it does, uttering it aloud will close the rift. Her true name…" His eyes cast towards the photograph. "How sad I shall not be around to hear it."

"You mean to say you don't even know her name?"

The governor looked sadder still. "Nobody does. She does not know it. How could you remember something given to you before time began? Some believe they have discovered it. Some refer to her as The Wanderer." Andrews shook his head. "A mistranslation. There is no word that we have for it, but the closest would be..." he thought, "something wondrous."

Camellia froze in place. The governor stood now behind him. Dark eyes blackened to the point where the irises bled into the white parts and became absorbed with something ancient, primordial. Whatever his wife gifted Andrews with, his human body had begun to lose the fight with it.

Cam realised something. "Porter knew." Things were beginning to make sense – in a strange sort of way. "That's what the assessments were for – the experiments. He was trying to find a way for you to survive long enough to find the cog."

The governor's head tipped back, mouth falling open. A voice came from deep within him, echoing as if cast from the depths of a cave. "Yes, that was regrettable. I did not mean for him to die, or any others. What a sad thing death is." Soft, female, the voice spoke the last words like the feeling was more curious than anything else. "I may be able to change what I appear to be, but I am not able to change what I am. What are you?"

Cam was not sure how to answer that anymore. A murderer, he supposed. There were documents in the drawers to claim that was the case. But like *Her*, Camellia had never chosen to kill a man. Some people were just born into it.

"A prisoner, like you. Serving my sentence."

Andrews closed his mouth, head falling forward. The black cloud beneath his feet began to rise and curl around him, skin growing grey and mottled. Camellia was numb to the fear. Something warm and comforting edged its way around his veins. Sliding his eyes to the table, he looked at the glass and wondered what manner of substance Andrews had crumbled into it, strong enough to battle any sense of fear or self-preservation.

Placing one hand on the governor's ailing chest, allowing the smoke to curl around his arm like a snake taking hold, Camellia closed his eyes and did not resist.

"Morning Guv'nor," Footsteps sounded across the room.

Governor Larkin opened his eyes. A guard carried a silver tray with his breakfast upon it; two slices of toast, two eggs, and a pot of hot coffee ground fresh in the prison kitchen. Larkin had not tasted eggs for eight years. But the guard knew nothing of that. Placing the food down, the young officer smiled. "Looks like it'll be a good, mild day today."

Spinning in his chair, Larkin glanced out of the window behind him. The sky was an insipid shade of unremarkable blue. Reaching up, Larkin felt the whiskers on his cheeks. Hands trailing down, he felt the soft, smooth silk of an elegant cravat and waistcoat. Turning back, he addressed the guard. "What day is this?"

The man seemed confused. "Tuesday, Sir."

Larkin nodded, dismissing him. Letting one arm come to rest on the desk, the index finger of his right hand trailed across the picture in its frame, a perfect image of a wondrous being, frozen in place. "Patience, my love. We have time."

EPILOGUE
THE FIRST STEP

He stepped through the portal and felt the crunch of dirt beneath his newly formed feet. It felt good, solid. As the rest of his body passed through the swirling purple energy that separated worlds, he felt energised.

Closing the portals had been a harder task than he had anticipated, but most of them had been shut. That fool on that mountain top had been lucky, escaping from the void so his little frost-casting friend could save him. Still, magic was not exactly science, a word he had learnt on his journey. Science required things to be performed precisely, whereas with magic there was always room for success despite a couple of errors.

As his new body fully formed in the world, he gestured behind his back and closed the portal.

The Wanderer, as the mortals had all called him, looked around to get his bearings.

He stood in a clearing of sorts, a large gothic building a few yards away. Around the clearing were several pedestals carved from the whitest of marble. Each one was home to an object, of which no two were the same. The Wanderer slowly moved from one pedestal to the next, examining each object in turn. There was an ancient knife, an old and tattered shoe, a silver tray, a water-damaged logbook, some armour caked in dried blood, a sounding bell and a hammer that had clearly ended the life of some mortal. Each object had a little inscription on a stone slate, but he decided not to read them. He knew exactly what they each were, trinkets from his journey to close the portals. It was surprising, amusing even, that the mortals thought these objects worth saving. This was clearly a place of worship for the people of this time. It would be the first thing he burned to the ground to show his followers who they should really worship.

In the sky above, the Great Portal still swirled, a maelstrom of magic and madness. It seemed to be smaller than it had at previous points in time. Perhaps closing the portals drained energy from it. The reason could wait until later, he felt. Now was the time to walk amongst his people and be worshipped as the god they so longed for.

"HALT!" a voice shouted from above.

The Wanderer frowned and looked up at the strange vehicle in the sky. It had no wings, nor propeller, and yet it floated in place like a cloud. A purple light pulsed from its base, a similar shade to the purple of the portals. Two helmeted heads looked down at him, red lines across them from where eyes presumably stared.

"Halt?" the Wanderer asked, confused. "Do you know who I am?"

Without saying a word, one of the riders in the silver carriage jumped over the edge and gracefully floated to the ground. He aimed a weapon at the Wanderer, pushing a button on the side that caused the barrel to light up.

"I won't ask again," the helmeted warrior said. "Don't move another muscle, false god."

He could not help but smile. The man before him may not have known much, but he at least knew that a god stood before him.

The Wanderer spread his arms out, nodding down at his naked form.

"I will forgive you for this trespass," he said. "For you are overly excited. After all, it is not every day that your god returns to you."

"My name is Tai Ch'lc," the helmeted man said, keeping the weapon pointed firmly at the Wanderer. "I am Commander of the Druidic Corp in this sector. We know exactly who you are and why you are here."

The Wanderer frowned. "The Druidic Corp?"

"It was formed shortly after your involvement with the Whale Riders. An order who would watch for your return to ensure it was the last time you walked this world. We are a peace-keeping organisation, funded by the nations you had contact with over the centuries so that we could finally put you down."

"Ha," the Wanderer laughed. "Druids with guns. Surely that goes against your peaceful ways."

Tai Ch'lc shrugged his padded shoulders. "You'd be surprised what compromises a person is willing to make to protect their world. Plus, our studies of the Great Portal meant we were perfectly positioned to use it in conjunction with technology. We got lucky, I suppose. You disappeared for nearly five hundred years."

The Wanderer looked up at the flying machine, then back at the weapon pointed towards him. It made sense if the last portal he had stepped through meant he had been transported five hundred years into the future. These were mortals who had grown up to worship technology. The sooner he disavowed them of that delusion, the better for everyone.

And then he saw it. A thin thread of purple energy drifting down from the sky and connecting with the barrel of the gun. He had not seen it before, perhaps because his body was still forming or maybe just an oversight after being distracting by these two modern Druids.

Regardless, something was happening here that he did not fully understand.

"I'm sure we can have a conversation before anybody takes an action they may live to regret," he said.

"Our orders are to neutralise you," Tai Ch'lc said, pressing a button on the side of his gun.

The thin purple thread grew thick and bright as energy from the portal streamed down into it.

"The Great Portal provides us with free, clean, power for whatever we need. Including this," the Druid said, looking down the weapon sight.

Tai Ch'lc pulled the trigger before the Wanderer could react. A beam of dazzling white light shot forth from the weapon, crackles of purple energy swirling around it.

It struck him directly in his chest, the pain of a thousand fires racing across his skin. The impact sent him flying off his feet and crashing into the ground. Everything hurt, bones broke and muscles tore. The Wanderer lay on his back, staring up at the Great Portal, in complete agony and utter confusion.

This was not his destiny. He had been thrown into The Void, escaped, and was meant to be a god. Clearly, all the portals had to be shut, including the one in the sky. Meaning his ascension had not happened, all because of that last swirling vortex above. It was the only explanation as to how a god could now be in so much pain. Footsteps to his left distracted him briefly. He turned to see Tai Ch'lc approach, his weapon aimed at The Wanderer as more portal energy streamed into it.

"What is this…?" he said to the mortal, wincing at the pain from speaking.

"This was the plan all along," Tai Ch'lc said. "You were put into a prison outside of this dimension, one our ancestors knew you would eventually escape from. The smaller portals were part of an elaborate distraction. While you jumped through each, trying to close them all, humanity would have time to come up with a solution that our ancestors couldn't. It was all about delaying you. You were never going to win, there was no path to ascension for you. You're not even powerful right now. You're mortal. We just really wanted to try out these guns on you, to be safe. Rest in pieces."

He did not feel the second shot. Strange, alien, thoughts entered his mind. He wondered if this was how Ewin had felt when the knife had been pushed into his chest. Pictured the look on Jonus' face when the zealot realised he had killed his own son because he had believed in a lie. As the weapon fired, the Wanderer thought about how Elodin had not wanted to die alone. Now, all the Wanderer could do was close his eyes and move to the Great Beyond – with nobody by his side.

THE AUTHORS

C.F. WELBURN

Craig Farndale Welburn is an award-winning author for his series: The Ashen Levels.

He was born in the year of Star Wars, in the birth town of Charles Darwin, and caught the fantasy bug as a child at the top of a faraway tree, in a hole in the ground and through a snowy wardrobe.

He left Shropshire to study literature, travel the lands and seek his fortune.

(He's still seeking…)

He currently lives in Madrid with his wife Jessica and son Otis.

Find C. F´s work here:

mybook.to/ISRWW

mybook.to/TAL-BOXSET

LEE C. CONLEY

Lee is a musician and writer in Lincolnshire, UK. He lives with his wife and daughters in the historic cathedral city of Lincoln. Alongside a lifetime of playing guitar and immersing himself in the study of music and history, Lee is also a practitioner and instructor of historic martial arts and swordsmanship, specialising in longsword. Lee is one of the founders of Bard of the Isles literary magazine and is now working on his debut fantasy series The Dead Sagas, which includes the novels A Ritual of Bone and A Ritual of Flesh, alongside generally writing speculative fiction and horror.

Want to get in touch with Lee?
www.leeconleyauthor.com

Facebook: www.facebook.com/LeeConleyAuthor/

Twitter: @LongswordLee or https://twitter.com/LongswordLee

Instagram: @LeeConleyAuthor or https://www.instagram.com/leeconleyauthor/

Goodreads: www.goodreads.com/author/show/14649012.Lee_Conley

Reddit: u/LeeConleyAuthor or https://www.reddit.com/user/LeeConleyAuthor

Sign up to Lee's mailing list!

If anyone would like to sign up for occasional (once or twice a year) email of news and updates on Lee's work, with the occasional competition or giveaway too, please sign yourselves up to Lee's mailing list.

https://mailchi.mp/ec0e4d5c30e7/leeconley-authlaningpage

H.L. TINSLEY

HL Tinsley is the pen name of indie author, blogger, and copywriter Holly Tinsley. Based in the UK, she is an author of Fantasy, Gothic Horror and Grimdark fiction. She has released two novels, SPBFO 7 finalist 'We Men of Ash and Shadow' and its sequel 'The Hand that Casts the Bone'. She is a regular contributor to gaming, TTRPG and pop culture websites and blogs.

You can find her on Twitter: @hollytinsl3y

Damien Larkin

Damien Larkin is an Irish science fiction and fantasy author. His military sci-fi novels Big Red and Blood Red Sand were longlisted for BSFA awards. He served for seven years in the Irish Reserve Defence Forces and lives in Dublin, Ireland.

FB:https://www.facebook.com/Damien-LarkinAuthor/
Twitter:https://twitter.com/Damo_Dangerman?
IG:https://www.instagram.com/damo_danger_larkin/
Website:https://www.damienlarkinbooks.com/
Booklink:https://www.damienlarkinbooks.com/shop

J E Hannaford

J E Hannaford is powered by coffee, dragons and whisky. She teaches Biology in the real world and invents fantasy beasts to populate her own. She lives in Suffolk, UK, and pines for the coast and mountains of Wales. A love of nature and the ocean washes through the pages of J E Hannaford's stories and pours out of the characters who live in it. Her debut series is The Black Hind's Wake, which begins with The Skin.

Website. www.jehannaford.com

For more details and social links; https://linktr.ee/jehannaford

DEREK POWER

Derek Power is the author of the Filthy Henry series. Hailing from Dublin, Ireland, most of his stories tend to involve Celtic myths and legends to some degree. His first foray into sci-fi can be found online with the sci-fi noir novel 'Duplex Tempus'. He has also featured in a couple of anthologies and spends most of his working day waiting for Hollywood to knock down the door for the movie rights. You can find all his books at

https://books2read.com/ap/xqkYXL/Derek-Power

and catch his tweets at https://twitter.com/dcpower_author

Several of his Filthy Henry books are also

available
at https://shows.acast.com/filthyhenry

DAVID GREEN

David Green is a writer of the epic and the urban, the fantastical and the mysterious. With his character-driven dark fantasy series Empire Of Ruin, or urban fantasy noir Hell In Haven starring Haven's only supernatural PI Nick Holleran, David takes readers on emotional, character-driven, action-packed thrill rides that leaves a reader needing their next fix. Hailing from the north-west of England, David now lives in County Galway on the west coast of Ireland with his wife and train-obsessed son. When not writing, David can be found wondering why he chooses to live in, and write about, places where it constantly rains.

Join his Facebook Group!
https://www.facebook.com/groups/davidgre-
ensreaderverseofmadness
Links: https://linktr.ee/davidgreenwriter

C. Marry Hultman

C. Marry Hultman is an expatriate Wisconsin-
ite currently living in Sweden. He is a writer
and podcaster. In his day-to-day life, he works
on various educational projects in Europe.
Together with a cadre of writers, he runs the
publishing house Nordic Press. As a writer he
has published three books; Face of Fear, These
Walls Will Fall and All the Children Shall
Lead. When not galivanting through Europe he
lives with his wife Marie, two daughters, and
the cats Nermal and Fizzgig.

More From Nordic Press

Novels/Novellas

Face of Fear by C. Marry Hultman
9789198671001

Dawson Junior G3 by Brian Wagstaff
9789198671049

Boy in the Wardrobe by Esther Jacoby
9789198684018

New Life Cottage by Esther Jacoby
9789198671056

The Wait by Esther Jacoby
e-book:https://books2read.com/u/4Dgz8Q

Liebe ist Warten by Esther Jacoby
9789198671070

Das Cottage by Ester Jacoby
978919868407

Musing on Death & Dying by Esther Jacoby
9789198671063

Earth Door by Cye Thomas
9789198671025

An Odd Collection of Tales By Cye Thomes
9789198684124

Graffiti Stories by Nick Gerrard
9789198671018

Punk Novelette by Nick Gerrard
9789198671087

Struggle and Strife by Nick Gerrard
9789198684049

Fake Escape by Natalie Hughes
e-book:https://books2read.com/u/bMXL5X

Hell Hath No Fury by Chisto Healy
9789198750706

True Mates by E.F. Vogel
9789198750713

CHRONICLES

Six Days to Hell by E.L. Giles
9789198684087

Cold as Hell by Neen Cohen
9789198684094

Murder Planet by Adam Carpenter
9789198671032

Generation Ship by Adam Carpenter
9789198684063

Sunshine by L.T. Emery
978-9198750942

<u>MYTHOS</u>
Antisocial Housing by Tim Mendees
978-9198750959

<u>ANTHOLOGIES</u>

Just 13
9789198684025

Lost Lore & Legends
9789198671094

Rise and Fall
9789198750911

Worlds Collide
9789198750928

Wicked West
9789198684193

Murder! Myster! Mayhem!
978-9198750980

THE MORTEM CYCLE

Death House
978-9198684117

Death Ship
978-9198684148

Death Beyond
978-9198684162

Death Cuisine
978-9198684186

Death Magic
978-9198750904

Find us at:
http://www.nordicpresspublishing.com

www.ingramcontent.com/pod-product-compliance
Lightning Source LLC
LaVergne TN
LVHW031322190726
843493LV00013B/3008